THE DEAD WILL RISE

THE DEAD WILL RISE

Chris Nickson

**SEVERN
HOUSE**

O'Neal Library
50 Oak Street
Mountain Brook, AL 35213

M

First world edition published in Great Britain and the USA in 2023
by Severn House, an imprint of Canongate Books Ltd,
14 High Street, Edinburgh EH1 1TE.

Trade paperback edition first published in Great Britain and the USA in 2023
by Severn House, an imprint of Canongate Books Ltd.

severnhouse.com

British Library Cataloguing-in-Publication Data
A CIP catalogue record for this title is available from the British Library.

ISBN-13: 978-1-4483-1019-7 (cased)
ISBN-13: 978-1-4483-1020-3 (e-book)

All Severn House titles are printed on acid-free paper.

MIX
Paper from
responsible sources
FSC® C013056

Typeset by Palimpsest Book Production Ltd.,
Falkirk, Stirlingshire, Scotland.
Printed and bound in Great Britain by
TJ Books Ltd, Padstow, Cornwall.

'For the trumpet will sound, and the dead will be raised imperishable, and we shall be changed'

—1 Corinthians, 15:52

Leeds, April 1824

I t was a balmy evening for early spring; after ten and still a faint, lingering hint of warmth in the air. Simon Westow turned to his wife and spoke into her ear, loud enough for her to hear over the press of people around them. Their sons, Richard and Amos, kept tight hold of her hands as they looked about in astonishment and disbelief at the spectacle of the Saturday night market. Simon reached down and ruffled Amos's hair. They exchanged a quick, happy grin.

It was the first time they'd brought the boys here. He'd arrived home in the afternoon with the seed planted in his mind. A treat for the twins. Not only letting them stay up long past their usual time for bed, but to go somewhere in the darkness.

Simon had been working relentlessly for weeks. From the turn of the year, crooks had been busy; there was plenty of demand for the services of a thief-taker to retrieve what had been stolen – always for a fee, of course. No sooner had one job ended than the next arrived. Simon and Jane, the young woman who worked with him, had made good money, but he was exhausted.

Finally, though, he'd returned the last items and collected his payment. There was nothing else waiting. More jobs would come soon, he knew that; crime never stopped. For now, though, he had a chance to draw breath. Simon was ready to celebrate, to do anything where he didn't have to consider work. Something different to carry him away. The Saturday night market in the space next to Holy Trinity Church on Boar Lane was ideal.

It was a patch of empty ground which was used for the circuses that regularly passed through Leeds. When they weren't in town, it became home to this.

The rich smell of roasting meat drifted through the air, stronger than the stink of smoke and soot that always hung over Leeds. A river of voices carried him along: loud, soft, shrill, deep. Candles guttered on some of the stalls, casting wild shadows high against the church walls. Bodies pushed against him, potent with the stench of drink and dirt, of sweat and hopelessness. Simon kept one hand on his knife, the other guarding his money as he turned his head to check that Rosie and the twins were with him.

It felt as if half the people in Leeds were crammed in here. The market opened at nine, after the factory workers had waited in the beershops for the foremen to come and pay their wages for the week. Wives stood outside, taking money for rent and food before their husbands could drink and gamble it all away.

Someone lit a torch. It hissed and flared, sending brilliant orange sparks curling up into the sky. For a single, short moment everything smelled of pine resin.

The Saturday market was part of Leeds. The faces changed, but one thing stayed constant: they were all filled with desperation. It was where people came to sell anything they could in order to survive for one more week.

He wanted his sons to see it. They were eight now, old enough to understand what the world was like for so many. They'd have their Saturday adventure, but also something to make them think.

Voices rose and fell, calling out their wares, as he eased a passage between people for his family.

'Eight a penny, grand pears! Come on and buy my pears here.'

'Fine walnuts! Sixteen a penny, none better!'

'Oysters from the coast. Fresh and tasty!'

The walnut girl hoisted her basket on to her shoulder as she tried to squeeze through the throng. As Simon slid between two men, he heard a stationer yelling a half-quire of paper for a penny as a lonely woman's voice tried to stand out, 'Won't someone buy my bonnet for fourpence? Just four pennies, please?'

On the far side of the stalls, a trio of street singers competed against a blind fiddler whose fingers flew as he blazed through a jig. Ann Carr the preacher pressed tracts on any soul who'd take one. Just on the edge of the bobbing circle of light a family stood, dignified and silent. A man with his wife and three daughters. All of them clean, dressed in their Sunday church clothes. His head was bowed, and the females silently held out the rush mats they'd woven for sale.

Simon stared for a moment at an old woman who'd lined up a row of shabby old shoes along the ground. She looked up with a soft, beatific smile. He took a coin from his pocket, pressed it into Richard's hand and told him what to do.

It wasn't much. Being here was a reminder that there could never be enough.

They moved around, buying a few small things they didn't need, and finally drifting away, leaving the noise to walk back to the house on Swinegate. Once the thrill of being out in the night faded, maybe the lesson would stay with his sons. Perhaps they'd learn a little humility. The reminder was no bad thing for him, either.

The boys were full of chatter, excited, slow to settle down and rest. Finally, the house was quiet. Rosie was already dreaming as he lay down beside her. Simon Westow felt content with his life.

ONE

Joseph Clark was one of the new breed of men. He was an engineer, his life wrapped in numbers and measurements. Clark's world was machines, everything powered by steam and turbines. All of it exact, calculated to the tiniest fraction of an inch.

He'd started just five years earlier with a small wooden workshop on Mabgate. Now the Clark Foundry was solid stone, sprawling along the street, eating up everything with a giant's appetite. The new buildings were permanent and commanding, shifts of men running all day and all night.

He stood in the kitchen of Simon's house on a Monday morning, looking awkward as he worked the brim of his hat through his fingers. Clark was barely thirty, but already his knowledge and patents had made him rich, a man with a fortune that grew larger each day. More wealth than many landowners. Yet money couldn't disguise his discomfort around people, Simon thought. They weren't as solid or reliable as numbers.

'Please, take a seat,' he said, but Clark gave a quick shake of his head. His suit was of the costliest wool, the linen of his shirt and stock starched pure white. But they might as well have come straight off the back of a beggar from the way he wore them. He carried the distracted air of a man who spent his life in another world.

Clark cleared his throat then began to speak, pausing often as he searched for the words he wanted.

'One of my assistants is named Harmony Jordan. He's been with me since I began the business. A fortnight ago, his daughter died . . . she was just ten years old. The family lives in Headingley . . . she was buried in St Michael's churchyard.' He took a breath and Simon studied the man's face. He was concentrating, marshalling the precise facts of what he needed to say. 'A week later, the family went to lay flowers on the grave. It looked as if it had been . . . disturbed. Jordan called the sexton. When the gravediggers opened up the ground, they discovered that his daughter's body had been removed from the coffin.'

Simon heard Rosie gasp in horror. He knew what she was thinking: Richard and Amos. On the other side of him, Jane sat silent, staring straight ahead.

'How long ago is it since they found the body was gone?'

'It happened on Friday. But they don't know when it was taken. Harmony told me on Saturday. That's why I'm here, Mr Westow. I want to hire you.'

Simon pursed his lips. 'I'm a thief-taker. You know that. I find items that have been stolen.'

'I do.' Clark looked directly into his face. 'Gwendolyn Jordan was stolen.'

'I understand. But I don't think I'm the person to help you.'

The man cocked his head, taken aback. 'Why not? It's your work, isn't it? Surely, taking bodies must be one of the worst things you can imagine.'

'I don't believe there could be anything worse,' Simon agreed. He sighed. 'You have to realize, Mr Clark: all I know about body snatching is what I've read in the newspapers. I've never even heard of it happening before in Leeds. You said Mr Jordan doesn't know exactly when it happened?'

'No. Just somewhere in the seven days between burial and discovery.'

Simon chewed the inside of his lip as he thought. 'The corpse could be anywhere by now. My understanding is that the surgeons and medical schools buy them to dissect for anatomy lessons. There are places in Edinburgh and London. Very likely a few other cities, too.'

'That doesn't help Harmony and his wife,' Clark said.

'No, of course not,' Simon agreed. 'Believe me, Mr Clark, I know that very well. I'm a parent too. What they're going through must be unendurable. But do you realize that even if I found the people who did it and they were convicted, they'd only go to prison for a few weeks? Months at the most. The law is very clear: taking a body is only a misdemeanour. It's not deemed to be property.'

He saw Clark's face harden. 'What? Why, in God's name?'

'I wish I knew the answer to that.'

'They also took the dress her parents had made for the burial.'

'Did they?' Simon pounced on the words. 'That could make all the difference.' A dress *was* property. If it cost enough, stealing it was a felony. The thieves could be transported, maybe even hanged.

'I imagine they'll have sold it in Leeds,' Clark said. 'I want you to find the men who did it.'

Simon glanced at Jane. Her face showed nothing, hands pressed flat on the table. He'd wanted a short break from work, but this was a job they could do. No, more than that. This was one he *had* to do.

'All right.'

'I'll pay you well beyond the value of the dress, don't worry about that,' the man continued. 'And believe me, I will definitely fund the prosecution of the men behind all this.'

'That's your choice.'

'I also want you to find out what happened to the body. Where it went, who bought it.'

'I can try,' Simon told him. 'I can't guarantee anything on that.'

'Just give me a name,' Clark said. 'That's all I need. I know people all over the country. Give me that and I'll be able to discover where she is and bring her home.' His expression softened. 'Harmony has been with me from the start. He's important to me.'

Loyalty, friendship. Maybe there was more to the man than numbers.

TWO

As she walked home, Jane kept reading words. Anything at all, everything she saw. She was eager for them. All the signs above shops, the advertisements pasted to walls and fences. Her lips moved silently, forming the words, hearing them in her mind.

When she was eight years old, after her father raped her, her mother had thrown her on to the streets. Survival became the only thing that mattered. Reading and writing couldn't help her find food or somewhere to sleep. Now, her life had changed. She was settled. She had her work with Simon, and she'd found contentment living with Mrs Shields, the old woman with a gentle soul who owned the cottage hidden away behind Green Dragon Yard.

The desire for change had arrived during the autumn. It had been growing through the year. An urge for something more in her life, something new. She'd asked Catherine Shields to teach her to read. As soon as she began to learn, she discovered she was hungry for it all, pushing herself, angry at her failure whenever she stumbled over a phrase or a spelling.

'There's no rush, child,' Mrs Shields told her with a soft smile. 'It's not a race.'

Jane drank it down, wanting more and more, to master everything. Rosie showed her numbers, how to add and subtract. One more thing she'd never had the chance to understand. A few times, when she was alone, she'd even scratched on some paper with a nib, trying to make her hand form letters and words.

Then, just three weeks before, as she strolled along Commercial Street, Jane spotted a bolt of muslin in a seamstress's window. She'd never paid attention to cloth or patterns. What was the need? Her clothes were old, they were garments for work, for wear and tear and dirt. She had money to afford better but she'd simply never had the urge. It was pointless, it was vanity.

But from nowhere the desire began to nag at her, imagining herself in a dress made from this material. For a week she denied it, telling herself it was frivolous and vain. She had no need of a new frock. Where did she ever go that demanded one? Yet finally she gave in, thrilled by the soft ring of the bell as she entered the shop.

When the dress was finished and she tried it on, she didn't recognize the young woman in the mirror. This wasn't the person she imagined; it was nobody she knew. Long dark hair and a heart-shaped face that led down to the point of her chin.

She ran her hands over the fabric. It was soft to the touch, rippling under her fingertips. A rich chocolate brown colour, with small designs the shade of ripe raspberries. Modestly cut, high over the bosom, nothing to draw attention. The first new garment she'd ever owned. Jane clutched the package under her arm as she walked up the Head Row.

As soon as she reached the house, she tucked it away in a chest, unopened, still tied in its brown paper. Suddenly she felt ashamed that she'd bought it. It was too good to wear for work. An indulgence. Money wasted on a pointless whim.

'I'll go and see the woman who made the funeral dress,' Simon said. 'There might be something to help identify it.'

'Let me do that,' Rosie told him. 'I'm going to be part of this.' There was a firmness in her voice that made him give way. 'Anyone who can do that . . .' Her words trailed away. A child; of course she'd feel that deep inside.

'I know.' He took hold of her hand. If it was one of his boys, he'd kill the men responsible.

'I'll talk to the seamstress,' she said. 'You don't know the first thing about dresses.'

'That's true enough,' he admitted.

He knew she'd be able to come back with a far better description than he could ever manage. Rosie had done it all before; until she became pregnant with the boys, his wife had worked beside him. 'We need a description and how much it cost.'

Alone, he sat at the kitchen table, scribbling notes and thoughts on a scrap of paper. He could hear the voice of the tutor drifting through from the parlour, teaching his sons mathematics. Division and multiplication. Tools to use in the world, but words he'd never heard as he grew up in the workhouse.

His boys enjoyed a better life than that. But Gwendolyn Jordan was a reminder that death could come to anyone at any time.

How must her parents have felt as they put her in the ground? He couldn't begin to imagine the pain. Then to discover her body had been stolen . . . The corpse almost certainly vanished from Leeds the day after it was taken. Packed into a box, labelled with an address in another town and placed on a coach. If he found the men, he might be able to discover where it had gone and who'd bought it. Anything more than that . . . even with Clark's influence, it was unlikely that her bones would ever come home again.

He'd believed Leeds had escaped the plague of body snatchers. He'd hoped so; he should have known better. If there was money to be made, people would do it. No matter how evil, how sickening, someone would do it.

'The seamstress did better than a description,' Rosie said. She sat across from him and pulled out a sheet of paper. 'She drew it for me.'

It was crude, thick lines of heavy pencil on rough butcher's paper. Still, it gave the shape and showed the panels at the breast, the lines of embroidery at the wrist and the hem. Enough to identify it.

'It cost almost two pounds,' she said.

His eyes widened in disbelief. 'For a burial gown? That's a fortune. Why?'

'They wanted the very best linen. The Jordans insisted on it. Pure white. That's not cheap. Then the seamstress was up for two nights straight, sewing all the embroidery.'

Simon studied the sketch. Almost two pounds; that was enough to make it a felony, enough to hang the thieves. 'I'll take it to the clothes stalls at the market tomorrow.'

She shook her head. 'There's no need. I've already been.'

He sat back, smiling in admiration. 'You're thorough.'

The bitterness ran under her words. 'I told you, Simon; I want the people who did this.'

'Did you find anything?'

'Mrs Harris recognized it immediately. She bought the gown and sold it the same day.'

Simon sat upright, attentive. 'When?'

'Last Tuesday.'

Six days ago. The Jordans had found the disturbance at the

grave on Friday, a week after their daughter was buried. That left four nights when the body could have been taken.

'Who sold it to her?'

'A man. She doesn't know his name, but she's seen him around before. A thick moustache that's mostly white. Keeps a grubby red kerchief tied around his neck. He's missing the little finger on his right hand.'

'How old is the man? Did she say anything about that?'

'She thinks he's probably around fifty. He claimed he found it.' Rosie snorted her disgust.

He had to be one of the men who'd taken Gwendolyn Jordan. Now Simon had somewhere to begin.

'Find them, Simon.' He understood the images playing through her head and pulled her so close he could feel her heart beating. 'Find them,' she repeated.

'We will,' he promised.

The little finger missing from the right hand. That was something, but not so much; too many men carried injuries like that. He only needed to walk along Briggate to spot five or six of them. Casualties of the machines, the mills, the mines, the wars. Scars, fingers, hands, arms and legs gone.

Jane shook her head. She didn't know him.

'I'll ask,' she said. Someone might be able to give her a name.

'You follow that one,' Simon told her. 'I'm going to see what I can discover about these other men who dig up bodies.'

George Mudie stopped turning the handle of his printing press. The last sheet glided out on to the pile.

'I heard about it.' His expression soured. 'Turned my stomach.' He walked to the desk, took a bottle of brandy from the drawer and poured a little into a glass. He held it up to the light, then downed the drink in a single swallow, trying to wash the taste of disgust from his mouth. He'd been a newspaperman once, an editor, used to seeing and describing brutal things. But those days had long gone, vanished in arguments and dismissals. These days he ran this printing shop.

'The girl was just ten years old.'

'Ten, eighty . . . the age doesn't matter, Simon.' He lowered his head in sorrow. 'They're all people. They had families. Nobody deserves to have their grave desecrated like that.'

'We agree on that.'

'When you find them, you'd better make sure no word goes around or people will hang them.'

No need for a trial; the mob would tear them apart in disgust. It was hardly a surprise; maybe he even sympathized. He knew Rosie would gladly see it happen. What mercy for a crime against the dead?

'First I have to find them. Can you think of anyone who might have information?'

'Not this time. I don't want the acquaintance of anyone who'd resort to that.'

'You know Dr Hunter at the infirmary, don't you?'

'I have done since he started there, yes,' Mudie replied cautiously.

'Could you ask him . . .?'

'They don't have a school of anatomy. Not even a medical school, Simon.'

'Can you ask anyway?'

'All right,' Mudie agreed. 'But the whole thing makes me sick.'

Everywhere was the same. Quick, angry looks before hurrying away. Even the temptation of a few coins made no difference. Nobody knew them; nobody *wanted* to know them. Body snatchers weren't criminals. They were barely human. As the clock struck noon, he had nothing. Not even a clue or a hint.

Hands pushed deep in his pockets, Simon strode down Kirkgate. How was he going to find them? How long had they been carrying on their trade in town? How many corpses had vanished, unnoticed?

He stopped at the parish church, staring across at the burial ground. Were the dead all still there, rotting in their coffins? Would he even be able to spot if they'd been taken?

With a creak, the gate pushed open under his hand. Ghosts walked here. He could feel them. While Leeds rushed and roared outside the walls, among the gravestones everything was eerie and hushed. The day always seemed colder here, as if something had leached away its warmth. There was no danger he could sense, but still he loosened his knife in its sheath, and another up his sleeve.

Everything looked quiet, undisturbed. He strolled, trying not to draw attention, eyes searching the ground for any sign of digging. In the area for new graves, the start of a hole and a pair of spades leaning against a tree. Where someone had been buried recently, the sod had been tamped down, the soil uneven.

'What do you want?'

The shout made him turn, raising his arms to show he was no threat. A man appeared, aiming an old fowling piece. Jack Lancaster, the sexton. Blinking, not wearing his spectacles, face set like iron.

'It's Simon Westow, Jack,' he answered. 'The thief-taker.'

'I know who you are.' But he didn't lower the gun as he approached. 'What are you doing?'

'Looking. I've been hired to find the men who took that girl in Headingley. You must have heard about it.'

'That didn't happen here.' A gruff reply. 'Everyone in this place is where they're supposed to be.'

'I'm sure they are.' Simon started to ease himself away.

'You'd do well to be careful where you tread, too. We're putting in a pair of mantraps, just in case anyone tries anything.'

Back on Kirkgate, he took a deep breath. If he'd arrived at dusk, there'd have been shots, not questions and warnings. People were fearful. Instead of this place, he'd do better to walk out to Headingley and see where it had all happened.

A few couples enjoyed the balm of a spring day on Woodhouse Moor. Away from town, the air was cleaner, clearer, sharp and sweet as he breathed it in. By the time he reached St Michael's, across from the ancient shire oak, the sun shone through branches thick with buds.

Simon found the sexton in the church, supervising a pair of workmen. When he explained the errand, the man gave a slow, sober nod and led the way into the churchyard. Mature trees shaded the dead, and a low wall protected them from the world outside.

'We're talking about making that higher,' the man said. 'But it's going to cost money that we don't have. We've had volunteers keeping watch at night instead.'

'How long can you manage that?'

'As long as we need.' He led the way between rows, scarcely

needing to glance down to know where he was. He was a rail of a man, wearing a black suit neatly mended at the cuffs and clean, well-washed linen; everything about him was tidy and exact. The sexton stopped in front of a grave that looked exactly like all the others. No headstone to mark it out yet.

'This is where Gwendolyn Jordan was buried. Her family have been coming to the church every Sunday since they moved out here two years ago,' His face fell with grief. 'She was a very bright girl, always lively and beaming.'

'What happened to her? How did she die?' That was something he hadn't heard from Clark.

'She started with a fever, poor little lass. A little more than a day and she went.' He paused and stared at the ground. 'The doctor couldn't save her. They have money – well, you know where Mr Jordan works – but that can't help when the Lord wants someone.'

But the Lord hadn't stopped the men who took her body.

'Do you have any idea when they stole the corpse?'

'I didn't know a thing about it until Mr and Mrs Jordan came looking for me. That was Friday. Gwendolyn had been buried the Friday before.' He pressed his lips together. 'I only live a few yards away and I hadn't heard any reports of strangers or noises in the middle of the night . . .' His voice trailed off and he gazed at Simon with helpless eyes. 'How could I have known? I keep asking myself that. How?'

'You couldn't. Don't blame yourself. Have you ever had any trouble before?'

The sexton shook his head. 'Nothing. Headingley is a small place, Mr Westow. We know each other. Unfamiliar faces stand out.'

Not always, Simon thought; he'd been here a few times in the past, careful to stay out of sight. It wasn't difficult to do.

'No gossip or rumours, nothing like that?'

'Not a thing,' he answered.

The grave appeared intact, the sod more or less level with the ground all around. Simon squatted, feeling the earth with his fingertips. After a few seconds he stopped. This was pointless; even if he found something, he'd have no idea what it was.

'We've put everything back properly,' the man told him.

'How obvious was it?'

'Hardly at all,' he answered after a moment. 'The body snatchers knew what they were doing. Difficult to spot. They cut out part of the sod and dug down to expose the top of the coffin. Then they cut that open, tied a rope around the body and hauled it out. Afterwards, they put everything back. It probably only took twenty minutes.'

So fast. Clever, too; he had to admit that. Everything achieved with a minimum of effort. The man was right; they obviously knew their business. This wasn't the work of fumbling amateurs. Above all, they'd known exactly *where* to go.

'Doesn't a spade make noise when people dig?' He'd heard enough labourers; there was nothing quiet about the work.

'I'm told the blade of the shovel is made of wood, not metal,' the sexton said. 'It hardly makes a sound. Nothing to travel in the darkness.'

Simon hadn't realized that body snatching was a trade, with its own tools. He looked around. The closest house was more than twenty yards away. The gable end faced the churchyard, no windows that could look down on the scene. With the low wall and a track beyond it for a cart, things could hardly have been easier for the robbers.

'Have you searched the other graves?'

The sexton nodded. 'Everyone who's been buried in the last three months. I couldn't see any signs, but . . .' He shrugged. Without digging all the way down, it might be impossible ever to know.

'Who knew she was being buried?'

'Plenty in the parish,' the man answered. 'It was no secret. The Jordans are popular. They give money to charity. Mrs Jordan is friendly, always willing to help.'

Simon had plenty to consider as he walked back towards Leeds. A low, grey pall of smoke and soot hung over the town. He felt the air grow thicker against his skin, grittier in his mouth as he swallowed. The price of industry and prosperity was all the factory chimneys throwing out their smoke, turning the buildings black and poisoning the people.

The body snatchers hadn't been lucky. They were organized, well-informed. In and out of the graveyard before anyone knew. Gwendolyn Jordan's body had probably been sold long before they began to dig.

He cut across the moor, following a track down the hill to the road that went towards Meanwood, then through Sheepscar, cutting down Skinner Lane to Mabgate and the Clark Foundry.

THREE

'**M**r Westow, have you found them already?'

Clark bustled in, a very different man from the one who'd appeared at Simon's house the day before. This place was his kingdom and he was its ruler. He was comfortable here.

He wore an old suit speckled with burn marks, covered by a heavy leather apron. His hands were dark with dirt and oil. But his face was alive with hope.

'Not yet,' Simon said, and the eager smile vanished.

'Have you made progress?'

'A little.' He listed the things they'd learned, then added, 'I came to talk to Mr Jordan.'

'Of course, of course. Let me find him for you.' He hurried away again.

The building was loud, ringing with the clang of metal and the pounding of steam hammers. Men shouted. Off around a corner, someone gave a long, barking laugh. The whole place had the air of dashing forward, of rushing full pace into the future.

Clark's desk was a mess of papers. They sat in neglected piles and jumbles, a thin layer of dust covering everything. After a few minutes the door handle turned and a man entered. He was as wiry as his employer, a few years older, eyes filled with a raw sorrow that he didn't try to hide.

'You're Mr Westow?'

'Yes. I'm sorry for all you're going through. I'm a father, too . . .' He stopped. Jordan would already have heard enough, listened to too much sympathy. No need to add to that weight. The man nodded but said nothing. What words could express the horrors in his head? 'I'm sorry, but I need to ask you a few questions.'

'All right.' Jordan examined his hands as if he wasn't certain what to do with them.

'When you discovered the grave had been disturbed, was that the first time you'd been there since the funeral?'

'No.' The answer came out dry and awkward. 'No, of course not. I'd stopped there every day on my way home from work.' The man paused, taking a breath and biting his lip. 'When we . . . that was the first time we'd all been there together. My wife and my other children,' he added.

'You hadn't noticed anything on your earlier visits?'

Jordan shook his head. 'I hadn't really looked. It wasn't obvious. My wife spotted it. She was clearing the grass and saw that the dirt had been disturbed.'

He'd hoped the man might have suspected something earlier. Some small clue as to exactly which night it happened. No luck. There were still four possible nights the body could have been taken, and it looked as if it might stay that way.

'Thank you. That was all I needed to know. Believe me, please, I'll do everything I can,' Simon promised him.

He stopped on Lady Bridge, staring down at the water of the beck as it flowed lazily along, shot through with patches of red and yellow from the dye works in Sheepscar. He didn't want to believe it. Yet however much he tried to deny the idea, this probably wasn't isolated. The gang of body snatchers could have been operating here for a while.

Jane frowned. She saw a word she didn't know on the notice pasted to the wall, and tried to sound it out in her mind, syllable by syllable. If she could say it, she might understand what it meant. She had work to do, but still stopped for a minute. It was important to her.

Finally she walked on, spelling it out in her mind once more so she'd remember it. Later she'd ask Mrs Shields; the old woman would know.

'He just wanted rid of that dress as soon as he could,' Mrs Harris at the clothes stall told her. 'Couldn't happen quick enough for him. He knew it was quality, good linen, mind.' She rolled her eyes. 'Not that he had any idea *how* good. The very best, you could feel it, like silk when you touched it. I told him what I was willing to pay and that was it. No haggling. Took it and dashed off as fast as he could.'

'Have you ever seen him before?'

'His face was familiar, but he's never sold to me. I'd remember that. I don't think he's ever bought anything, either.' Her mouth tightened. 'Why? Why are you and that other woman asking about the gown?'

'We want to find him, that's all. If he comes back, send someone for Simon Westow, the thief-taker. He'll see you're paid for it.'

The name was enough to make Mrs Harris narrow her eyes. 'What's going on?' Her voice sharpened. 'I don't want to end up in court or in prison.'

'You won't,' Jane assured her. 'Nobody will ever know your name.'

'All right, I suppose,' she agreed. But it was a grudging acceptance.

Kate the pie-seller pursed her lips as she shook her head. 'It could be anyone. It's impossible to know from a description like that.'

That was no surprise. A missing finger was almost as common as breathing among working men. Most of them wore moustaches and kerchiefs around their necks.

'If you see someone who might fit . . .' Jane passed across six pennies, money for food and information; they vanished into Kate's pocket.

'Don't you worry, I'll see that you hear.' She selected three of the pies and passed them over, the crusts still warm.

Jane ate one, gave another to a group of children who were watching the barges being unloaded by the river. A word, a promise of money, and they scattered to search for the man.

She knew most of the beggars along the streets, dropped coins in their tin cups and stopped to talk to them. They noticed more than anyone expected, but none of them recognized the man.

Except for Dodson, the old soldier with the wooden leg. He cocked his head when she asked and ran his tongue over his lips.

'I can't be sure,' he said, 'but I might have seen someone just like him.'

'When?'

'I don't know. Last week, maybe. Or it could have been at the start of this.' He looked up with an apologetic smile. 'It's hard to tell. The days all blend into one another.'

He was a sober man, reliable, not given to fancy or lies. He'd lost his leg nine years before, at Waterloo. With no trade and no pension for a soldier, he'd had no choice but to end up a beggar.

'Where was he?'

'Right over there.' He nodded to a spot across the street. 'If it's the same man, he was talking to someone else.'

Jane felt the lurch of her heart in her chest. 'This one he was talking to. Who was he? Do you know him at all?'

'I've seen him before,' Dodson replied. 'I don't think I've ever heard his name. But he's the type who stands out. Very big. Broad, plenty of muscle.' He closed his eyes to conjure the man into his mind. 'He had a top hat, all worn and battered at the front. Fawn trousers with a stain down the left thigh. No buckle on one of his shoes.' He smiled at her, proud of his memory. 'Does that help?'

'Very much.' Jane put the last pie in his lap and sent a small shower of coins into his cup. 'Thank you.'

Dodson was good; that should be exact enough to trace him. She talked to the children by the market too. Someone would find the information.

He heard Rosie and the twins in the kitchen. While the boys worked on their sums, she was chopping onions and throwing them into the pot to sizzle. As Simon entered, she turned her head and pushed back her hair.

'You've been popular,' she said. 'Two different boys have delivered notes for you.'

'Who sent them?' He was looking over the boys' shoulders, inspecting the homework their tutor had set.

'One's from George Mudie. He says he talked to Hunter, who's certain that no dissections are happening in Leeds.'

Simon nodded. That was one small blessing; at least the body hadn't been cut up by a surgeon here. 'What about the other one?'

'It's from Mrs Parker.'

'Who's Mrs Parker?' He frowned as he tried to place the name.

'Mrs *Amanda* Parker.' She raised her eyebrows. 'You know. *That* one. She requests that you call on her tomorrow morning. With Jane; she was insistent on that.'

He chuckled. *That one.* Of course, he should have guessed. Amanda Parker was notorious. Still in her thirties and already a widow twice over, the woman was a scandal in what passed for society in Leeds. The story circulated that she'd grown up poor on Quarry Hill. Some claimed she'd been a whore when she was young. Maybe it was true, maybe not; she'd never said. Somehow she found an old, rich man to marry. Bewitched and seduced him, the gossips claimed. He died four years later and left her wealthy. Then she found another with just as much money. His heart gave out within two years, making her richer still. These days the rumours swirled that she found her lovers among the grown, gilded sons of the merchants and millowners.

'What does she want?' He pointed out a mistake in Richard's work, then praised his work on some subtraction.

'I don't know. There's only the invitation. Or maybe she believes it's a command.' He heard the cold, distant note under Rosie's voice. Well, well, Simon thought; another one who didn't like the woman.

'I'd better go and warn Jane. I'll see what she's managed to find out, too.'

'I did a little cleaning today,' Mrs Shields said.

'There's no need.' Jane looked at her. 'I've told you I can do that.'

'You know I like to help when I can. It makes me feel useful.' She gave her soft smile. 'I'm not an invalid.'

'Of course you're not. But please be careful.' Gently, she squeezed the old woman's fingers. The woman was family. Not her blood, but more like kin than any of them had been. Mrs Shields had given her a place that was home. She felt safe here. Loved. For the first time in her life, she was happy. She never wanted that to change.

'Don't you worry, child. I am.' Her eyes twinkled, and a teasing edge crept into her voice. 'A curious thing happened. While I was busy, I looked in that chest by the fire. There's a parcel inside, still tied up with string. It doesn't look like it's been opened.'

Jane straightened her back. 'It's mine.'

'What is it? You don't have to hide anything from me.'

It was a long moment before she could answer. 'A dress.'

'A dress?' Mrs Shields stared in complete disbelief.

How could she start to explain when it no longer made any sense? Jane took a deep breath and tried to find the words.

'I saw the material in the dressmaker's window. It . . . I . . . I liked it. I don't know why.'

'You never need a reason, child. You liked it, that's enough.'

'I went in to look at it. When she held it up against me, I could imagine a dress made from it.'

'Why shouldn't you?' Mrs Shields asked. 'You have the money. I don't think I've ever seen you spend anything on yourself.'

'But I don't *need* it,' she said.

'No, you don't,' the old woman agreed. 'Still, there's no sin in owning something pretty. You deserve to treat yourself.'

Did she? It felt frivolous, an indulgence. A waste, as if she'd been carried away by some small madness.

'Put it on for me,' Mrs Shields said. Her eyes twinkled. 'Please. I want to see what this material looks like.'

She was hesitant. More than anything, Jane felt ashamed of spending the money. But finally she removed the old work dress and stood in front of the mirror, adjusting her new frock. The pattern still made her beam with pleasure.

'You look so beautiful,' Mrs Shields said. It was more than an empty compliment, she knew that. The woman's face was filled with joy; for a second Jane could believe she'd done the right thing. Then she was aware of herself again, the short sleeves displaying her arms with their uneven ladder of scars. The sense that people might look and notice her. 'It's beautifully stitched. Turn around. Let me see you properly.'

She did it, feeling foolish, suddenly hating the dress again.

'You're right, child, that is a wonderful pattern. Those colours suit you perfectly. The brown sets off your eyes. I hope you'll wear it often.'

Jane said nothing. They both knew what would happen. Where did she go that needed a good dress? For work, old clothes served her well, and there was no need to put on something special for the market or the butcher. It wasn't as if she had any social occasions, and she didn't want any. Gratefully she slipped away and changed back. A sense of relief flooded through her body. The clothes hid her. Like this, she was invisible. No sense that people were looking at her. But she still folded the new dress carefully and wrapped it in the brown paper.

As she tucked it away in the chest, Jane said, 'I saw a word today that I didn't know. Can you tell me what it—'

The knock on the door stopped her. She turned the handle, fingers tight around the hilt of her knife. No danger. Only Simon.

*　　*　　*

He listened closely as she told him about the man Dodson described, then shook his head.

'No, I don't know him. Have you told people?'

'Yes.' Tomorrow someone might have a morsel for her. A day, two at most, and they'd track him down.

'We have another job, too. Mrs Parker sent a note; she wants to see us in the morning.'

She blinked. 'Us?'

'She was very specific. Both of us.'

Jane didn't know what to say. No one ever asked for her. Why did the woman need anyone there besides Simon? He was the thief-taker. He made the decisions.

'If that's what she wants,' she agreed after a moment.

'I'll come around nine. I doubt she's the type who rises early.'

She'd heard of Amanda Parker; probably everyone in Leeds knew the woman's name and reputation. But how could someone like that know about *her*? Why? What did she want?

She didn't like people knowing her name. A life in the shadows was preferable, to stay unknown and unremembered.

After Simon left, she began again: 'I saw a word I didn't know today. What does *exterminate* mean?' She sounded the word out slowly and spelled it. 'It was on a poster when I was out.'

'Sit down, child, and I'll tell you.' Mrs Shields's voice was soothing, always comforting. 'After that, you can read to me. We'll see how you're coming along.' She held up a book. Jane read the title: *Pride and Prejudice*.

Traces of the day's spring warmth lingered into the darkness. Simon took his time, moving from inn to beershop to tavern. A pair of coaches passed, one arriving, the horses flecked white with sweat as they slowed to turn under the arch into a courtyard. The other was departing, the driver cracking his whip and shouting encouragement to the animals to make speed along Briggate and the road going north.

He found familiar faces, spent a few moments talking, then moved on again. Twice he stopped and took a drink, deep in conversation. It was late when he passed George Mudie's printing shop out beyond the Head Row, but a light was still burning inside. Simon knocked on the door.

'A rush job,' Mudie explained as he walked back to the press. 'Secret, too.'

'I hope it pays well.'

The man laughed. 'Do you think I'd be here at this time of night if it didn't? What are you doing out and about?'

'Trying to find our body snatchers. Thank you for the information from Dr Hunter.'

Mudie's face soured. 'I told you how I feel about that business.'

'What do you know about it?'

'For once, not a damned thing more than anyone else, and I'm quite happy to leave it that way.' He took a bottle of brandy from the table and poured a little into a glass. 'What I loathe is the way they defend it by saying medical students need to dissect bodies in order to learn and there aren't enough available legally.' His voice grew tighter. 'That's their justification for violating graves. For taking someone's family without consent. Can you accept it?'

'No,' Simon agreed. There could never be a reason for that. Even if the families never learned the truth, the body was still gone. Cut up, disposed of far from home.

'I wonder if there have been more here and we just don't know,' Mudie said.

'It was very well done,' Simon told him.

'Not amateurs?'

'No,' he replied. 'No, I'm sure they weren't. That concerns me.'

Mudie took a drink. 'Bastards. Found any names yet?'

'Descriptions, that's all.' He went through them but Mudie shook his head.

'I can ask, I suppose. You never know . . .'

'Do you think you'll find them, Simon?' Rosie snuggled against him in bed. He felt her soft breath on his neck.

'Yes.' He had no doubt. They'd be prosecuted for the gown. Transported to Van Diemen's Land if they were lucky. But he doubted they'd ever recover Gwendolyn Jordan's body. That had gone.

'I keep thinking about the parents of that poor girl.'

The picture of Harmony Jordan's bereft face flickered in his mind. 'I know.'

'Just make sure I'm involved in the hunt. I want them caught.'

FOUR

Burley House was grand, standing alone beyond the far end of the Head Row. Jane had passed it often, but at the gate she paused to study it properly. Everything was neat and symmetrical, perfectly in proportion. It appeared simple and straightforward, but there was something more, she decided. The word sprang into her mind: elegant. Three storeys, with a drive that led around to a coach house. A man in livery with a hard, arrogant face stopped polishing the carriage to stare straight at her. Inspecting her.

It was the type of building that should have stood farther from town, she thought, deep in its own grounds; it had probably been that way when it was first built. Now Leeds had spread around it and the town's smoke had turned the stonework as black as everywhere else.

Mrs Shields had urged her to wear the new muslin, but she shook her head. Mrs Parker wanted to hire them; wearing her work clothes was the right thing to do. In the dress she'd have felt awkward, attracting attention that she didn't want.

A maid led them through the hall to a parlour that overlooked the small garden. A few early flowers brought splashes of colour against the brown of the earth. The grass was carefully tended, cut close, a bright, brilliant green.

Five minutes passed before Mrs Parker entered. She was a tall, plump woman, dressed in a fashionable gown of dark blue silk that rippled and cascaded around her body, cunningly cut to hide her weight. Her skin was pale, her eyes grey. Jane felt the woman's gaze and returned it.

'I'm glad you came,' Mrs Parker said as she settled into a chair and perched a china cup and saucer on her lap. 'Both of you.' She turned to Simon. 'I want to engage your services.'

'You understand what we do?' Simon asked. 'We find items that have been stolen and return them.'

Mrs Parker gave a short, impatient nod. 'Credit me with some intelligence, Mr Westow. Of course I know exactly what you do. I'm also very well aware of the fee you charge. Believe me, if I hadn't heard excellent reports of your work, you wouldn't be standing here.'

Jane watched Simon give a small bow and try to hide his frown.

'What do you need from us? What's been taken?'

Mrs Parker took a sip of coffee before she answered. 'I was foolish enough to let my guard down around a gentleman I believed I knew well. His name is Thomas Rawlings and he took advantage of me.'

'How much?'

'Almost fifty pounds.' The woman gave a rueful smile. 'It's a very great deal to most people, I know that. It was my own fault. I was too ready to believe him on many things. When he asked to borrow the money until the allowance from his father arrived, I agreed. He took it and left me.'

Jane tried to make sense of what she'd just heard. Fifty pounds was a fortune to most people, but she treated it like barely more than a few coins. Why would he leave a woman who would provide for him like that? Something rang hollow in it all.

Mrs Parker raised her head. 'I'm sure you're aware of my reputation, Mr Westow.'

'I've heard rumours,' Simon answered after a long pause.

The woman smiled. There was something behind Mrs Parker's eyes, Jane thought. Coldness. Cruelty. 'Very tactfully put. I daresay much of what you've been told is true, and I don't regret a single moment.' Her voice hardened again and her expression changed. 'But I refuse to be played for a fool by a braggart and a liar.'

Simon was slow to respond; even then his words were hesitant. 'We have a great deal of work at the moment, but we can spend a little time looking for him. Is that acceptable?'

A lie and Jane knew it. Their only job was finding the body snatchers. This was his way of accepting it without completely taking it on.

'If you're as good as people claim.'

'Do you intend to prosecute?'

'No,' she told him. 'What I want is for the pair of you to find him, then come and tell me where he is. Nothing more than that.'

'Why?' Simon tried to hide his astonishment. 'Usually we recover the—'

She cut him off. 'I'm quite sure you have your way of doing things. But if you work for me, then you'll do it as I wish. Is that clear?' Her voice was calm, but hard as steel.

Jane could feel Simon start to bristle. For a second, she wasn't sure if he'd stay or walk out.

'I see.'

'Do your job and leave the rest to me. I want my revenge on Thomas Rawlings.'

'Do you intend to harm him?'

'That's none of your business,' Mrs Parker said.

'Yes, it is. If it's part of your plan, we won't be taking this job,' he told her.

'Then let me put your mind at rest. I don't intend to hurt him. Not physically, at least. I want my money back, and I want him humiliated.'

'If people know what he's done, they'll find out he . . . eased the money from you.'

'Let them.' Her tone was sharp, tinged with anger. 'It'll hardly be the first time people have talked about me. But he needs to realize there are consequences, so he won't try it again with someone else. And,' she added, 'no one else will try to see me as an easy touch.'

'Do you know if he's still in Leeds?'

'I haven't heard a word about him since he left. That was a week ago.' She considered for a moment, impatiently tapping a fingernail against her teeth. 'I imagine he must have stayed in town. His friends are here and he has long credit with the tradesmen. I can't see him going anywhere else.'

'You said his name's Thomas Rawlings?'

'Yes.' She gave a small snort. 'He likes people to call him Tom.'

Jane cleared her throat. 'Why did you want me to be here?'

'I wanted a look at a girl who does this type of work,' Mrs Parker told her. 'People have told me you're dangerous.'

She shrugged; she couldn't control what others said. She didn't like Mrs Parker.

'Tom' – the woman stretched out the name – 'has a weakness for a certain type of young woman.'

'What type might that be?' Simon asked. She could hear his ominous tone, but the woman didn't seem to notice.

'Someone from the street. When he was drunk, he liked to boast about bargaining whores on Briggate down from sixpence to twopence because they were desperate.'

Jane had met plenty of men like that. Sometimes they'd try to stop her as she walked. She always ignored them. If they persisted, she'd show her knife. That was usually enough to send them scurrying away.

'I—' Simon began, but Mrs Parker held up a hand to silence him and turned to Jane again.

'He might take a fancy to you. You have the look of a stray. It might be a good way to lure him—'

'No.' Simon's voice rode over her words.

'No?'

'We work in our own way,' he said. 'If you want our services, then you let us do our job.'

Mrs Parker raised an eyebrow. 'What do you say, girl? He allows you to think for yourself, doesn't he?'

'Simon just told you.'

'I know Tom Rawlings,' the woman said. 'I know how his mind works. Believe me, he'd come sniffing around you.'

Without another word, Jane stood and began to walk to the door. She heard Simon's footsteps behind her on the polished floor.

She was reaching for the door handle when Mrs Parker spoke again.

'If you're going to insist, then try it your way. See if it works.'

'I told you, we're busy.' He paused. 'I'm willing to give it two days, putting in time when we have it. But you give us free rein,' Simon told her. 'No interference.'

A long pause.

'Agreed,' she said reluctantly.

'As you only want us to find him, our fee will be due when we give you that information.'

'I understand.'

Outside, Jane blinked in the sunlight. 'We should just have left.'

Simon glanced back at the door. 'I don't trust her.'

'Why did you agree to do it?'

He rubbed his chin. 'She's up to something. I want to see what it is.'

People who used their services wanted their stolen items returned. That was all. They rarely asked questions or made demands. Fifty pounds, he thought . . . even for someone as rich as Mrs Parker was supposed to be, that was a large sum.

Simon followed, walking slowly as Jane started to march back into town.

She stopped and turned, looking at him. 'Do you believe her?'

'I believe she's looking for him,' he answered after a moment, trying to form his thoughts into words. 'I'm willing to accept that.' People rarely told him everything; he'd learned that over the years. There was always something they held back. 'As for anything more, I think it's mostly lies. There's a lot she hasn't said. It makes me want to know what it is. Why did she pick *us*? Why does she want us involved?'

'She's playing a game. I still don't see why she wanted me there.'

'No,' he admitted. 'Maybe Mrs Parker thinks she's being clever. I don't know. But if she's making us part of whatever game she's playing, I want to find out so we can protect ourselves.'

'When we were about to walk out . . .'

'I noticed. She was quick enough to give in.' He frowned. 'Two days,' he said. 'We can fit it in around hunting for the body snatchers. If we find him, then we'll decide what to do. If not, I'll tell her we're stopping and she can hire someone else.'

Jane nodded. The day held the promise of spring, but the thought of the woman made her shiver. It wasn't just her: as they left, the coachman had been there again, standing with his arms folded, eyes on her, never looking away when she turned towards him. 'Where do you want to begin?'

Simon shrugged. 'She said he likes prostitutes. Why don't you talk to some of them?'

But most of them wouldn't appear until the shadows lengthened. Before that she'd see if there was any news of the man who'd sold the burial gown, or his companion.

Simon walked, feeling the anger burn in his belly. The woman had a plan of some kind. As if she was trying to trap him into something. Trying to use him. She didn't have quite enough guile to hide it properly.

Why did he agree to work for her? A good question. He should have followed Jane's lead and walked away. Too late now. But if he could find out what she was planning, he could stop it. Protect himself.

Two days. A few small hours squeezed around the rest of their business. Long enough to see how things stood, at least. Maybe he'd discover the truth. Then he could decide what to do about it.

As he asked around town about body snatchers, Simon felt like a man hunting for the key to a lock he couldn't see. Nobody he talked to would admit to knowing a thing about stealing the dead. They all claimed that they'd never met anyone who did. He believed most of them. There were always a few who glanced furtively away as they answered, not willing to look him in the eye.

What did that prove? He had no choice but to carry on, going around and around, asking his questions, hoping that somewhere he could find his way into all this.

By late afternoon his voice was hoarse. He'd recited the same phrases so often that he didn't need to think about them. Every time he came up with nothing. As he left the small, smoky dramshop on Kirkgate, a man slipped out behind him. Simon started to reach for his knife, but the man hurried past. As he turned into a ginnel, he glanced back.

That was enough. Simon followed. The man was waiting where the passage opened into a yard, careful to keep his face half in shadow.

'What you're asking about . . .'

He had a thick accent. Not from Leeds, or any town he knew. Somewhere out in the country, perhaps.

'What about it?'

'How much is it worth?'

'That depends on what you can tell me.'

The man was silent, eyes moving nervously as he made sure no one was watching them. 'A name or two.'

Simon shook his head. 'Anyone can pass on a name. It doesn't mean a thing.'

'I could tell you where they took their last two.'

Two. Two bodies. He breathed deep.

'How many have there been in all?'

The man chuckled. 'Willing to pay now, are you?'

Three shillings. A very generous sum. Simon placed the coins in the man's palm. The skin was hard, cracked and ingrained deep with dirt. A raw chuckle as he tipped the money into his pocket.

'You need to find Harold Ackroyd and Peter Kingsley. They're the ones who do most of it. They have someone else who does the heavy work for them.'

'Who?'

A shrug. 'I don't know his name. Everyone just calls him the Irishman. He's big, very strong. You'd do well to watch out for him, though. He could crack your skull without trying.'

'How do you know them?'

The man shook his head. 'Your money doesn't buy you that.'

Simon hesitated. He didn't want to ask the question again, but he couldn't stop himself. He needed to know.

'How many have there been?'

'Seven. Maybe even more by now.'

FIVE

Seven. He felt dizzy, off-balance in the world. Seven corpses stolen from their graves. Seven. He knew about one: Gwendolyn Jordan. That left six families who believed they still had a father, a mother, a daughter or a son under the sod.

Resurrectionists. That was the name one writer in the newspapers had given the body snatchers. But there was no eternal life waiting after the corpses were pulled from the ground. The only thing that remained was the brutality of dissection, then back to the soil, nameless and alone.

Simon felt the bile rise again and forced it back down. Seven. Seven, for the love of God.

Harold Ackroyd. Peter Kingsley. The Irishman. Now he knew who he was hunting, they should be easy to find. One of them would have sold the burial gown. They'd pay. Joseph Clark had the power to make sure of that.

Dr Thackrah was standing in the afternoon sun on King Street, looking at the flowers blooming in the small park outside the infirmary as he smoked a cigar. He was the town surgeon, one of the few doctors who gave any consideration to the poor and the factory workers.

But he'd trained pupils, several of them. His students. They might need bodies to learn their trade.

'Westow?' He rolled Simon's name around his tongue. 'I've heard your name before. From Dr Hey, perhaps?'

'It's possible. I know him. I'm the thief-taker.'

Thackrah had a vivid, intense air. Short hair, a thin, hooked nose and small, steel-framed spectacles. His shirt collar was stiff with starch and his stock was a brilliant white.

'That's right, I remember now. What can I do for you?'

'I'm curious if you know anything about body snatching.'

Thackrah narrowed his eyes. 'I hope you're not accusing me, Mr Westow.'

Simon shook his head. 'Nothing like that. I believe there are

schools of anatomy where pupils are . . . encouraged to supply
their own bodies for dissection.'

'That's what I've heard,' the man said. His voice was even,
non-committal. 'But I can assure you there's nothing like that
here.'

'I'm certain there's not,' he agreed quickly. 'But *if* bodies were
taken in Leeds, where might they be sent?'

'Are they being taken?'

Simon looked at him and said nothing.

'My God.' The words hissed out of his mouth. 'They are.'

'I'm not going to say one way or another, doctor.' Seven. The
anger burned through him.

'I see.' Thackrah hadn't known, that was obvious. His expression slid from shock to disgust to thought. 'There are medical
schools in London and Edinburgh. I've heard stories – probably
everyone in the profession has – but I didn't know they were
real or just sensation.'

'They're real. You have pupils, don't you?'

'My apprentices, yes. We don't have a medical school of any
kind here.'

'Do you train them in anatomy?'

'As best I can. Without human bodies, it's difficult. But—'

Simon held up his hand. 'As I said, I'm not accusing you,
doctor. Not for a minute.'

Thackrah glared at him before nodding. 'I'll take you at your
word. But be very careful what you suggest, Mr Westow.'

'Has anyone ever approached you, offering bodies for sale?'

'Once. Back in January. I turned him away. I didn't believe a
word of it.'

Just three months earlier, Simon thought. Interesting. 'Do you
remember what he looked like?'

'Not really. He wasn't especially clean. Dark hair, I think. He
said he could get me a body, but he wanted three pounds in
advance, another five on delivery. I told him to leave.'

Eight pounds in total. A very tidy sum.

'Seven bodies have been dug up in Leeds and sold.' He paused
long enough for the words to sink in. 'At least seven.'

Thackrah looked down at the ground, frowning. It seemed like
a long time before he spoke.

'I see.'

'One of them was a girl aged ten,' Simon continued. 'Her name was Gwendolyn.' He wanted the man to know, to understand that each body had been a real person and that a family mourned them. 'Her mother discovered that the grave had been disturbed.'

'Is that who hired you?'

'In a manner of speaking.' It was a good enough answer. 'I'm going to find the people responsible.'

'I hope you do. But I'm sure you know they'll spend very little time in prison. Six months, most likely less.'

Simon tried to make out his tone. But Thackrah's voice was flat, giving little away.

'Believe me, doctor, I'm very aware of that. Gwendolyn's parents had a burial gown made for her. The body snatchers stole it and sold it. *That* is a felony.'

'I wish you luck, Mr Westow. It's an horrific crime. As I told you, it had nothing to do with me.' He tossed his cigar on the ground and ambled back towards the infirmary.

Jane drifted around Leeds. Nobody noticed her as she walked with a shawl over her hair. No messages waiting with Kate the pie-seller. The groups of children she asked hadn't managed to find the man who'd sold the burial gown or his friend.

She'd given up, walking home along the Head Row when she sensed someone behind her. Just a presence, no real threat or danger. Still, she twisted the gold ring on her finger, the one Mrs Shields had given her, for luck, reached into the pocket of her dress and took hold of her knife, then slipped into a ginnel and waited.

It only took a few seconds for him to appear, and he stopped and raised his hands as soon as he spotted the blade. The boy was no more than ten, barefoot and dirty, wearing a pair of threadbare trousers and a shirt that hadn't been white for many years.

Jane recognized his face. He was always there, around the other children. Someone who remained on the edges, standing a little apart with a serious, intent expression on his face, never close to anyone.

'What do you want?'

He looked straight into her eyes, not afraid or hesitant. 'You're looking for two men, aren't you?'

Jane looked back at him. No guile; he wasn't hiding anything. 'That's not a secret. Do you have something to tell me?'

'I know who one of them is,' he said. 'Not his name, but what they call him.'

'Which one?'

'The big man.' He waited.

She placed three pennies on his palm. 'Go on.'

'Everyone calls him the Irishman.'

That was something useful. 'What else can you tell me about him?'

'He wears a top hat that's all out of shape.' Dodson the beggar had mentioned someone like that. 'I've seen him a few times by that hill beyond Marsh Lane.'

'Near the York Road? Is that where you mean?'

'Yes.'

'Does he live there?' she asked.

The boy shook his head. 'I don't know. I've only seen him walking, that's all. Sometimes he carries a spade and an axe over his shoulder.'

He might be a labourer. Or they could be tools for digging up corpses.

'Anything else? What's your name?'

'Walter.' He thought for a moment. 'I heard him speak once. The way he talks, I couldn't make out more than a word of what he was saying.'

'Why?' she asked. 'Does he have a problem with his voice?'

He shook his head. 'No, I don't think it's that. The man he was with seemed to understand him easily.'

An Irishman; it would make sense for him to have an accent. Jane smiled and took out three more coins. Walter had earned them; he'd given her a start when nobody else seemed able to help. 'If you can find out anything else, look for me. I'll pay you.'

His eyes widened as if he'd never owned so much money. Jane remembered what it was like to survive outside, to scramble through each day. Sixpence would keep him alive for a while.

'I will.' He ran off as quickly as he'd arrived.

He was earnest; there was nothing light-hearted about the boy. The type who meant everything he said or did. She believed what he'd told her.

*   *   *

'The Irishman,' Simon said. 'Interesting. Someone else gave me the name, too. If he wears a hat like that he should be easy enough to spot. I was told that he's the one who does the digging. He works with a pair called Harold Ackroyd and Peter Kingsley.'

'One of them must have sold Gwendolyn Jordan's burial gown,' Rosie said.

It had to be. They wouldn't want anyone else involved; too much danger from loose tongues.

Jane sat on the other side of the table, staring down at the wood. Simon could hear the boys in the yard, Richard arguing loudly with Amos, then quiet again before they began to laugh.

'The man who gave me the names told me something else.' He hadn't said it yet. He'd tried to force it away, but it wouldn't leave his mind. Simon rubbed the heels of his hands against his eyes. Seven. Impossible to believe. But they needed to know. Maybe everyone in Leeds should hear it.

'What is it?' Rosie asked. 'Simon?'

'He claims they've taken seven bodies around town. Possibly more than that.'

Silence filled the room. What words could measure the horror? Nothing that could begin to do justice to the dead.

'Seven,' Rosie said finally. The word fell like a tear.

He stood, his chair scraping across the floorboards.

'Let's find them,' he said. 'We'll put a little work in on Tom Rawlings for Mrs Parker, too.'

'I'll talk to the women tonight,' Jane said.

A nod and she was gone into the evening.

'Seven.' Rosie gazed out of the window, watching their boys playing. He came up behind and wrapped his arms around her waist. The twins were so quick, so filled with life.

'We know who to look for now. That's a start.'

'I meant what I said, Simon. Don't keep me out of this. They have to pay.' Her voice was winter.

'You'll be there,' he promised.

'Watch out for Amanda Parker,' she told him.

'I will. Believe me, I will.'

A few of the whores were already out and shouting for custom. Flirting, teasing; this wasn't a trade for the shy, Jane knew that.

The women laughed and joked; they looked as if they were enjoying themselves, but underneath all that they had to possess an iron core to survive. Too many had been murdered or injured by men who didn't want to pay for what the women were selling, who believed they had a right to it. Once they were in the shadows, every customer could be a killer.

The women had all seen Jane before. They accepted her; she came around with her questions and offered money for solid information. It was an easy way to earn a few pennies.

'Do you know a man called Tom Rawlings?'

A shake of the head, an empty look. It was no surprise. Most men who came sniffing down here never gave their names, certainly not their real ones. But someone might be able to point her in the right direction.

She'd been going around for half an hour when a woman cocked her head.

'Fancy fellow, is he? Flash?'

'Yes,' Jane replied. She didn't know. Very likely, if he was with Mrs Parker.

'There's one I've noticed a few times. Once I spotted him walking with that woman.' Her voice dripped with a sad mix of hope and envy. 'You know, the one who started out down here and ended up rich.'

Jane smiled at the description. Short, to the point. She could only mean Mrs Parker. 'That's him. Have you seen him lately?'

The woman shook her head. Her hair hung in dark curls, but they were greasy, unwashed, and the strain of hunger showed around her mouth. She kept careful hold of her left hand to try to stop it from shaking. 'I don't think so. Not in a few weeks. Why do you want him?'

'Someone's looking for him, that's all.'

The answer seemed to satisfy. She shouted to a woman who leaned against a wall on the other side of Briggate, holding a fan in front of her face, 'When did you last see Betsy?'

'Which Betsy?'

'The one with the cast in the corner of her eye.'

'Don't know. A week, maybe. It could be longer.'

'Who's Betsy?' Jane asked.

'That man, he liked her,' the woman replied. 'She's pretty enough, I suppose, apart from her eye. But if you look at her from the left side, you don't see it. He spent the night with her sometimes, maybe longer. Always paid her well. She'd have a little money to treat us to a pie the next day.'

'Where does she live?' Jane brought money from her pocket.

'I don't know.' The woman closed her fist around the coins. 'Why don't you come back in two hours? I might be able to find out more.'

She had a name now, a small description. Some of the others knew Betsy with the cast, but there was little else they could tell her. Finally, as the clock struck ten, Jane returned to Briggate.

'She lives near the York Road. That's what I was told.'

'Anything besides that?'

She shook her head. 'You know how it is. We like to keep our lives separate from all this.' A few more coins. The woman's hand was steady now. Jane could smell gin on her breath.

'Look for me if you hear anything more.'

Enough for one night. It was a good start. As she made her way home, she thought about Mrs Parker again, trying to imagine what else the woman could want with them.

Early business was brisk at the coffee cart outside the Bull and Mouth on Briggate. A clear morning, a bracing chill in the air that would soon fade. Men queued, grateful to pay for a tin mug of something hot to drink and a slice of bread and dripping to line their bellies before they went to work.

It was a good place to hear gossip, too. Rumours and whispers always floated through the air here. Often it was nothing, but some-times . . . sometimes Simon heard things that were important.

Not today, though. He drank and listened and asked a few questions, hoping that someone might know the Irishman. But half an hour brought little. He drifted away, down Kirkgate and across Timble Bridge, over to Marsh Lane and the hill beyond.

There were plenty of houses on the bank of land between Mill Street and Richmond Road; more were going up all the time. Terraces of them, still so new that the bricks didn't even have a patina of soot yet. Quickly thrown together, cheap and shoddy, each one a quick profit for the builders. Some looked as if a strong wind might make them topple. The landscape was changing every day in this part of town.

Rented out, a family packed into each room, a landlord could

make good money here. The streets were unpaved, only a runnel
for sewage down the middle of the road, brimming with the stink
of old piss and shit. A couple of feral dogs roamed, eyeing him
warily.

As he passed, Simon could hear people talking inside one
house. Elsewhere the cry of a baby, voices raised in arguments.
He strode along the streets, making a map of them in his head.
If the Irishman lived up here, it would help to have a good idea
of the place.

An hour and he was home again. Rosie was bustling around,
feeding Richard and Amos and making sure they were prepared
for their tutor. He quizzed them on the homework they'd been
given, satisfied with the answers. A few more years and they'd
move beyond any learning he possessed. Good, that was what
he wanted for them. A proper education to give them a founda-
tion in the world.

Their lessons had begun by the time Jane arrived and told him
what she'd learned about Rawlings and a prostitute named Betsy.

'Off the York Road?' Simon said with interest.

'Yes. I'll go up there and ask.'

'I was over that way earlier this morning. I wanted to see
if I could get a feel for the Irishman.' He rubbed his chin. 'Both
of them in a small area. That's quite a coincidence.'

'Why would there be a link?' Jane pursed her lips.

He sighed. 'There probably isn't. The housing's cheap. I'm
probably seeing things that aren't there.'

'I'll try to find out if anyone knows this woman Betsy or the
Irishman up there.'

'While you're doing that, I'll hunt for a sniff of Harold Ackroyd
and Peter Kingsley.'

He needed to be careful. Simon didn't want word to reach the
men that someone was asking about them. Nothing that might
scare them off.

Barnabas Wade was standing by the bar in the Talbot, waiting
for the Newcastle coach to arrive with passengers he could
persuade to buy his worthless stocks. Once he'd been a lawyer,
until he was disbarred. Now he survived on a glib tongue and
careful contracts that protected him. But he had sharp ears. He
heard plenty of things.

'Harold Ackroyd? I don't know the name,' he said with certainty.

'What about Kingsley?'

'I think someone might have mentioned him last week. I'm just trying to remember what they said.'

Simon bought him a brandy and waited. This wasn't a trick for free drinks. Wade didn't need that. He knew something.

'That's it,' he said with a satisfied nod. 'He seemed to be spending money, buying drinks for people.'

'Very generous of him. Where was this? Who told you?'

Wade shrugged. 'I've no idea. I talk to a lot of people, Simon. It was just chatter; I didn't pay it much mind.'

'Do you know him at all?'

'Kingsley? I've met him once or twice, that's all. He likes to play cards, although he's not as good as he imagines. You know the type, believes he's cleverer than he really is.'

He knew, all right; he'd met enough of them in his time. So many looked to crime. It was a quick way to make money. Most of them were easy to catch. They were the bread and butter of his trade.

'What does he look like?'

'There's nothing much about him,' Wade answered after a few seconds. 'His hair is light brown, almost fair I suppose. He's not especially thin or fat or tall or small.'

'How old?'

Wade shrugged. 'In his late twenties, at a guess. I doubt he's any older than that. Why do you want him, anyway? What's he done?'

'It might be nothing,' Simon lied. 'But I won't know until I talk to him.'

SIX

Jane had been through these streets so often that she didn't need to think where she was going; she simply *felt* the way in her bones.

It was easy enough to ask questions. The women who ran the small shops all knew their customers. If Betsy didn't spend her money at one place, she'd buy her food and tea at another. With the cast in her eye, people were certain to remember her.

She found what she needed in the third shop she tried. It was small, poor, barely room enough for four people, just a few goods scattered on the shelf and half a sack of flour on the flour that looked as if it had been nibbled by rats.

'I know who you mean, right enough,' the woman said. She pulled the shawl closer around her throat, as if she needed its protection. 'I don't think I've ever heard her name, though. But I've seen her and I know what she does. You only have to look at her to tell.'

Jane placed three pennies on the counter. 'Where does she live?'

The woman nodded down the hill. 'Goulden's Yard. Don't ask me whereabouts in there, I couldn't tell you. I tried to be friendly, but she's not one for talking.'

'Have you ever seen her with a man?'

The woman sniffed. 'I have. A right one, too, always looking down his nose when he walks around here. Like he doesn't think we're good enough for his sort.'

Rawlings, she thought, it had to be. 'Have you spotted them together lately?'

'I might have.'

Another couple of pennies. 'When?'

'Must be three days back, or maybe it was four. Not twenty-four hours before that, she'd been standing talking to another man, too, friendly as you like.'

Jane felt the pulse quicken in her wrist. 'Another one? Who was he? Anyone you know?'

'Course it was.' She gave a withering look. 'Everyone round here knows the Irishman.'

'The Irishman?' She could scarcely believe what she'd just heard.

'That's what we all call him, any road. He told me his name once, but I forgot it. He's from over there, Ireland, you can hardly make sense of a word he says. Him and the girl, they have an understanding.' She pursed her lips, disapproving. 'When she's not got that other man with her, the Irishman looks after things. He takes care of affairs if someone gives her a problem.'

'He lives nearby?'

'He moves around a lot.' The woman shrugged. 'Not settled, like. I suppose it's just his way.'

For a moment Jane couldn't speak. She was trying to think, surprised to have learned so much so quickly, scarcely believing the way the pieces seemed to click together. It didn't seem possible. Then she put down two more coins, thanked the woman and hurried out.

Goulden's Yard. She stood by the entrance, staring at the buildings. A pair of small warehouses, a workshop and two houses surrounded a cobbled yard. The doors were open at the businesses, men moving about, the hammering of a machine. She glanced around. There was no place out of sight where she could easily watch as people came and went.

Jane turned and started to walk back along Marsh Lane. She had plenty to tell Simon.

He had to force himself to remain quiet until she finished. Sometimes Jane didn't understand just how good she was at all this, he thought. Not only could she follow without being seen, she brought back information that was pure gold.

The Irishman. He was there with the body snatchers, and now he was connected to Betsy and Rawlings. He was the linchpin. But why would those two things come together? Where was Mrs Parker in this? It seemed impossible that she'd be involved with body snatching. Why would she do something like that?

'What do we do next?' Jane's voice interrupted his thoughts.

'Rawlings,' Simon answered. 'He and this woman Betsy should be able to lead us to the Irishman, whoever he is. I'd like to be prepared by the time we meet him.'

'If we're going into her house, there are men working in Goulden's Yard during the day.'

'Tonight, then.' Better if there were no onlookers who might remember them. 'Meet at dusk.'

He had the afternoon free to take Richard and Amos out, to run on the moorland west of town. Each year, Leeds crept farther and farther; it was becoming impossible to keep track of it all. He'd go to an area he hadn't visited in a few months and find it filled with new streets, all freshly risen from the ground and bustling with people he didn't know. The face of the town was constantly shifting from week to week.

Simon watched the boys run, wondering if he'd ever had that much energy. It didn't matter; let them enjoy it. He watched and wandered until they were beginning to flag, then shepherded them back home again. There were far worse ways to spend a few hours.

Goulden's Yard was dark. The workshops were closed up for the night, and the warehouse offered a blank face.

'The houses are over there,' Jane said quietly. No lights showed in either of them. The first was locked. Simon took out his picks, tried one, then a second, feeling it slide in easily. He held his breath as it caught, then gently turned and they were in.

A man lived here, he thought. The smell gave it away. Tobacco, the ripeness of sweat. A single room in front of them as they entered, another above. Jane hurried up the stairs as Simon walked around, lifting things and putting them down again. No trace of a woman.

He waited by the door until Jane reappeared.

'Nothing,' she whispered.

It had to be next door. As long as Jane had been told the truth. He touched the handle. It turned in his grip and he hesitated. Cautiously, he pushed it open. The angry buzz of flies came from somewhere. A strong stink of decay drifted across the air. Simon halted for a moment, breathing through his mouth. Jane nodded and slipped past him.

She picked her way up the stairs as Simon searched below. The detritus of a life: a broken comb, chipped and worn. A sliver of mirror resting on a table. Not a single thing to identify the person who lived here.

'Come up here.' Jane's voice was low.

He kept his tread soft. In the bedroom the shutters were open, offering a little light. This was where the flies had gathered, loud, crowded across the corpse in the bed. He waved them away and peered down at the face.

Not Betsy. He was looking at a man. Simon swatted the flies again, reached out and touched the cheek. From the texture of the skin, he'd been dead for a few days. Maggots were crawling in his mouth and nostrils. Good features, thick, dark hair. Simon pulled down the sheet and another swarm of flies rose up around him. A single cut on the chest, between the ribs, and a puddle of blood dried under him. Gold rings on the first and little fingers of his right hand.

He'd never seen the man before, but he knew full well who it had to be.

Tom Rawlings.

'Betsy must have taken her clothes,' Jane said. 'I don't expect she had many.'

'No.'

Time to go, he thought, before someone came and discovered them here. A few seconds at the door with the picks, making sure he left it locked tight. That would slow anyone trying to wander inside. Then they were moving through the darkness, out on to Marsh Lane and back across Timble Bridge into Leeds. Finally he felt he could breathe again without tasting the stench of death.

'Are we going to tell the constable?' Jane asked. 'It's murder.'

'No,' he said to her. 'We're not going to tell a soul. Not even Mrs Parker.'

'But—'

'I know.' The woman was the whole reason they'd been in Goulden's Court. Strange that their first glimpse of Tom Rawlings should be his corpse. Did she know he was dead? Was this part of whatever game she was playing, trying to drag them deep into a mess? He didn't know and he wasn't about to give her any kind of hold over him. Sooner or later, someone would discover the body. For now, Simon intended to stay silent. 'Safer if we were never here.'

'All right,' she agreed.

Who'd killed him? The Irishman? He had to be the obvious

candidate. Betsy? Equally possible. Why, though? Something bigger was going on, and that was another reason to stand back and watch what happened. Murder wasn't a thief-taker's business. It belonged to the law, and if Constable Porter learned Simon had been here, he'd be arresting him and dragging him off to gaol.

'Go home as if nothing had happened,' Simon told her. 'We'll talk about it tomorrow.'

'What about you?'

'I need to find a body snatcher who likes to gamble.'

Simon was right, she thought. There was no need to invite trouble; it always arrived of its own accord.

As Jane walked, she tried to make sense of the day. It was a tangle, lines that curled and wove around each other. She couldn't straighten them. Not until they knew much more.

Briggate was busy, men spilling out from the inns and beer-shops. She drifted by; hardly a soul glanced at her. As she turned on to the Head Row, she had no sense of anyone following, and by the time she reached Green Dragon Yard, she knew she was completely alone. Through the gap in the wall, then she was home.

Mrs Shields had banked the fire. The room was warm. She checked on the old woman, tucking the covers around her, then settled near the hearth. Jane opened the book that lay on the table and started to read. Slowly, she traced the words with her fingertip and soon she was caught up in the story of the Bennet sisters. Their lives were utterly different from hers, but the writer made it seem so real. She was there with them. How could anyone do that?

Simon stood with a mug of beer, leaning against the wall in the Yorkshire Grey on Kirkgate, idly watching a group playing cards at one of the tables.

He'd heard one of them called Peter. After a few minutes he turned to another of the spectators. 'That man on the far side,' Simon said. 'The one called Peter. I'm sure I know him from somewhere. What is his surname?'

'Kingsley.' He turned away.

He had his man. Easier than he dared hope. But he certainly

wasn't the one who'd sold the burial gown. He was much as Wade had described him, in his twenties, wearing a shirt and stock.

For the rest of the evening Simon sat in a corner, out of sight of the man. Sipping, patient, thinking about poor dead Tom Rawlings. He considered what to do. Tomorrow he'd go and see Mrs Parker, tell her they hadn't found a trace of the man yet and bow out of things. What would happen when the body was discovered? When Constable Porter came to Mrs Parker with his questions, she'd tell him how she'd employed Simon and Jane to hunt for Rawlings. But the longer it took, the murkier the waters would be. And it might give him time to discover the real murderer.

He waited. Kingsley loved his cards. Hand after hand after hand. Winning a few, losing more. The man wasn't a heavy drinker, only two glasses of gin in an hour. Finally he stood, swallowing the dregs and placing a billycock hat on his head.

Simon waited for half a minute, then followed him into the night.

Kingsley idled along, hands in his pockets, unaware that anyone was behind him. Up Kirkgate, turning on to Vicar Lane. Simon was happy to keep distance between them, close enough to keep him in sight, but not near enough to rouse suspicions. It was a chance to think more about Rawlings.

As Kingsley vanished on to Wood Street, Simon began to walk faster. The lane was barely wider than a ginnel, winding through to Briggate. But before he could reach the turning, a man stepped out of the shadows.

'In a hurry, friend?'

He was smirking. Lanky, thin, dressed in clothes barely better than rags. A knife dangled from his hand. Simon cursed himself. He'd let his mind stray, hadn't been alert.

'I am,' he replied. 'You'd better step aside.'

The man shook his head. 'There's always a toll to pay when I'm here, friend.'

Just a robber, out for anything he could take. Not someone sent after him. Be grateful for small mercies, Simon thought.

'No,' he said.

The man pushed his lips together. Simon could smell the beer on his breath. 'Then you don't give me any choice. I'll have to hurt you before I take your money.'

He extended his hand. His blade was dull, rusted. He was slow, as if he believed simply owning a weapon gave him power. Too slow. In the time it took him to advance a single pace, Simon had grabbed his wrist and twisted it. The knife clattered on to the flagstones.

'Never threaten to hurt,' Simon told him, 'unless you're sure you can win.'

The man tried to wriggle away. More pressure and he gave a cry of pain that echoed off the buildings.

'I'll find you, friend.'

A final push, and Simon felt the man's bone crack. He let go and pushed him down to the ground. He'd be in no state to rob anyone for a while.

'You do that. I'll even save you the trouble of looking. Have you heard of Simon Westow, the thief-taker?'

'Yes.'

'That's me. Friend. I'll be waiting for you.'

The man scrambled to his feet and ran, clutching his broken wrist. A few seconds and only the echo of his footsteps hung in the night air. Simon could feel the blood pulsing in his temples and the fast, heavy thud of his heart. Damn the man. It was too late to catch up to Kingsley now. He could have gone anywhere. No matter, he thought; there would be another time.

SEVEN

The morning was heavy with sound. Traders trundled slowly up and down Briggate, squeezing either side of the old Moot Hall that stood like an island in the middle of the street. Coach drivers waited impatiently to go by and make speed.

Simon stood at the coffee cart outside the Bull and Mouth, listening as people talked. Always the freshest news in Leeds, better than the *Intelligencer* or the *Mercury*. There were mutterings of this and that, the scandal of a woman seen out and about with a fellow who wasn't her husband, the rumour of a man who'd gambled his fortune away. No one mentioned Tom Rawlings.

He walked, feeling the freshness of the day vanish as smoke from the factory chimneys began to cloud the air. He knew he'd been fortunate last night. The robber had been inept and Simon had been quick and decisive. But it wouldn't always be that way. Sooner or later someone would decide to try his luck, to see if he was a better fighter than the thief-taker. Eventually Simon would lose; that was the way of the world. Until then, the more he could use his tongue instead of his blade, the longer he'd stay alive.

Machines were thumping behind brick walls, looms whirring in the mills, making the music of Leeds. Tonight he'd go out again and find Kingsley. This time he'd discover where he lived. For now he wanted to hunt down Harold Ackroyd, the other body snatcher. The man with the white moustache and the missing finger. He had to be the one who'd sold the burial gown.

By noon he'd learned a little more. For a few months, Ackroyd had shovelled coal into a boiler at a factory. Then he'd started a fight with the foreman and left him dazed and bloody on the floor. He'd worked as a porter on the river, supervising others who hauled heavy sacks on and off the barges. But not everything listed on the bill of lading reached the warehouse; Ackroyd had something going on the side. After a while he became too greedy, and the owners let him go.

It wasn't that much information, just enough to build a vague impression of the man. Strong, with a brittle temper. One of life's natural criminals, eager for some easy money.

He had a sketch of Ackroyd's past. A useful beginning, but it didn't help him find the man now.

Simon stayed clear of the area beyond Timble Bridge, nowhere near Goulden's Court or the streets that ran off the York Road. It would be helpful to know more about Thomas Rawlings and what his body was doing in a house there, but he wasn't going to start asking questions people might remember. Let it lie.

Finally he gave up and went home. Time for a rest before he hunted the gambler again.

Jane wandered. She covered the area between Marsh Lane and the York Road, from Sexton Street and Marton Lane, past Paley's Galleries and down to William Street, all the way over to Muck Lane. With the shawl covering her hair, she was just one more figure moving through the day; completely unmemorable.

She stopped in a few of the shops dotted around the area, spending a copper or two in each, just on ordinary things – a twist of tea, a slice of cheese. Unimportant items. A chance to ask a question or two.

'You're new round here, aren't you?' The women behind the counter always began with the same question. They knew every face on the nearby streets.

She had her lie prepared. 'I've been working up at Burmantofts Hall, except they don't have anything for me today.'

The words fell so naturally that they surprised her. For a moment she could almost believe them herself.

'When I was passing yesterday evening, I saw a woman on the next street over. I could have sworn I knew her.'

'Oh?' the shopkeeper asked. 'What was she like?'

'She's not old. We worked at the same mill a year or two ago. She has a cast in her eye.'

The first three times brought nothing. The fourth woman, with a tidy little place on the corner of New Row, had an answer.

'Oh aye, she was in here yesterday, buying bread and butter. Not seen her before, mind. There was a man waiting outside for her. Big bruiser, he was. She told me they'd just moved in round the corner.'

Jane felt her heart beating a little faster. She was close.

'Did she tell you her name? For the life of me I can't remember it.'

'No, and I didn't ask.' She sniffed, slighted. 'It's not my place, is it?'

'No,' she agreed. She'd learned enough. Anything further would be pressing too hard. She wished the woman good day and left. She could return another time. If the shopkeeper had learned more about Betsy, Jane knew the woman would pass it on, happy to share the gossip.

Simon put the twins to bed and made up a story to lull them into sleep. Finally, he doused the oil lamp and stood in the doorway to gaze at them. Proud of who they were and fearful of what the world might do to them. Gwendolyn Jordan had only been two years older than his boys when the fever took her. No matter what he did, how hard he tried, he couldn't protect his family from everything.

A kiss for Rosie, then he was off into the night. He tried the Yorkshire Grey first; maybe Kingsley had gone there again. Tonight, though, there was no sign of him. The same in the other places along Kirkgate, from Briggate down past the parish church.

If he'd kept his senses sharp, he'd already know where Kingsley lived. Instead, he'd let his guard down and found himself in a fight with a robber. Stupid. He'd been in this trade long enough to know better.

Off in the distance the clock struck eleven. Simon felt weary, his senses dulled. Time to go home, he decided. Kingsley might not even have come out. Or he could be involved in the other business with Ackroyd and the Irishman. There was a sliver of moon, maybe just enough light to dig up a freshly buried body.

The eighth. Maybe even more than that, and he'd never know.

A fitful sleep. He dreamed of corpses and faceless men digging, clods of earth, panicking as the dirt began to fill his mouth. By the time he woke, Simon hardly felt rested. Another hour or two would have been welcome.

But it was a new day, there was work to do. At the coffee cart, no rumours of any dead men found in Goulden's Yard. He ambled back towards the house on Swinegate. Close to Byrd's Court,

Jane fell into step beside him. Quickly, she told him what she'd managed to learn about Betsy and the Irishman.

Simon listened carefully, smiling to himself. The straightforward girl he'd originally taken on had grown into a woman who could tell a convincing lie to discover the things she needed. She still possessed all her old skills, she still kept the world away, but now there was more depth to her. She was growing, hungry for knowledge, learning to read, asking Rosie to teach her to add and subtract numbers. He was able to rely on her more and more. It wouldn't be long before she was better at this work than he was.

'I think it's time to see Joseph Clark again,' he said.

'Seven.' Simon looked at Clark's face. 'That's what I was told. Seven bodies taken. It could be more by now.'

'I see.' The man closed his eyes for a moment and pressed his fingernails into his palms. The colour had drained from his face. Only the three of them in the office. There was no need for Mr Jordan to endure this. He already had enough pain pressing down on his heart.

'We know who the men are, but we still have to find them, I hope before they can do anything else. The hard part will be trying to prove it. When it comes to taking the bodies, that might be almost impossible unless we catch them in the act or with a corpse.'

Clark grimaced. 'What do you need from me?' he asked.

'Nothing for now,' Simon answered, and saw the man's eyes widen in surprise. 'Just tell me that you're satisfied for us to carry on.'

'Of course I am. This is why I employed you in the first place. I told you, I'll prosecute.'

'You might hear things.'

He cocked his head. 'What kind of things? Are you within the law?'

'We are. But there could be things it's better you don't know. You'll have to trust us to do our job.'

'Mr Westow, I hire someone for their ability and let them work. Is that a good enough answer for you?'

'It is.' He smiled. 'Thank you.'

'How long until it's over, do you think? I can see the way it's preying on Harmony. I don't like to see him like that.'

'As soon as we can.' It was the best Simon could offer.

A nod. 'Then it has to be that way. Please tell me as soon as you learn something.'

'I will.'

He'd wanted to give a warning. Now Clark would be prepared for any news; Simon felt certain the man wouldn't grow fearful and back off. Simon wanted these men, not just for Gwendolyn Jordan, but for all the others they'd taken. Rosie had been right: they needed to pay.

'What about Mrs Parker?' Jane asked. 'We should see her, too.'

'I know.' He sighed. He'd intended to go yesterday, but in the end he'd decided to wait. Let her believe they'd been putting in more hours for her. 'We might as well do it now, so we'll still have the rest of the day.'

She looked as if she'd barely finished preparing for the morning. Amanda Parker glared as Simon explained that they'd been unable to find any trace of Rawlings. From the angry glint in her eye, she didn't believe a word.

'I expected more from you.' Her tone was sharp, cold. 'People said you were good at this work.'

'Not everything goes quickly or smoothly.'

Mrs Parker turned her head to consider Jane. 'You might have had more luck if you'd used the girl. There's not much to her, but he'd have risen to the bait. It's not too late.'

'You agreed to our terms,' Simon reminded her. 'They haven't changed.'

She arched an eyebrow. 'Your methods obviously haven't worked so far.'

'We searched for three days in the end.'

'That ought to be long enough, Mr Westow. Leeds isn't that big.'

Exactly what he'd been hoping to hear. 'I'm sorry you feel that way. However, as you do . . .'

'What?'

'Perhaps it would be better for us both if you found someone else. You don't seem happy with our services and you don't believe in the way we work. I think it would be easier if we parted ways now.' Simon gave a small bow and turned towards the door.

She hesitated for a moment, taken aback. Mrs Parker narrowed her eyes, as if she was trying to peer into his mind. Her mouth turned down. 'Isn't that very drastic, Mr Westow? Has Rawlings paid you to stop working for me? Is that it? You found him and now he's employing you.'

'No.' He kept his voice even and steady. 'I've never spoken to him.' That much was true.

'I'm not sure I believe you.'

Simon gave a small shrug. 'Your choice, of course. But it's another reason we shouldn't work for you.'

'I trust you won't regret this decision, Mr Westow.'

'I don't believe I will.' He gave a small bow. 'I wish you well. I'm sure you'll find someone who will do the job you need. I believe this is the best thing for us both, Mrs Parker.'

Outside, he exhaled. Relief. It was done.

'I still don't trust her,' Jane said. 'Not an inch. She's not finished yet.'

'Maybe not,' he agreed. 'But she can't prove we found Tom Rawlings.'

'That one's going to make trouble, though. Count on it.'

Trouble. The thought kept lurching into her mind throughout the day. Jane spent her time on the far side of Timble Bridge again. Walking with the shawl raised over her hair, watching. Nobody noticed her; she had no sense of anyone following.

She went into two shops. The women who ran them could have been sisters: both with pinched, wrinkled mouths and quick, angry gestures. Jane managed a fleeting question about Betsy and the Irishman between their complaints about the weather and the way neighbours had argued long into the night. Both the women had plenty to say, but nothing she wanted to know.

Darkness was falling as she made her way through the town. Men were drinking and singing, their shifts done for the day. A few called out to her. One offered her money. She pushed his arm aside and strode on, hand tight around the handle of her knife.

Jane had barely turned on to Lands Lane when the tingle rose up her spine. Someone behind her. She slipped through the warren of yards, round by the Angel Inn, but the feeling remained.

She couldn't let strangers discover where she lived. She wasn't going to put Mrs Shields in danger. Five more minutes and he hadn't gone. She couldn't see him; she wasn't even certain she heard his footsteps. But he was there, no doubt about it, and he meant her harm.

Jane walked a little faster; not a run, nothing to show panic, just enough to allow her the safety of distance. She slipped into a patch of deep shadow beside a building and held her breath. A quick twist of the ring for luck.

He passed, gazing around with a fierce hunter's glare, and crept on. Light glinted on a knife in his hand. She knew the face. She'd seen it just a few days before. Then, though, he'd been polishing Mrs Parker's coach when he eyed her.

He was here to hurt her. Why? Was this his own doing? Had the woman sent him? The timing seemed too curious for it to be anything else. But what reason could she have?

Another few seconds and he'd realize he'd lost her. He'd retrace his steps. She had to decide: confront him or flee?

Jane knew she could kill him in a moment, before he even had the chance to defend himself. Her palms itched to do it. She felt the desire, the tightness in her chest. But her problems would begin as soon as the body was discovered. Mrs Parker would set the constable on her. Then, if they found Rawlings . . . no, this time it was safer to run. In the morning she'd talk to Simon and they'd decide what to do.

EIGHT

'**A**re you certain it was the same man?' Simon asked. Immediately he regretted his words. Jane never said something unless she was sure. 'I'm sorry.'

'Why would she send him after me?'

'Maybe she didn't. You said he was staring at you when we went to the house.' He had a blurred recollection of the man working on the coach, but couldn't have described him for twenty pounds.

'He was.'

'It might have been lust,' Rosie said.

Simon saw the doubt in Jane's eyes. Whatever they said, they both knew he'd probably been sent by his employer. Revenge for them walking away? Then why not go after Simon? Or did Mrs Parker mistake Jane for easy prey?

'No,' she said finally.

'You did right,' he told her. Keeping a distance was the best course. He'd been to the coffee cart just after first light; still no mention of anyone finding a body in Goulden's Yard. But it was only a matter of time.

'What if he comes back?' she asked.

'Do exactly the same thing,' Simon told her, and saw the flash of anger in her eyes. 'Disarm him if you want. Humiliate him. But don't hurt him unless he attacks you. Whatever happens, just make sure you don't kill him.'

A moment, then she nodded her agreement. Good, Simon thought. Two years ago Jane wouldn't have held back. The man who'd followed her would already have been dead; she wouldn't have hesitated.

'He probably won't return. There's no need to worry about it unless he does.'

'What do you want me to do today?'

'We still need an address for Betsy and the Irishman.'

She gave a nod and drifted away, quickly vanishing down Swinegate.

* * *

He was unlikely to have a sniff of Kingsley before evening. Gambling in the public houses, snatching bodies; the man seemed to be a creature of the night. Maybe he could catch up with the other one today. Harold Ackroyd.

'I want him,' Rosie said when he told her his plans. 'He sold the burial gown. I want to see his face when he's arrested.'

It was Saturday; the boys would be with their tutor all morning. 'Then come with me.'

She shook her head and gave him a dark grin. 'You go and talk to the men. I'll ask around some of the whores. See if they know him.'

Ackroyd had worked in a warehouse once; Simon decided to start asking questions down by the river. Along the wharves, in the little beershops that served the men labouring there.

Some of them nodded when he described Ackroyd. One claimed to have seen him looking for work just a few days before. But none of them knew where to find him. The south side of the river brought more of the same until he reached the sloop builder's yard, close to the weir.

A carpenter took a pull from a jug, swilled the liquid around his mouth and spat it out, then drank again and swallowed. The air held the sweet tang of wood shavings. All around, men were busy, concentrating on their tasks. Sawdust clogged everything. Simon could feel it catching in his throat.

'I used to know him a few years ago,' the man said. 'Sly as the devil.'

Another dead end. The past was no use to him. 'Thank you.'

'You might talk to Jemmy Williamson, though.' He pointed with his chisel. 'The one with the fair hair over there. He was mentioning Harry Ackroyd just yesterday.'

Simon suddenly felt very alert. 'What did he say? Do you remember?'

A shake of the head. 'I wasn't listening. I just recall the name, that's all. A lot of us over here used to know Harry. Why do you want him, anyway?'

'He owes some money.' A convenient lie, but one people would believe.

The man chuckled. 'That sounds like him. See what Jemmy has to say.'

* * *

'What about him?' Jem Williamson asked. He'd been studying a set of plans, then turning back to the long block of oak in front of him. He studied Simon with suspicious eyes.

'Money.' Maybe a single word would be enough.

'You wouldn't be the first.'

'Someone said you were talking about him.'

'Saw him two nights ago in that dram house right by Pitfall, wetting his whistle. He bought me one, so if you're after a debt you'd better hurry up and catch him before his money's run out. Didn't stay long. Said he had some work to do. Wouldn't say what it was, though. Just tapped the side of his nose.'

After dark, a job he didn't want to discuss. Whose body had they taken?

'Did he say where he was living?'

Williamson shrugged. 'Never asked.'

'Thank you.' Damnation.

'No, wait. I take that back. There was something.' The man drew a hand across his face, showing pale skin under a fine coating of sawdust. 'He did mention something about some friend of his up around Sheepscar.'

'Anything more than that?'

'That was it.' He returned to his work, starting to measure out lengths on the wood.

Sheepscar. It had the dye works and the rape oil mill. A few places along Skinner Lane and the barracks by the road out to Roundhay. But very few dwellings. He should be able to find Ackroyd in a place like that.

Out along North Street. After a series of new streets where houses were rising, Leeds became a straggle of dwellings that gave way to orchards and fields. Young lambs played, watched by their mothers. A few months and their wool would become someone's new coat or dress.

Stone farmhouses dotted the hillside. No close neighbours to ask questions. An ideal place to keep a body, Simon thought. He carried on, past a small cluster of buildings all the way to the bridge and the toll house at the start of the turnpike.

The man who took the money had little to do all day but watch. A coin or two loosened his tongue.

'I've seen someone who looks a little like that,' he said. 'White moustache, kerchief around his neck.'

'What about the missing finger?'

A hard shake of the head. 'Not close enough to tell. But he looked about fifty.'

That was Ackroyd. It had to be.

'Where was he?' Simon asked. When no answer came, he put down two more coins.

'You see that place, about a hundred yards away?' He pointed at a whitewashed brick house, two storeys tall. A low stone wall set it back from the road. Simon had noticed the place as he passed, neatly kept but unremarkable.

'Does he live there by himself?'

'No. He must be a lodger. I only started seeing him a couple of months ago.'

'Who owns the place?'

'I couldn't tell you. It had been empty for a while, then someone moved in last autumn. A clerk, from the look of him. Black suit, a decent pair of shoes and a hat. I see him walking off into town every morning.'

'Do you know his name?'

'No.'

'Anything else about him?'

The man raised his eyebrows. He was enjoying this, passing the time and making some extra money. Two more coins, but worth every penny so far.

'He's not that old, probably not even in his thirties, fair hair. I've never seen him up close. He's over there and I'm in here. Mind you, the night man in this booth, he says that sometimes there's been some comings and goings at the house in the evenings, after it gets dark. Not often, but enough for him to notice.'

That was what he needed to hear. Now Simon knew where they took each body once they lifted it from the ground. Bring it back to the white house, fit it into a box, then off to the coaching office the next day.

'Have you ever seen anyone leaving there with a box on a cart?'

'I suppose I have, now you mention it.' The man was wary now, suspicious. 'Why, what are they up to? Who are you, anyway?'

One more coin, worth more than the others together. He kept

a finger on it. 'I'm someone who was never here asking questions. Do we understand each other?'

The man gave a broad, amiable grin. 'I don't think I've seen you before.'

As he ambled back towards Leeds, Simon glanced over at the house. It stood on the opposite side of Sheepscar Lane from the entrance to the dye works, across from a beershop. There was a handcart in the small yard. Wooden planks stacked against the wall, enough to make several boxes.

He was careful not to linger. Nothing to draw the attention of anyone who might be watching. But he'd found the right place, he felt it in his bones. Seven bodies had come through there, most likely more than that. Ackroyd was living in the house. He'd bet good money that Kingsley and the Irishman both knew the place well. Simon still had plenty of questions: who rented the house, and what was his role in it all? Who owned it? He needed to find out, but he had to do it discreetly, so nobody ever knew he'd been asking. He didn't want to risk frightening them off before they paid for what they'd done.

'If you wanted to know who owned a building, who would you ask?'

He sat by George Mudie's desk, raising his voice over the sound of the press as the man cranked the handle and turned out sheet after sheet, an advertisement for a balm to cure most known ailments.

'Go to the Court House. They'll have a record of the deeds. I'm surprised you don't know that by now.'

Of course: he should have known it. It was where the deed to his own house was lodged. But it wasn't knowledge a thief-taker needed from day to day.

The Court House was a grand stone building at the bottom of Park Row, close to the Coloured Cloth Hall. Ten years old and already the pale stone was gritted and grimed with soot. Two tall columns either side of the entrance, and heavy wooden doors, as if justice needed to be protected. Inside, the building felt cool after the warmth of the day.

First Simon had to find the right clerk. Then the man had to pore over ledgers until he found the one he needed. His finger trailed down the entries and stopped. Selecting a small piece of paper, he picked up his nib, dipped it in the inkwell and wrote. Blotted the words, folded the paper and looked up in expectation of a reward.

Everyone craved a little extra. It was the way of the world. He took out a few pennies and placed them on the desk. Smiling, the clerk handed over the paper.

Simon waited until he was out in the air to unfold it. The name was written in beautiful, flowing copperplate: Mr Robert Parker, Burley House. The man had been Amanda Parker's second husband. After his death, the property in Sheepscar would have passed to her.

He felt a chill pass through his body as he stood staring at the paper. A river of questions tumbled into his head: Was this something to do with Rawlings? Could Mrs Parker be involved with body snatchers?

So much that he needed to know and he didn't have the beginning of any answers. The only fact was that someone rented a house she owned and used it for the crime. She could easily deny all knowledge of that, and people would believe her. Rawlings? It seemed that no one had found his body yet. Even that link between her and the body snatchers was tenuous, and he wasn't going to offer any evidence.

The connection was as flimsy as gossamer. Would Amanda Parker take a risk like that? If word ever spread that she was somehow involved in stealing corpses, she'd be cast out; no one in Leeds would want to know her. It couldn't be the money; everyone said that both her husbands had left her rich. She had that grand house and everything in it, and who knew how many other properties?

Still, a few careful enquiries might be a good idea.

Simon crumpled the paper, thrust it in his pocket and began to walk.

Jane stroked her knife across the whetstone time after time, until she was lulled by the rhythm, doing it without thinking. The weather was mild enough to sit outside, perched on a stool with the April sun on her face as Mrs Shields worked in the containers that made up her garden. Liquor barrels that had once held brandy, cut in half and filled with soil. Now plants were starting to bloom again. Another year.

Jane didn't know what they were, couldn't call any of the flowers by name. She only knew that the old woman took pleasure in caring for them. Pruning, encouraging, watering. She'd make up compounds to sprinkle on the soil, to treat them for diseases.

Holding up the blade, she ran it against the ball of her thumb. Perfectly sharp. Ready in case the coachman returned. She'd had no more sense of him, but what could she do if he came and confronted her?

Why had he come at all? Was it for himself? Or was he doing his mistress's bidding, and carrying out some strange urge for revenge she might have?

She'd only learn the truth once she had him helpless and begging to stay alive. If he showed himself again, that was what she'd need to do. Make him confess and then walk away. Leave him unharmed, exactly as Simon said.

Jane put the knife in the pocket of her dress and ran her hands along her forearms, feeling the scars where she'd cut herself. They were starting to fade, to vanish into history. They were reminders of a distant lifetime, when she'd needed to do that. She tried to picture that girl, but the image was too ghostly. Probably better that way.

She stood and stretched, gathering the shawl around her shoulders. A brief kiss on Mrs Shields's head and she was through the gap in the wall and out into Leeds.

Simon was home before the boys finished their lessons. They tumbled out of the parlour, relishing their freedom until Monday. He cut bread and cheese for them as he thought about what he'd learned during the morning.

It was another half-hour before Rosie returned, arriving home with a satisfied smile. She'd worn her everyday clothes to go out, a plain, worn dress and well-washed apron, hair under a shawl.

'He lives in Sheepscar,' she said after she'd pushed the boys into the yard to play.

'The white house not far from the toll booth.'

Rosie nodded. 'That's the one.' She smiled. 'Ackroyd has a lady friend he sometimes entertains there. According to her, the place stinks.'

'I'm sure it does. It's where they take the bodies.'

'Ah.' Her eyes widened. 'I saw the cart.'

He stopped and looked at her in admiration. 'You went there?'

'I knocked on the door and asked if they wanted someone to cook and clean. Told them my husband was hurt and couldn't work, so we needed money.'

She'd changed her voice, giving it a pleading note, looking out from under her eyelashes. Very convincing.

'Did you talk to Ackroyd?'

'No. Someone younger. He told me they weren't hiring.'

'Thin? Dark hair?'

'Yes.'

'That sounds like Kingsley,' he said.

'When are we going to take them?' she asked.

'Soon,' he promised. 'When we can catch them with a body.'

Jane wandered across Timble Bridge and into the streets beyond once more. She kept out of sight, hugging the shadows as she walked, keeping her eyes alert for any sign of Betsy or the Irishman.

Afternoon was bending towards evening when she caught a glimpse of a couple who could be the ones. Jane hurried around the block until she was walking towards them on the other side of the street. No mistaking the cast in the woman's eye. It was her. The man was tall, with thick, muscled shoulders under his old coat. A battered top hat, and a dark stain on the left leg of his trousers. Exactly as she'd been told.

She followed at a distance, careful to make certain they didn't spot her. Down three more streets, then he took out a key, unlocked the door to a house and they vanished inside. As she passed half a minute later, Jane noticed the faded and flaked green paint of the wood.

Now she knew where they were living. There were two good, hidden places to stand and keep watch. Tomorrow, she thought, and hurried off to tell Simon.

His skin tingled as he listened. Anticipation. They were coming closer.

They knew where Ackroyd and Kingsley were staying. Jane had found the Irishman and Betsy. He sat at the kitchen table and tried to form a plan.

'How are we going to stop them?' Rosie asked. She stood with her back against the dresser that held the plates, frowning.

A thin smile crossed Simon's face. He'd come up with an idea during the afternoon. 'We're not.'

Jane turned her head and gave him a sharp look. 'What? Why not?'

'We know the only way to convict is if they're caught in the act or with a body. We'll let them do the work and damn themselves. We'll follow them when they go out, then watch them dig. They'll take the body back to Sheepscar so they can pack it. That's when we'll tell Constable Porter. I know it's not a felony, but it might be the best we can manage. We'll still have the testimony about Ackroyd selling Gwendolyn Jordan's burial gown. That will convict him.'

He could see the doubt in Rosie's eyes. 'We're going to need plenty of luck to make it work.'

'I know.' The scheme barely held together. But how could it be anything more? It was all they had, and they needed to make the most of it.

'What about Mrs Parker?' Jane asked.

He sighed. She was the piece that didn't seem to fit anywhere. 'I don't know. That's still a mystery. I can't make head nor tail of what she's doing or why she's tried to involve us.'

'You said she owns the house in Sheepscar,' Rosie said

'All her lawyer has to do is claim that it's pure coincidence and there's nothing to contradict that.'

'She's part of it,' Jane said. There was no doubt in her voice.

'For what it's worth, I think so, too,' he agreed. 'But we need evidence. We daren't accuse her without that. She'd sue us for slander.'

Amanda Parker had the ear of too many influential people in Leeds. Enough people liked her, men still looked at her with longing. Some of them admired the way she'd risen in the world, and that she did exactly what she pleased. She was their local scent of scandal and they enjoyed that. He'd need something solid to damn her.

'The man who rents this house, does he have any connection to her?' Rosie asked.

'I still need to find out about him,' Simon said. 'He has to be involved in the body snatching. Once I find out what he does it might make more sense.'

'What about the coachman?' Jane asked.

'If he comes back, make him tell you what he knows,' Rosie said.

'Sooner or later, someone is going to find Rawlings's body, and Mrs Parker will make sure the constable looks at us,' Simon told her. 'We need to be prepared.'

'Yes.' Jane's voice was tight. 'I'll start watching the Irishman. If anything is happening, he'll lead me there.'

Simon had been searching for more than an hour before he finally caught up with Barnabas Wade. He was at the Talbot, deep in conversation with a traveller who still had a heavy bag between his feet. Wade signalled the potboy to bring more drinks.

He was close to the kill. It was written on Wade's face, easing towards the perfect moment. Finally, the handshake. Wade brought the contract from his coat and wrote in all the details while his victim stood, pleased with the bargain he'd made.

A few more minutes and it was all complete. The man ambled away, satisfied, and Wade put the bank notes in his pocket and rubbed his hands together with pleasure.

'By the time he realizes, he'll be in Bristol or somewhere a long way from Leeds.'

'You'd better hope he doesn't have friends round here,' Simon told him.

'He'll consult with his lawyer and see that everything was legal. He won't have a case to bring against me.' Wade was beaming with the pleasure of success. 'What can I do for you, Simon? It must be important; you've been standing there for the best part of half an hour.'

'Amanda Parker.'

'What about her?'

'Is she as wealthy as everyone says?'

Barnabas narrowed his eyes, suddenly very curious. 'As far as I know,' he said. His expression began to sharpen with possibilities. 'Why, have you heard something?'

'I want to know, that's all. Can you ask a few questions? Do it very, very softly,' he added. 'I don't want her knowing.'

'I can try.'

'I can pay you for it.'

'I'll look for you the day after tomorrow,' Wade told him. 'I should know something by then.'

It was night when he eventually left the Talbot. Time to go home.

Jane found a cramped space between buildings to watch the house Betsy and the Irishman rented. Stinking soot from the bricks rubbed off on to her dress and shawl. She had a good view of the door; no one was likely to spot her hidden away here in the shadows.

They appeared as dusk turned into night, the darkness growing around them as they ambled down the street. Talking softly, not in a hurry. Jane followed, keeping to the other side of the road, letting the distance spin out until she could barely see them.

Over Timble Bridge, then up Kirkgate, where the clamour and din of the evening rose from the beershops. They parted on Briggate. Betsy turned left, down towards the bridge; the Irishman went the other way.

The woman was going to work. Something changed in her walk as she moved off alone. She held her back straighter, desiring attention, putting herself on display.

Jane stayed behind the Irishman. With his size and his battered top hat, he was easy to follow. He didn't go too far, just a tavern set back in Bay Horse Yard. The windows were frosted, she couldn't see inside. It was the type of place where a woman's face would stand out. Safer to find somewhere to wait.

Jane passed the time by reading the advertising posters pasted to the walls. She sounded out the words she didn't know, going over everything again and again until she believed she understood it all. It fascinated her, the way the words fitted one after the other.

Two hours. She heard the church bell toll the time. People came and went, figures moving through small hanging pools of lantern light. The warmth faded, and she felt the bite of the night chill, shifting her weight from leg to leg to keep warm. The tavern door opened and she was ready. The Irishman, alone. He called something over his shoulder and headed towards Briggate.

He turned in the direction of the bridge. She trailed behind, eyes fixed on the man who stood out, far taller than most around him. Close to the river he met Betsy and the two of them set off along the Calls.

Going home. For a moment, Jane wondered whether to follow. Instead, she turned and started the walk to where her own bed lay. Her legs ached from standing so long, she was ready to sleep.

NINE

Even on a Sunday morning the coffee cart was busy. Some still had to labour on the Sabbath, and there was a profit to be made from them. Simon noticed a few familiar faces enjoying the early bustle of gossip and idle chatter. Simon took a drink, relishing the hot bitter liquid as he listened to what people were saying.

Someone had spotted a body in the river at first light. It was downstream, near the old ferry crossing out beyond Far Bank. That seemed to be the only fact. A man or a woman? Nobody was certain, turning to every new arrival in the hope they'd heard more. He didn't pay it much mind.

Finally Simon left. An hour or two and it would all be common knowledge. There was hardly anything unusual about someone in the water; it happened at least once a month.

He had things to do. Now he knew where Kingsley and Ackroyd were living, he wanted to try to identify the clerk who rented the house in Sheepscar. Tomorrow, once offices opened for the new week.

Constantly niggling at the back of his mind was the thought of Amanda Parker. She was part of this. She had to be. But how? He couldn't work that out. Nor could he understand *why*. However he approached the question, he couldn't see an answer. Maybe Wade would be able to tell him something useful. One more thing that would have to wait.

Seven. The number kept coming back to him. It haunted him, taunted, begging him to do something.

Every night the body snatchers remained free, that number could rise. Another family could lose someone and never even know. It was his responsibility. A duty he owed.

Rosie was off visiting neighbours with the boys. Jane was sitting at the kitchen table, slowly reading a tiny book she hurriedly pushed into her pocket as he entered. Five minutes and they'd exchanged the little they'd learned.

'What about today?' she asked.

'Let's start out together,' Simon answered. 'If something happens, one of us can follow it up.'

A teasing haze of chimney smoke kept the sun away. She could feel the tightness in her chest, the sharp taste in her lungs. The soot seemed to cling close to the ground. Jane watched the faces of the people they passed, only half-listening as Simon talked.

At the corner of Briggate and Boar Lane, she saw Dodson the beggar sitting on the ground in a small patch of sun. Jane dug a coin from her pocket and placed it in his tin cup.

'Did you hear about the body in the river?' the man asked.

'This morning,' Simon said. 'Do they know who it is yet?'

'One of the whores who works down towards the bridge,' the beggar said. 'I heard the constable say it as he went past with one of the watch. On his way to where they'd found her, by the face on him.'

'What was her name? Did they mention it?' Jane asked. She felt fear starting to rise from the pit of her belly and forced it back down. Her mind swirled, going over every detail from the night before.

'No.' Dodson's expression changed, suddenly concerned. 'You've gone pale. Are you all right?'

'I'm fine.' A lie. She put another penny in the cup and began to walk away.

'We need to find out,' Simon said.

'Yes.' It was Betsy. She was as sure as if she'd seen the body herself.

'It might not be her.'

'It is.' She didn't look at him. She didn't need to; they were both thinking the same thing.

'Where did you last see her and the Irishman?'

'On the Calls.' The street ran right by the river. So many places to put a body into the water. 'I thought they were going home.'

'Why would you think anything else?' Simon asked.

There was nothing. No hint. No arguments, no raised voices. The man had done nothing unusual. Betsy hadn't seemed fearful. Nothing at all to make Jane suspect.

'If I'd followed them a few minutes longer . . .' She could have stopped a death.

'How were you to know what was in his mind?'

She didn't answer. Instead, as she walked, she rubbed the old scars on her arm. The litany of all her failures and mistakes. She hadn't added to them in a long time. She wouldn't now, but they would always be her reminder.

There was a small crowd gathered on the shore, a rowing boat pulled up on the mud. The body lay on the bank, covered by an old sheet. Jane kept her distance as Simon drifted close enough to approach a man who was walking away from the others. They talked for a minute before the man nodded and disappeared.

The sun was shining, warm on her shoulders and arms. A gentle breeze blew from the south, barely enough to ruffle the hem of her dress. She glanced down at the water. This didn't seem like a day for death.

Simon passed her, moving back towards Leeds. He inclined his head. She followed. They'd walked a quarter of a mile before he spoke.

'Someone recognized her.' He drew a breath. 'It looks as if she drowned, but there's a wound on the back of her head. She might have hit it in the water—'

'Or the Irishman did it.'

'Yes. None of them seem to know about him yet.' He turned to look at her. 'Time?'

She didn't need to think about it. 'Yes.'

Simon brought his fist down on the wood, hearing the echo inside. Houses always sounded different when they were empty. Another knock. Nothing.

The lock was flimsy, a few seconds with his picks. They were inside, closing the door before any neighbours might notice. He sniffed. A stale smell of cooking, tobacco.

'I'll look upstairs,' Jane whispered. He heard her move softly up the steps and began to search.

The Irishman had been thorough. For all he could find, the place might have been empty for months. No scraps of paper dropped behind the few sticks of furniture or wedged in corners. Nothing to identify the tenants. They wouldn't have owned much, but even so . . .

'Everything's gone,' Jane said. 'Everything.'

Not the actions of an innocent man. He must have vanished in the middle of the night, flitting away after he'd murdered

Betsy. Round here, they would be used to people disappearing in the darkness; even if they saw, they wouldn't pay it any mind.

'When he'd finished drinking, did anyone see them meet?'

She thought. 'I don't think so. It wasn't on Briggate. It was round the corner, just by Pitfall.'

Yes, Simon thought, the Irishman had planned this. Where would he go? He was a big man, very noticeable. It wouldn't be easy for him to hide.

A thought came to him: the house in Sheepscar.

Jane was quiet, he noticed. Even more than usual. She was walking beside him, but he knew her mind was elsewhere. Damning herself as guilty for something she couldn't have foreseen. In the past she'd balanced the whole weight of the world on her shoulders. He thought she'd finally managed to leave that behind.

What could they do about the Irishman? He'd murdered Betsy. Simon knew that. So did Jane. But there had been no witnesses to the act. Nothing anyone could prove.

Why kill her now? What was the plan?

They sat in the kitchen: Simon, Rosie beside him, Jane on the other side of the table. They needed to decide what to do next, to understand what was happening.

Rosie stayed quiet for a long time after he recounted everything.

'Betsy was a connection,' she said finally. 'With Rawlings dead, she was the only link between Amanda Parker and the body snatchers.'

'Did Mrs Parker order the killing?' Simon asked.

Rosie peered into the distance. She grimaced before she spoke. 'It's possible. We'll never be able to prove it, though.' After a moment she added, 'The man who rents the Sheepscar house must be part of all this. He might even be the one who arranges the sale of the corpses and takes payment. Do any of the others look capable of that?'

'I don't know enough about Kingsley to say,' Simon replied, 'but I doubt Ackroyd or the Irishman could manage it.'

Rosie nodded. 'Tomorrow we need to find out about the clerk.'

Jane sat, frowning. 'Why didn't they try to sell Rawlings's

body after they'd killed him?' she asked. 'Or Betsy? They had them both.'

'The Irishman would have had to move Betsy,' Rosie said. Her words came hesitantly at first, then faster as she thought it through. 'A dead body weighs a lot. And it's a big risk. Someone could have seen him carrying it. The same with Rawlings. If they're caught with a corpse that's been buried, that's one thing. The worst they'd get is a few months in prison. Probably less. Someone they'd murdered? They'd hang, no question about it.'

In the dusk, Simon and Jane strode to Sheepscar, hunting in the half-light for a good place to watch the house. But the ground was too open. Keeping out of sight was impossible.

'The only worthwhile spot I can see is over there, the far side of the toll house,' Jane said and pointed. They'd looked at it earlier. A hollow in the ground beside a tree, fringed with tall, wild grass. It was hidden, that was true, but it was two hundred yards away and they'd have no view into the yard.

'We'll have to make do with that,' he said. 'Or only come out here at night.'

'It's growing dark now.' Her statement was a question. He nodded.

'Stay if you want. Make sure they don't see you.'

By the time he reached the bottom of Briggate it was full night. A question had worried at him since they'd sat and talked: why hadn't anyone found Rawlings's body yet?

He looked towards Swinegate and home. But the pull was too strong. He turned the other way, keeping a quick pace past the parish church as the bells rang for the end of Sunday evening service, then crossing Timble Bridge. The sounds of the town began to fade.

He gazed around, alert for any sounds or footsteps. Any sense that someone might be following him. Nothing at all. At the entrance to Goulden's Yard, he drew his knife, comforted by the weight in his hand.

One minute, two. Not a hint of movement anywhere. Somewhere in the far distance a dog barked. Silently, he crossed the cobbles, staying close to the walls, in the shadows. A hurried moment to pick the lock and he was inside, closing the door, barely daring to breathe.

The stench of the body should have been overwhelming, but there was hardly anything. Only a quiet perfume of decay. Upstairs, enough light came through the window for him to see the bed had been stripped. The mattress folded, no bloody sheet left.

No Thomas Rawlings.

A few flies still buzzed around, the only reminder that there had ever been a murdered man here.

What was happening? He truly didn't understand.

Simon hurried out, back across the cobbles of the court. To the entrance. Something moved. A man, his shape blacker than the night.

'You shouldn't have come out here.'

TEN

Simon didn't know the man's voice. In the darkness he couldn't make out his features. He kept a tight grip on his knife and eased a second out from the sleeve of his coat.

The man moved. Simon slid to the side, deep into the shadows. No light could catch his silhouette there. Now they were both blind. Invisible. He listened intently, hearing the man's breathing, each scuffle of his boots on the cobbles.

His eyes began to adjust; he could make out more. An outline. Then a sudden reflection of steel. Just enough time to turn before the knife would have cut him. Dancing away on the balls of his feet.

Close. Far too close.

Simon crouched. A smaller target. Easier to spring and evade. The man lunged again. Where Simon had been standing, not where he was now.

It was an opening. He darted forward. The tip of his blade ripped through cloth and hit flesh. A tiny moment of resistance, then into the skin. The man cried out and was still for a second. Simon brought his other knife down into the man's right arm.

Another howl. The man let go of his weapon and it clattered to the ground. He was no danger now: wounded, blade gone. Simon felt him turn and lope away, a black blur in the night. The sound of his feet on the road echoed off the buildings as he went.

Simon bent over, hands pressing down on his knees as he tried to catch his breath. Panting hard, gulping down air. He was sweating, starting to shiver as it cooled on his skin. The fight had only lasted a few seconds, but each one had felt like a lifetime.

'*You shouldn't have come out here.*' That was what the man had said. It had to be one of the body snatchers. Not the Irishman: too small, and he'd spoken in a clear Leeds accent. Ackroyd? Kingsley? He'd find out tomorrow. One of them would be in pain and carrying his arm in a sling.

Simon took a deep breath and started towards home. Trudging,

placing one foot in front of the other, as he tried to make sense
of tonight. Rawlings's body gone. Someone trying to kill him.
By the time he unlocked the door it was still a mystery.

Simon stood by the coffee cart. Morning and he was weary, body
heavy and slow after a night of broken sleep. There was little
fresh gossip, hardly a word about Betsy; she was just another
dead whore who'd drowned in the river. He was sipping hot
coffee when Jane appeared. A final gulp, then he put down
the battered tin mug and started to walk.

They stood on Leeds Bridge, staring down at the water. The
coloured swirls from dyes, the sharp stink of piss. Logs carried
in the current. A dead animal.

He told her everything that happened after he left her in
Sheepscar. He saw the questioning frown on her face as he said
the body had vanished.

'Do you think he followed you?' Jane asked.

'No.' Simon was certain of that. 'He must have already been
around. Saw me go in and waited.'

'I stayed for two hours. Nobody came or went from the house
in Sheepscar.'

But they didn't know who was living there. The clerk who
rented the place. Ackroyd, it seemed. Perhaps Kingsley? The
Irishman?

'If Rawlings's body has gone now, why didn't they just take
it when they killed him?'

'I don't know,' he told her. He'd tried to pick his way through
that as he lay awake in the darkness. But it was a puzzle that
was beyond him. 'The only possibility is somebody wanted him
left there.'

'You mean Mrs Parker.'

'Yes.'

'Why would she do that?'

'Maybe she believed we'd find it and come running to tell
her.' It was the only reason he could imagine. He gave a long
sigh. 'Let's start by discovering who attacked me last night.'

Jane needed a better spot in Sheepscar. Somewhere closer to the
house. Finally she found one, off the road towards Leeds. Just
a dip in the ground, but sheltered by bushes. The early sun had

warmed the earth; she arranged herself to watch the people who passed.

She ignored the husbands and wives together, the groups of men, someone travelling with a packhorse. A man hurrying on alone could be the clerk, but she didn't know his face.

An hour passed, with no one to catch her attention. Then she saw them, approaching from the distance, heading towards Leeds. One in his early thirties, perhaps, with a loose-limbed, carefree walk. The other was older, a white moustache and red face. His right arm was caught up against his chest in a sling and he grimaced with each step, other hand rubbing the side of his body. That had to be Ackroyd. Now she knew who'd attacked Simon the night before. And with him, Kingsley.

Jane waited until they'd passed, giving them a good fifty-yard lead, then she eased down the slope and raised her shawl as she followed along the road.

Closer to town she narrowed the distance, keeping a careful eye on the men as people began to crowd around. All the way down Briggate, then along Kirkgate and over Timble Bridge.

Fewer people around now, and she stayed back. The men turned, following the river along New Causeway, past Near and Far Bank and beyond Fearn's Island. The track became a towpath for the barges, flat and hard.

She found places behind trees to watch them, hoping they wouldn't turn and see her. But they seemed oblivious to the world. They were talking, minds on other things. Past the place where Betsy's body had been pulled from the water. Farther still, out beyond the ferry.

Suddenly they disappeared. There when she looked, gone when she raised her eyes again. For a moment, her heart seemed to stop beating. All she could do was stare. A few moments later she caught a small movement. A man moving through the tall grass next to the river.

Jane crouched, slipping behind a tree. After a moment she sidled a few more yards up the slope, deep into the shadow of a willow tree. The men were only twenty-five yards away now, close enough for her to pick out their features. The yellow tobacco stains on Ackroyd's white moustache. The patch of dried blood on his coat, the way his mouth tightened each time he shifted his weight.

The other man was pulling away branches that covered a handcart and tossing them into the undergrowth. A quick heave and he'd dragged it out.

They began to walk back along the track. Ackroyd was speaking as the other man pushed the cart. She stayed absolutely still as they passed. Not even a flicker to catch their eye. The trundle of the wheels had faded into the distance before she moved. No need to follow all the way; she knew exactly where they were going.

Jane scrambled down the hillside, keeping a wary eye in case they turned back, then ran across to the place they'd hidden the cart. A small inlet, dirty water lapping softly against a low bank. A heavy branch, ten feet long, bobbed in the reeds.

She could imagine what had happened. They'd brought Rawlings's body here after dark and launched it into the river. It was far enough from Leeds that it was unlikely to be seen. By the time the fish had nibbled at the corpse he'd be unrecognizable anyway.

Easier to leave the cart than bump over the ruts all the way to Sheepscar in the middle of the night. Ackroyd must have returned to Goulden's Yard and found Simon.

It fitted together. Jane looked along the river. No shape that looked human that she could see.

She caught up with them on Kirkgate. After the quiet of the river, all the voices fell around her in a blaring cacophony of sound. Jane gathered her shawl at her throat and walked with her head down, trying to shut it out.

Up Briggate and out towards Sheepscar. She settled into the hollow on the hill to watch.

Two hours and nothing. She stretched out her legs and stood. For now she had ample to tell Simon.

He was standing outside the Moot Hall, reading the notice that someone had pasted up. Demolition of the old building, and a new corn exchange to go up in its place. Finally. About time.

Leeds was changing. There was a market on Kirkgate now, a new large bazaar just off Briggate, and a shambles for the butchers to kill and cut their meat. The town needed it. Leeds had grown too big for life to continue the old way. Progress, Simon thought grimly as he looked at the haze of factory smoke and tasted the soot in the air.

He began to walk. The roads were clogged with carts and coaches. People packed the pavements. Glancing around, he saw Jane with her determined stride on the other side of the street. He ducked across the road, almost caught by a wagon wheel, boot sliding in a pile of horse dung, and caught up to her close to the corner of Duncan Street.

He chewed on his lower lip as she told him about the cart and Ackroyd with his arm in the sling.

'This other man—' he began, but a voice cut him off.

'Well, well, the pair of you together.' Constable Porter's voice, sounding pleased with himself. 'You're saving me a lot of trouble.'

Simon turned. The man was grinning, two members of the watch standing stone-faced behind him.

'Are we? Why?'

'I want to talk to her.' He nodded towards Jane. 'People have been telling me things about you.'

'What things?' Simon asked.

'Not for you, Westow,' Porter told him. The man was relishing this, a chance to show his authority. 'Her.'

A nod from the constable and his men took hold of Jane, one to each arm, clamping her firmly. Simon studied her face. Set hard, not letting herself show a thing. No anger, no fear.

'I'll fetch the lawyer,' Simon said as they marched her off.

They pushed her through to the cells. A warm day, but the room felt cold, the old stone chilly and damp under her touch. The key turned and the sound of voices faded.

Jane was alone. A little light came through the high window. Impossible to escape with iron bars there. Where would she go, anyway? They'd know where she lived.

Why had Porter taken her and not Simon? Did he believe she'd break once he began to ask questions?

What did the constable want? Rawlings's body was gone, drifting down towards the ocean. It had to be something to do with Betsy. He'd discovered she'd gone around asking questions.

In her head, Jane pored over every tiny detail. There was nothing to show she'd ever found the woman. They could ask. She'd be safe.

She heard the footsteps, the key turning, the groan of the old hinges as the door opened. One of the men from the watch pulled her to her feet, hand sliding over her breast and squeezing.

She wouldn't let herself show anything. Nothing at all. She wouldn't feel it.

He dragged her to the main room and pushed her down into a chair. The place stank of age and hopelessness and fear. She could sense the ghosts of all the men and women who'd come through here. Years of them.

The constable sat on the other side of the ancient wooden desk, picking at something between his teeth with a fingernail, then wiping his hand on his trousers.

Jane could feel his eyes on her. She stared back. Inside, the fear and fury mixed. In the cell she'd been terrified. What if the door never opened again? What if she was left there, to starve and die?

It couldn't happen. She knew that, but it didn't stop the terror. Out in the room, at least she could breathe.

'You were on Briggate, asking questions about a whore,' Porter said.

'No,' she replied, seeing his eyes widen in surprise. 'I was asking about a man.'

'Who?'

'Thomas Rawlings. Mrs Parker had hired us to find him.'

He sat and stared for a moment, then nodded. 'She told me she'd employed you and Westow.'

'She claimed he'd borrowed fifty pounds from her, then disappeared. She wanted us to find him.'

Porter chuckled. 'That's a pretty tale. But it's not what she said to me. She insisted he stole it.'

Jane gave him a blank expression. 'All I know is what she explained to us. In the end, we spent two or three days searching for Rawlings.'

Inside, she was terrified, pressing her hands down against her thighs to stop them shaking, digging her nails into her flesh. She wasn't going to let him see any fear. Refused to let him smell it on her. She couldn't do that.

'Did you find him?'

'No.'

A nod. 'That fits. She said you and Westow went back and

told her you were giving up on the job because you couldn't find him.'

'It's what I just said.'

'She said she wondered if you'd found him and he'd paid you to say you couldn't.'

Jane shook her head. 'If he'd needed to borrow fifty pounds from her to pay his way, does that sound likely? Did she give you a scrap of proof for her idea?'

Porter remained silent, glaring. Reluctantly, he said, 'No.'

'Have *you* managed to find him?'

'Not yet. The watch has searched, but we haven't come up with him yet.'

She said nothing, feeling safer in the silence.

'Tell me about the whore. How did she come into it?'

Jane knew she was on surer ground here. 'Mrs Parker had told us that Rawlings liked prostitutes. She thought he might go for me. That was why she wanted me with Simon at her house. One of the women on Briggate knew Rawlings. She told me he liked to spend time with someone called Betsy. Said she had a cast in her eye. But no one had seen her for a few days.'

Let him make of that what he wanted.

'Did you ever find her?'

She shook her head again. 'No.'

'Don't lie to me, girl.' His voice hardened and he started to rise.

She didn't waver. Her voice stayed steady. 'We never found her. After that, Simon told Mrs Parker we wouldn't be continuing with the job.'

'You know we pulled her body from the river.'

'I heard about it.' That was all she was going to say on the matter.

He kept his eyes on her for a long time. 'Your name is Jane, is that right?'

'Yes.'

'You live with Mrs Shields, behind the Green Dragon.'

'I do.'

The constable sat back and gave a sly smile. 'What's your surname? You must have one.'

She kept her mouth firmly closed. She didn't want to say it. A name was power. She didn't want him to have any over her.

She'd given up that name long ago, when her parents abandoned her. Both of them were dead now, but she felt no loss, no regret.

'Well?'

Jane shook her head. She wasn't going to tell him. A small nod and one of the other men moved, slapped her face so hard she crashed to the floor. The chair toppled beside her. She started to reach for her knife. It wasn't there. Of course; the constable's men had taken it when they put her in the cell.

ELEVEN

Her eyes burned with rage. She barely noticed the pain in her cheek. Jane crouched, her head still spinning, looking from one man to the next as the door opened.

Pollard the lawyer. Simon had kept his promise. With one glance he took in the scene and extended an arm to help her up.

'I think you've finished here, Constable,' he said.

'We—'

'What? Are you trying to say you haven't finished beating her yet? Is this a new type of law I haven't discovered?'

Porter shook his head. Jane steadied herself, unsure of her balance for a second. Her tongue moved inside her mouth, tasting blood, feeling for loose teeth. Everything was firm.

'My knife.' Her voice was thick and heavy. Speaking felt like an effort.

The man from the night watch placed it on the desk. Jane slid it into her pocket as she studied his face. Sometime, somewhere, she'd see him and take her revenge for that blow.

Simon was waiting outside, pacing and frowning. He hurried over as they emerged. 'Did he hurt you?'

She shook her head.

'What did he want?'

Quickly, she told him, hurrying as she felt the world beginning to tumble around her. Tears were starting to form in her eyes.

'Thank you.' Jane turned her head away as she raised her shawl. Crying was a weakness; she wouldn't allow anyone to see her do that. Not even Simon.

'Why don't you go home? I'll walk with you if you like.'

'No.' She was staring along Briggate. That way, Simon and Pollard couldn't see her face. The knife appeared in her hand. 'I'll be fine.'

Simon watched as she walked away. Less than ten paces and she blended into the crowd, invisible.

'She was on the floor when I went in,' Pollard said. 'It looked as though they'd hit her.' He grinned. 'They didn't dare try to stop me when I escorted her out.'

Simon had seen the red mark on her face. Bullies. Bullies with positions and power. He'd seen them all his life. Workhouse masters, factory overseers. Some men just craved the chance to hurt. They'd taken her rather than him because they thought they could intimidate her. That only showed they didn't know a single thing about her.

'Good timing.'

'Why did they take her in?' Pollard asked.

'Come over to the Rose and Crown. I'll tell you and see if you can make anything of it.'

'You were looking for this man Rawlings because Mrs Parker employed you?' Pollard asked.

'Yes.'

'What the devil is the woman doing, do you think?'

'I was hoping you might have a suggestion,' Simon said.

The lawyer shook his head. 'No. But I can say you did the right thing when you walked away from her.'

He sighed. 'It was a mistake to accept the job in the first place.'

'It's a little late for regrets.'

'I wanted to see what she was up to. It seemed right at the time.'

'She'd hardly be the first person to play games with you, Simon.'

Over the years, a few clients had tried to use him. But this felt different.

'There's more, isn't there?'

Simon cocked his head, lifted his mug and drank. Pollard knew there was something, but . . . no, for now, he'd keep his own counsel about any connection between Amanda Parker and the body snatchers.

'No.'

'It's your choice,' the lawyer said with an exasperated sigh. 'Just try not to be a fool. One of these days the constable might come up with a charge that sticks. Either against you or Jane.' He stood and looked down. 'Whatever it is you're involved in, think about that.'

*   *   *

Jane barely noticed the streets or the people. She walked in a daze, placing one foot in front of the other. Going home, going to safety. She could feel the skin flaming where she'd been slapped, and kept her shawl over it. If anyone saw the redness, she believed they'd know exactly what had happened as clearly as if they'd seen into her soul.

She felt a prickle rising up her spine. Someone was following her. At the corner she turned left, going from the Head Row on to Lands Lane, then slipping through the courts and ginnels until she came out on Albion Street. He was still there.

Jane had the knife in her hand, pressed against her thigh, ready. The only thing she wanted was to walk into the little house behind Green Dragon Yard. To close the door and keep the world away for a few hours.

The gaol had scared her. She knew it was nothing more than stones and wood, but it felt like a place where a person could vanish forever. In there she was powerless, at the mercy of men. The fingers on her breast, the imprint of the palm on her cheek. Men had done that. Whoever was following her, he'd come at a dangerous time. She was overflowing with anger. Ready to kill.

Into Short Street, then Butts Court. Jane could feel him edging closer, waiting for his opportunity. Three yards past the corner she turned, ready.

He followed, stopping as soon as he saw her. His eyes widened as he took in her blade.

Mrs Parker's coachman. Here once again. Wearing an old jacket with dark stains on the lapels. Even with the brim of his hat pulled low, she could read the hunger in his eyes.

He could die so easily, so quickly. A blow or two and she'd finish him before he knew what had happened. But she remembered Simon's instruction. She wasn't going to return to the gaol. But she'd make him hurt. Make him wish he hadn't come sniffing after her. She'd take out her fury on him.

'What do you want?' Her voice was cracked and bitter; she scarcely recognized it as her own.

'Nothing bad.' A lulling smile. 'Don't worry, nothing bad.'

He held his knife low, inching closer. She watched.

'Did she send you?'

'Who?'

'Mrs Parker.'

'I don't know anyone called Mrs Parker.'

For just a second, Jane doubted herself. Had she mistaken him for someone else? She hesitated too long. He started to spring forward, raising his arm.

But the man wasn't a real fighter. Not quick enough, not deadly enough.

She wanted to catch him in the armpit. At the last moment he turned his body and the knife sliced into his shoulder, deep enough to make him grunt. A single cut. She wanted to make more. Dozens. Hundreds.

No. If she carried on, she might never stop.

He groped for the wound with his left hand, only taking his eyes off her to see the blood on his fingers.

'Get out of here,' she told him. 'You'll live.'

She wiped the knife clean on her dress as he backed cautiously away. Staring in case she pursued him. But she was done.

The anger still raged. None of it had helped.

'Child,' Mrs Shields said when she saw her. 'Child, what's happened to you?'

She opened her arms and Jane felt them around her, as light as a bird's wings.

'This was while you were on your way home from the gaol?' Simon asked.

Jane nodded. What more was there to say? She'd told him everything. It was still alive in her head; it had been all night. The look on the coachman's face, her own hesitation. At least she'd done what Simon asked: she hadn't killed him.

'He must have been waiting for you to come out. She was the one who told Porter about us.'

'Yes,' Jane said. 'But she must have known he couldn't keep us there. Why would she send her servant otherwise?'

'The timing is interesting,' Rosie said. She stood at the head of the kitchen table, arms folded. On either side of her, Richard and Amos were gulping down their bread and dripping. 'The body snatchers dump Rawlings's body in the river, down where no one is likely to find it. The next day Mrs Parker talks to the constable and he takes you in.' She looked at Jane. 'She even gave him a different story from the one she told you, and nobody can prove anything either way. He had nothing to keep you in gaol.'

'What would Amanda Parker gain from that?' Simon asked. All they could do was shake their heads.

'Why would she lie to Porter about lending Rawlings money?' Rosie asked.

'Innocence,' Simon replied. 'If Rawlings takes fifty pounds and leaves without a word, she's a woman who's been abandoned. That's the kind of thing that might appeal to some men. If she let him have it, she becomes a fool. It's easier to dismiss her, especially given her reputation.'

'We don't know which of her stories is true . . .'

'She ordered his death,' Jane said. Not an ounce of doubt in her voice. Not after the gaol, and the coachman following her.

'I agree,' Simon said. The thought gave him a spark. 'From the feel of his skin, he was dead before we even began to look for him. If we'd told Mrs Parker we'd found him, she could have accused us of murder—'

'But when nobody discovered his body, he lost any worth he ever had.' Rosie continued the idea. 'She tells them to get rid of him, and still informs the constable. There's no murder charge, but it makes her look honest.'

'It doesn't matter now.' Jane raised her head and looked at them, thinking of the body going down the river. 'No one will ever find him.'

'Where do we go from here?' Rosie asked.

'Let's find out who this clerk is who rents the house in Sheepscar. One of the men has to find information about burials, so they know where to go. He seems to be a good possibility. Let's see if we can discover any more connections between body snatching and Mrs Parker.'

Jane glanced out of the window. 'It's full light. He's probably already at work.'

'Later, or tomorrow. There are still things we can do.' He laced up his boots. 'Come on.'

'Where?' Jane asked.

Simon grinned. 'We're going to stir things up a little and see what happens.'

'The gaol . . .' Simon began once they were out in the air. But as soon as he said the words, he saw the change in Jane's face. Her expression closed, as if a door had slammed. But he had to speak. 'Porter has nothing. He has no idea who killed Betsy or why. He probably believes she drowned. I don't think he knows about the Irishman.'

She didn't answer, darting away to kneel by the beggar she'd seen the day before, the man in an old army jacket. Below the knee, his right leg was made of wood, chipped and battered. Simon noticed the way the man's face came alive as he saw her. The pair talked in low voices for a minute, then she placed some coins in his tin cup and rose.

'The Irishman came past here about half an hour ago.'

'Which way?'

'Down towards the church.'

They both knew what that meant. Easy to cross Timble Bridge and into the streets beyond. Simon and Jane were the only people pursuing him. Half an hour . . . too late to catch him.

Where could they go? What could they do?

'What's the best way for the body snatchers to learn about any recent deaths?' Simon asked.

'From gravediggers?'

Possibly, he thought. How many churches were there in Leeds, though? They'd all have their own sextons and church-wardens, their own men to dig the ground for coffins.

'Let's go to Headingley,' he said, and she narrowed her eyes in a question. 'It's the only place where we're certain a body's been taken. The sexton didn't have many ideas when I talked to him the last time. Maybe he's had a few more thoughts. I know more now, too,' he added. 'I have a better idea of what to ask.'

The sexton seemed uneasy at Jane's presence, casting glances towards her and keeping his distance. She stayed close to the wall, well away, looking around, silent.

'I told you before, Mr Westow, we notice strangers here. We have our own gravediggers. They do labouring jobs around the village. I wouldn't even know where to find someone from outside.' He gave a brief smile. 'We're a small place. Not many die, thank the Lord.'

'I'd like to speak to one of the gravediggers if I might.'

The sexton thought for a moment. 'I saw George Harris a while ago. We have a funeral tomorrow and I needed to arrange things with him. Let me see if he's still nearby.'

'Have you seen anything interesting?' Simon asked Jane as they waited.

'The man you were talking to.'

'The sexton? I saw the way he looked at you. Women make some men uneasy.'

She shook her head. 'It's not that. I've seen him before.'

'Where?'

She grimaced. 'I'm trying to remember.'

Jane listened as Simon questioned George Harris. He was in his fifties, body a little stooped, hair grey and tangled. Every answer came slowly and deliberately, in a single tone.

'Me and my brother Charlie, we do all the work at the church,' he said. 'We cut the grass in the yard and dig all the graves.'

She watched the man's face as he spoke. He was intent on finding the words. He didn't have any guile; the man couldn't lie to save his life. She glanced at Simon and shook her head. A few more questions and he thanked the man. They watched him amble away.

'It wasn't him.'

'No,' she agreed. 'But who was it?'

The sexton waited in the church porch, writing in a small notebook that he thrust into his pocket as they approached.

'Was he able to help?'

'I'm afraid not,' Simon told him. 'Thank you, anyway.'

The man's gaze flickered away when he saw Jane studying his face. She'd seen him, she *knew* she had. But she still couldn't place where. As they walked back towards Leeds, she worried at herself, trying to make the memory come to her.

She'd just finished supper when she remembered. A gulp of Mrs Shields's special cordial and she rose.

'You look flustered, child.'

'I need to go and see Simon.'

'What's happened?' The old woman was suddenly worried.

'It's just something I realized. But it's important. I need to find him.'

It was his turn to keep watch in Sheepscar. Unless the men had gone after a body, he should still be out there. She hurried, not running but walking quickly, with the shawl gathered around her throat. Close to the house, she vanished deep into the shadows. Out of sight of anyone who might be looking out of a window.

She couldn't see Simon. He was hidden away in the darkness. Jane let out a low whistle, stopped and listened. An answer came, a spot somewhere away from the toll booth. As she neared, he whispered, 'Over here.'

'Nothing tonight?' she asked as she settled beside him.

'I can't see the whole place, but no one's come or gone from the house. Why are you here, anyway?'

'I remembered where I saw the sexton.'

He said nothing, waiting.

'It was when I followed the Irishman and Betsy into town, the night he killed her.'

'Go on.'

'After she left him on Briggate, he went up to a beershop in Bay Horse Yard. I stayed outside. I'd been there perhaps five minutes when the sexton went in. He came out about half an hour before the Irishman.'

A church sexton was supposed to be an upright man. Not a drinker, certainly not someone who spent time in places like that. Even more, if he wanted a drink, why traipse all the way into town when there were good places closer to home?

'Are you absolutely sure?' She knew he had to ask; she didn't mind his doubt.

'I'm certain.' She'd gone through it as she walked out here. It was the same man. She'd swear on it if she had to. 'Do you remember what he said to us?'

'There's going to be a funeral tomorrow.'

TWELVE

Barely first light and Jane was already in Headingley; she'd spent the night there. The dawn chorus was still busy, birds filling the sky with their songs. Jane had come here after leaving Simon, and squeezed herself into a small space. She'd spotted it when they were there during the day, a hidden little opening most eyes skipped past.

It offered a good view of the sexton's house. He hadn't gone out in the evening, although she'd been alert when he finally extinguished his lamp. She was still in the same place when he lit it again early the next morning. An hour later the man glanced up at the sky before striding over to the churchyard.

Ten more minutes and George the gravedigger arrived with his brother, a man who stood a few inches shorter, a little broader, but moved with the same slow deliberation. The sexton gave them instructions and marched off, back towards his house. But he didn't stop. He glanced over his shoulder and carried on walking, picking up his pace as he left the village.

It was still early, very few people around. The sexton was wary, checking over his shoulder as if he was scared someone might follow. Jane had to be careful. She stayed off to the side, moving silently from tree to tree across Woodhouse Moor.

He was on his way into Leeds, no doubt about that. At first she was surprised; she'd expected him to head down and over the ridge to the house in Sheepscar. Now . . . she didn't know, but she had to find out.

Simon's questions had obviously worried the man yesterday. She'd seen it in the way his body stiffened and his face tightened. He was the one who'd told the body snatchers about Gwendolyn Jordan's burial. He'd probably informed them of the one happening later today, thinking nobody would expect them to strike twice in the same place.

After yesterday he must be panicking, hurrying to call them off. As soon as he reached town, he was easier to follow. So many people, and with the shawl over her hair, she knew he'd never notice her.

Briggate, Kirkgate, he hurried along with his shoulders hunched, his head down. He crossed Timble Bridge and she let him push ahead, crossing the road and just keeping him in sight. Along Mill Street, then down New Row. By the time she peered around the corner he'd gone. Not enough time for him to have disappeared round the next one; he'd vanished into one of the houses. Only six on each side.

Nowhere for her to hide here. She walked back to Timble Bridge and found a place behind a filthy wall where she could wait. He'd have to come this way.

A quarter of an hour and the sexton hadn't returned. She grew chilled standing in the shadows. He couldn't be too long; he still needed to walk back to Headingley and prepare everything for the funeral.

Rosie passed, carrying a bag. Jane watched as she pushed open the door of the butcher's shop. Two women together would be a perfect disguise; the sexton would never pay them any attention. She was standing outside as Rosie emerged. A few hurried words of explanation and they lingered on the bridge, idly talking as the beck flowed a few feet beneath their feet.

'He's coming,' Jane said quietly.

'What do you want to do?'

Just a moment to decide. 'I'm going to confront him.'

She'd see how he reacted. Jane took the knife from her pocket. The man couldn't outrun her. Would he dare to start a fight? She didn't think so; still, she was prepared, and Rosie was by her side.

As the sexton approached, she stepped out in front of him. He was a worried man, Jane thought. A terrified one. He seemed to notice the shape of a woman at first and tried to move around her. As she followed, he looked into her face and recognized her. His mouth opened into a broad O.

'Have you been to see the Irishman?' she asked. It was a guess, but she knew the name would unnerve him.

His head moved wildly, looking around for help of any kind. His eyes were full of panic, mouth opening and closing but no words came out. After a few seconds his shoulders slumped and he nodded.

Jane turned to Rosie. 'We need Simon here.' As she hurried off, Jane looked at the sexton. 'You stand over there.'

'But—' he began.

'Over there.' She let him see the tip of the blade. He obeyed. No danger in him, she decided. He wouldn't fight, wouldn't suddenly try to flee. He'd been caught, and he knew it. She gazed up Kirkgate, hoping to see Simon. Jane didn't notice until too late that the sexton was staring over her shoulder, eyes widening.

She turned just as the Irishman charged into her. He was big, powerful. She'd never even sensed he was close. The force hurled her back against the bridge parapet. Jane felt the stone crunch into her spine. Pain roared up and down her body. Her arms flailed as she tried to keep her balance. He'd knocked the breath from her; she couldn't even cry out. Jane tried to bring her knife around, to slash at him. To catch his head, his body, anything at all. But he was too strong, gripping her arms, pinning them. Jane smelled foul breath as he brought his face close. Very slowly he was beginning to push her backwards, forcing her feet off the ground. He wanted to hurt her. Her spine was bent so far over the parapet she thought it was going to break. Her head was hanging in the air. Somewhere below, she could hear the water flowing. Loud. Too loud. Jane kicked, trying to hurt him with her feet. He didn't even seem to notice. His legs were as solid as wood. She tried to shout, but no sound came. The Irishman pressed harder. His eyes showed nothing. No pleasure, no victory, no anger. Just flat and empty. Without any warning, the pressure eased. He let go. She started to come up towards him, ready to attack. But it was only a short moment of freedom. Before she could push forward, he took hold of her. His hands were big enough to span her waist, so large that the fingertips almost touched. The Irishman lifted her. She felt herself rising. She seemed to weigh nothing at all. One final chance. She brought her knife down and caught him across his left eye. Then he threw her and she was flying into the air.

Simon ran down Kirkgate, Rosie close behind him. His feet pounded over the cobbles, weaving in and out between carts and coaches. His heart was racing, his breathing ragged. As he passed the parish church, he could see a crowd at the side of Timble Bridge.

Christ Almighty. Something had happened. Something bad. He sprinted the final hundred yards as if his life depended on it.

He caught a glimpse of Jane. She was kneeling on the bank of the stream, soaked. Bent over, retching into the water. She looked so small and frail, little more than a twig. No sign of the sexton.

The crowd began to leave. The excitement was done, no one was dead. As he ran by, Simon caught snippets of talk: 'Threw her over.' 'Picked her up and tossed her.' 'He ran off with the other one.'

Jane was still on her hands and knees as Rosie pushed people out of the way to scramble down beside her. Her dress was torn. She had cuts on her face and hands. Rosie took hold of her arms and gently helped her to her feet. Simon watched, not sure what he could do. Jane opened her mouth, but Rosie shook her head.

'Not yet,' she said. 'Take your time.'

Jane was unsteady, holding on to the two of them, trying to catch her breath. It was a good ten feet from the top of the bridge to the beck, Simon guessed, and the water looked to be about three feet deep. Sharp rocks at the bottom. She was lucky. Finally she began to move, shuffling her feet. He took her weight as they climbed the bank, and Rosie kept her hands around Jane's shoulders. Simon darted into a dram shop, bought a glass of brandy and made her drink, watching as she coughed then swallowed.

'It'll take away the shock and the taste of the water.' With the tanneries out towards Meanwood, the dye works and rape seed oil plant in Sheepscar, the fulling mills and Clark Foundry on Mabgate, the beck had to be foul. Probably poisonous.

As they reached the road, Jane tried a few steps. She limped at first, favouring her left leg. Within a minute that seemed to pass. Her face gave nothing away. It was shuttered, closed. Rosie kept hold of her arm.

A few paces and Jane looked over her shoulder as if she expected another attack. Suddenly she stopped and patted her dress in a panic. 'My knife.'

'You must have lost it in the water.' Simon pulled a blade from his boot and offered it to her, hilt first. 'Take that until you find one you like.' It was good steel, sharpened every day. She hefted it, feeling the balance in her palm, and a small smile flickered across her lips.

She was in agony; it was obvious. Every bone in her body must hurt. Her hand clutched Rosie's sleeve so tight that her fingers were white. Each step had to be painful, but she didn't stop moving. She never would. It would be an admission of weakness, and she could never show that. Jane would keep going, no matter how much it cost her, or that it might kill her. That was her way. She'd never change.

People stopped and stared. A wet, bedraggled girl holding on to a woman, a man on her other side. As soon as Simon gazed back, they turned away.

Slowly, Jane began to tell them what happened. It came out in shards. Long gaps as she forced down the pain inside, until she was able to speak again.

'The Irishman was just there,' she said, as if she could still scarcely understand it. 'I don't know where he came from. I didn't even hear him until he was too close.'

She was beginning to tremble as the shock set in. Her teeth were chattering. Her fingers clutched the wet shawl tight around her head.

'You said you cut him?'

'Yes.' The word came out tentatively, then again more firmly. 'I know I did. Right here.' Her fingertips traced the spot over her eye. 'That's the last thing I can remember until I came out of the water.'

He saw Rosie shake her head. No more questions for now. They guided her through the gap in the wall to the small cottage. Mrs Shields saw them and bustled out, wrapping Jane in her arms.

'Child, child.' A moment to look at the cuts and bruises on Jane's face. 'Go inside and take off those wet clothes. I'll be there in a moment.'

Rosie gave a bare explanation, short and simple; Jane could add more later if she wanted.

'Nothing's broken,' Simon said.

'Nothing we can see,' the old woman replied. Her voice was calm. 'I'll look after her.'

'I'll help you,' Rosie said.

Where first? Headingley? Sheepscar? He chose the church.

Woodhouse Lane felt endless. He hurried along, sun on his

face, pushing himself to walk faster and faster. Sweat trickled down his back, more gathered in the stock around his neck. His lungs hurt, burning, almost ready to burst.

George the gravedigger and his brother were working steadily in the churchyard, a jug of ale waiting in the shade of a tree.

'Where's the sexton?' Simon asked breathlessly.

'He was here with another man. A big one. He said they were going over to his house.' He nodded in the direction of the building.

Simon felt panic grip at his belly. 'How long ago?' he asked. 'How long?'

George shrugged. 'Less than half an hour.'

Could they still be here? He took a minute, long enough for his breath to steady, then drew one knife from his belt and the other from his sleeve. The sexton looked like he had no fight in him, but when a man was cornered . . . and even wounded, the Irishman sounded like a brutal opponent.

He studied the window of the house, trying to judge if anyone was watching him. No sign, but that meant little. Simon tried the door handle. It turned easily, unlocked, and he pushed at it. Light flooded the room. There, on the floor, his neck bent at an unnatural angle, lay the sexton. No need to check if he was dead; it was obvious.

Simon looked upstairs. Empty. The Irishman had murdered and left. 'We need the watch here,' he told the gravediggers.

It took too long. But it always did. The watchman fumbled around, a man who'd never seen a killing before. He didn't know what to do after he'd questioned the gravediggers and Simon.

'Get Constable Porter up here from Leeds. Tell him Simon Westow said he should come. W-e-s-t-o-w. He'll understand.'

The man bobbed his head, looking grateful that someone else might take over.

'He knows where to find me,' Simon said. A final glance at the corpse and he left. At least the body snatchers wouldn't dare visit the graveyard tonight. A blessing for one family.

Over the moor, slithering and sliding down the dirt slope of Woodhouse Ridge to the Meanwood Road. Rushing along the track beside the beck and kicking up gravel.

He was certain they'd have already left the Sheepscar house.

Abandoned the place. But if not . . . there were three of them there. Ackroyd was wounded, his knife arm useless. The Irishman? Simon had no idea how badly he'd been hurt, but he'd killed the sexton since Jane cut his eye. That left Kingsley whole and healthy. But it was still one man against three. Part of him hoped they'd gone, a trail he could begin to follow. The other part wanted them there, to find some justice. They'd already murdered three people: Rawlings, Betsy, the sexton. Jane was lucky not to be the fourth. If she'd fallen differently . . . no, she was alive, that was what mattered. Bruised, bloody, but in time she would be fine.

It was impossible to be careful approaching the house. There was nowhere to hide. He was in the open. Knives appeared in his hands as he slipped over the low wall.

No handcart in the yard, nothing more than a pair of wheel tracks in the dust. A few planks of wood still propped against the back wall. Simon approached the house slowly, alert for the smallest sound or movement. Nothing to worry him.

The back door was open, hanging a few tempting inches from the latch. He pushed and let it swing back. Someone could be waiting inside, ready for him. Simon stood. The place *felt* empty, no sign of life, of anybody breathing inside the walls.

Silently, he moved from one room to the next, then up the stairs, testing each to make sure it didn't creak. Nothing.

They'd left in a rush. There was still clothing scattered around. Only one room was untouched, everything still neat. That had to belong to the clerk who rented the house. They'd abandoned him.

The body snatchers wouldn't be returning. They were looking for a new lair. Maybe they had one ready, a quiet, isolated place to hide. He had time to search properly.

As Simon opened the door to a small outbuilding, the stink of decay hit him in a wave; this must have been where they kept the corpses. He turned away, gagging, bile rising. For the love of Christ, how could anyone stand that, he wondered, as he tried to spit the taste from his mouth. The stench must have seeped into the walls.

Sawdust on the floor of the yard showed where they'd been cutting lumber for shipping boxes. The edges were still bright, almost white, as if it had just been sawn. Preparing everything for the body they'd intended to snatch tonight. At least those plans had vanished.

Simon kicked at the ground. How many boxes had they made? Still seven? Eight? Nine? More?

He wouldn't find the men today. They'd be careful to remain out of sight. But he'd catch up with them. He'd make them pay. For Gwendolyn Jordan, for all the others they'd taken.

Then there was the Irishman. Jane would want her slow, cold revenge for what he'd done to her.

It was still only the middle of the afternoon. The clerk wouldn't return from his job for a few hours. Mabgate was close. Clark deserved to know what had happened.

'The sexton?' He seemed to explode out of the chair, face red with fury. 'I met him at Gwendolyn's funeral. He seemed so . . .'

'Meek?' Simon asked. 'He had another side. Making a little money for himself.'

'He's definitely dead?'

'There's no doubt about it. One of the body snatchers killed him. Someone called the Irishman.'

Clark shook his head. This wasn't his world. Not a place where everything could be measured. It was dirty, bloody. Evil.

'I'll have to tell Harmony. He'll be . . .' He fumbled for the words but they were beyond his reach. 'You said they're looking for somewhere else?'

'If they don't already have it. There are three of them. I wounded one the other day. Jane cut the Irishman's face this morning. He tried to kill her.'

Clark drew in breath and stared down at the desk.

'You warned me it would be bloody, but I don't think I expected this. You live a violent life, Mr Westow.'

'These men are brutal,' Simon told him.

The man looked up with sorrow across his face. 'I hope you can stop them. For everyone's sake. What are you going to do now?'

'They won't dare do anything for a little while, so we have time to find them.'

'You said you need to catch them with a body.' Clark grimaced at the thought.

'Or in the act.'

'Can you do it?' A blunt, simple question.

'Yes,' Simon answered after a moment.

He hurried back to Sheepscar. The afternoon was slipping away. But no one had been there since he left. He examined the only room that sat undisturbed. A few clothes, none of them new, nothing to draw attention. Letters in a drawer, all addressed 'My dear son' and signed 'Your loving father'. Bank notes clumsily hidden in a box under one of the floorboards. Simon counted them and put them back. Twenty pounds. More than any clerk could have saved from his wages.

He found nothing to tie Amanda Parker to the business that had gone on here. All he had was the fact that she owned the house. But she was involved. He knew it. He could taste it.

Dusk had fallen when he heard the key in the front door.

The man entered, mouth opening as he saw a stranger in the house.

'Sit down,' Simon told him. 'Don't try to run.'

THIRTEEN

By the time the women had eased Jane into the house, she was shivering, teeth chattering. Shock. She knew that, but she couldn't stop it.

'We'll be fine,' she heard Catherine Shields tell Rosie. 'Your boys will be wondering where you are.'

'Are you sure? I want to help.'

'I'm certain. Thank you for bringing her home.'

The old woman warmed water, stripped off Jane's sodden clothes, washed her with soap that smelled like rosemary. She dried herself and pulled a brush through her hair as Mrs Shields brought out her medicines.

'Let me take care of those cuts first,' she said. 'Make sure they don't become infected.'

One, across her back, was deep. With patient hands, Mrs Shields sewed it shut. Jane felt little through the numbness in her mind. She was warm now, but lost in a chaos of thoughts.

'That's done. Now, rub this all over yourself.' She held up a pot of ointment. 'This way you won't ache as much later.'

The flesh was tender under her fingertips. Every inch hurt. Bruises were already beginning to bloom across her skin. Tenderly, she put on fresh linen, stockings, and finally the new dress. Jane had looked up, doubtful, as the woman held it out to her. But it was there, it was clean. She took it, slipped it over her head and pulled it down. Then she huddled inside a blanket, clutching it tight around her shoulders.

Perhaps she dozed; she wasn't sure. Outside it was a spring day, but in the room a fire burned in the hearth, its heat so welcome.

'Drink this,' Mrs Shields said, handing her a mug. 'Men have put plenty of poison in that beck. This will keep you safe.'

She felt like a child. Helpless. The shaking finally subsided until it became no more than a shudder that racked her body every few minutes. Still, she kept the blanket tight around her. It was protection. Jane sipped the liquid, tasting fruits and herbs she didn't recognize. It was pleasant; the gentle scent reminded her of summer days.

She hadn't let herself think again about what happened. She'd pushed it away. Now she was safe, she had time to consider it.

The Irishman had come out of nowhere. By the time she realized the sexton was staring at something, it was already too late. She believed she'd been alert; she was always careful. Yet she never felt him. She hadn't been good enough. Something had been missing in her awareness. This time she'd had no edge.

The Irishman had been running, he had the speed. The height and the weight. Barging into her, stealing all the breath from her body. For a moment she was certain he intended to break her back over the parapet.

He was in control every moment. Each move he made was sure. Then when he lifted her . . . it was as if she barely existed. Something to be plucked and tossed away. Cutting his eye had been sheer luck.

Falling. Flying. The cold, sharp sting of the beck. She'd landed flat on her back, the slap of her body against the water. Down, down, hitting the jagged rocks. After that, time began to flicker and jerk. Jane remembered gasping, opening her mouth and swallowing water, gagging at the foul taste, retching as she tried to stand. Her legs refused to support her. She saw that people were watching. Nobody came to help. She had to use her hands to crawl up on to the bank.

She was going to find the Irishman and hurt him. Kill him for what he did to her. It was the only way to feel in charge of her life again. Because of him, her knife was gone. She'd spent a long time on that blade, hour after hour of honing and grinding it until it felt absolutely natural in her hand. Until it was a part of her.

Jane stood. Slowly, carefully. She was weak. It would pass. Mrs Shields looked up with worried eyes.

'Are you all right? Do you need anything?'

'I'm fine.' It was partly true. She was battered, every fibre of her body was painful and aching. But she was alive. Nothing broken. Filled with fury at herself for failing, for losing. Next time . . . next time she'd make sure she had the advantage of him. She started to prowl around the room. Slow, every movement jarring and hurting, but the ointment was working. The pain seemed to exist on the other side of a veil.

In the bedroom, Jane eased a brick out of the wall and took a little of the money hidden there. There was plenty of it tucked away; more than three hundred pounds. Everything she'd saved from working with Simon.

Her boots were still sodden as she pulled them on, the leather damp and clammy.

'You can't go out, child,' Mrs Shields said, alarmed. 'You need to rest.'

'I have to,' Jane replied, giving a gentle smile and keeping her voice soft.

'Why?'

Jane shook her head. 'I won't be long. I'll be very careful, I promise.'

She tucked a dry shawl over her hair and glanced in the mirror. In the new dress she felt she was on display. The market had finished for the day, all the stalls packed away; no chance to buy any old clothes until tomorrow. But the knifesmith on Briggate was still open. She tried a dozen or more until she found one that felt as if it had been made for her hand. Simon's blade was good, but it was his. She needed her own, one she could trust, one she'd worked herself.

While the man put a keen edge on it, she went to the boot dealer. That was quicker. He had the right size, comfortable when she tried them on her feet. A stout sole that would last, lacing up with a strong leather thong. Back for the knife, testing it on the ball of her thumb. So sharp she never felt it break the skin. Perfect. Slowly, cradling her pain, Jane hobbled home again.

Her body still screamed as she walked, but she felt better now. Safer. She was taking control again. She was ready.

As dusk arrived, the day caught up to her. She'd been reading *Pride and Prejudice*, feeling as if she was a part of the story, observing everything. Even though the people were unlike anyone she'd known, she understood them. She was there, tangled up in the writer's magic.

She must have dozed. Like an old woman. Jane never even realized Mrs Shields was standing by her until she was gently shaking her shoulder and saying, 'Drink this. You need to sleep, child. It will help you.'

*   *   *

The clerk still had one hand on the door. He turned, poised as if he was ready to bolt.

'Don't,' Simon told him. His tone was enough to make the man pause. 'Sit down. Your friends have all left you.'

He craned his neck, looking around as if he might spot the others. 'Who are you?'

'My name's Simon Westow. I'm a thief-taker.' He saw the man's body tense. 'I told you, they've gone. They've abandoned you. I thought we'd have a talk before I bring the constable. Now sit down.'

The man blinked as he obeyed, eyes never leaving Simon's knife. He was in his late twenties, his face and clothes clean, no dirt ingrained around his fingernails. Ink stains on the side of his hand.

'What's your name?'

He hesitated, then answered, 'I'm Paul Glover. But I don't understand. What do you want here?'

'Everything.'

The story came haltingly. Fearfully. It had begun because the clerk had been complaining of having no money in spite of working. One night he was out drinking and met Kingsley. The gambler had cultivated him, told Glover he could do well if he was willing to look the other way at some things.

The clerk worked for an attorney with his office on Briggate. He knew the law, all its subtleties and gaps. But he craved silver in his pocket, enough to enjoy a few good things in life. Kingsley had drawn him in with promises that fed his desires.

By the time the man told him to rent this house and advanced him the amount, he was already snared. He didn't even ask what they were planning. He didn't care. All he wanted were the coins jingling as he spent them.

The first body they brought horrified him.

'I had . . . I don't know, visions of hell. I'm not religious, but how could it be right? I begged them to get rid of it. The next day, it was gone.'

The second was a little easier. By the fourth, he barely noticed the stink.

'I had nothing to do with any of it.' He was craven, almost begging. 'That was the three of them. They paid for the house and gave me some money, that's all . . .'

'How many did they take?' He wanted the confirmation. He needed the truth.

'Eight,' Glover replied after a second. 'But I think there might have been one or two before I met Kingsley and they moved everything here. I'm not sure, just a hint in something they said, and they seemed to know what to do.'

As Simon considered it, the idea made sense. A trial run or two, experimenting and refining. Testing the potential, and becoming serious once they discovered the possibilities.

But eight at least. For the love of God . . . they had to pay.

'Who found this house?' he asked.

'Kingsley. He said it would be perfect.'

'Why did he need you? He could have rented it himself.'

'He told me it was easier this way. I don't think he wanted his name on any papers.'

That was perfectly believable.

Simon cocked his head. 'You're a clerk. You have some education. Once you discovered what they were doing, why didn't you leave?'

He hung his head. 'I began to like the money.'

At least it was an honest answer. Not good, but truthful.

'The money's disappeared now. You should, too, before Constable Porter arrives.'

Glover's eyes grew wide 'But I thought—'

There was no corpse here. No proof of anything at all. Porter wouldn't waste his time taking the young man into custody. There was nothing to gain by it. But with luck he'd be too scared to realize that.

'Which of them found the bodies?'

Glover shook his head. 'I don't know. I never asked. I stayed away from it.'

Simon believed that. He sounded so desperate.

'Here's what I'll do. I'm going to catch up with the others. But I can guarantee you that when the constable arrests them, they'll all be singing your name, saying you were the leader. You could end up transported. Or there's even the noose.' He saw the shadow of terror cross the clerk's face. 'Do you know what would be best?'

'What?' He stammered out the word.

'Pack up what you have and go. Now. Today. Leave Leeds.

I'll give you an hour before I go to the gaol.' Simon picked up the knife. 'After that . . .' He shook his head, slid the blade into its sheath and moved towards the door. The man was scared; he'd leave. One fewer to consider. 'One last thing. What kind of dealings have you had with Mrs Parker?'

Glover frowned. 'Who?'

'Mrs Parker. Amanda Parker.'

'I don't know anyone called Parker.'

It was no act. He was genuinely puzzled.

'What about a man named Tom Rawlings or a whore called Betsy?'

The clerk shook his head. 'I've never heard of them.'

Still the truth. 'You said Kingsley knew about this place.'

'Yes. I had to see a lawyer to sign the agreement.'

'Did you ever ask how he came across it?'

'No.' He looked confused. 'Why would I?'

'Are there any instructions for what you should do if something happened here?'

The clerk shook his head. 'No. I never thought . . .'

'Good day, Mr Glover. Remember, you have an hour.'

'But the rent is paid until—'

'An hour.'

Simon walked up North Street towards Leeds. Near the crest he stopped, turned and looked over his shoulder at the house. He wasn't going to take the constable there. All Porter would care about was proof, and Simon had none.

The body snatchers had vanished. But they hadn't gone far; Simon was convinced of that. They weren't likely to give up a trade that paid well for very little work. They needed to be in a place with a regular supply of bodies. Where death was commonplace. Somewhere they knew, where men like the sexton could be bribed. A town like Leeds.

Eight. They hadn't finished. Not even close.

The knock came after nine. Simon had been about to give up on the man. Better late than never, he thought, as he slid open the bolts on the front door.

'Right, Westow, you'd better tell me what's going on. I've just come back from examining the sexton's body in Headingley.'

Porter listened, face growing redder and angrier as Simon and Rosie explained about the body snatchers. He made no mention of Mrs Parker; no need to turn over that stone again. Not until he had something definite to offer. Even without her, there was plenty.

'As soon as you knew where they were, you should have come to me,' the constable said.

'Why?' Rosie's question caught him by surprise. 'What could you have done?'

'We'd have gone and arrested them.'

'You'd have found no corpse there. You wouldn't have been able to charge them with anything,' she said.

He glowered at her. 'We'd have run them off.'

'They've gone,' Simon told him. 'I went to the house in Sheepscar after I found the sexton. Nobody there.'

'How long have you known we had body snatchers here, Westow?'

'A week,' Simon replied. 'Maybe a little longer.'

'I see.' The constable glowered. 'Do you know how many they've taken?'

'Eight.' He saw the horror grow on Porter's face. 'Maybe even more.'

'I didn't know any of it.' The man looked up, sorrowful. 'Eight?'

'Eight,' Rosie repeated. 'One of them was just ten years old.'

'Dear God,' Porter said.

'We know who they are.'

'Who's employed you, Westow?'

Simon smiled as he shook his head. 'You know I'm not going to tell you that. But we can work together. We'll find them again, and when they have a body, I'll tell you. You come and arrest them and take all the glory.'

The constable eyed him suspiciously. 'What's in it for you?'

'Justice,' Rosie said. Her eyes glittered. 'And our fee.'

FOURTEEN

Jane hurt. Thick bolts of pain knifed through her with each tiny movement. She forced herself up from the bed, to stand in front of the mirror. Broad bruises had started to develop all across her body and legs. But the ointment Mrs Shields made would keep them down and stop much of the aching. The cuts on her face and arms would heal, even the deep one on her back. The tincture the old woman had given her the evening before had brought a good night's sleep, deep and thankfully dreamless. No memories to haunt her through the night, no ghosts chasing her. Her mind was fresh as she woke and dressed, then slipped out of the house. Walking took time, but she forced herself to keep going.

Jane took Simon's knife from her pocket and placed it on the kitchen table. He slid it back inside his boot.

'Did you find yours?'

'I bought a new one,' she replied, holding it in her palm.

'How do you feel?' he asked. 'Do you need to take a day or two to rest?'

'No.' She wanted to hunt down the Irishman, to cut him. To kill him. 'I'm fine,' she lied. She knew how to keep pain at bay.

'That dress,' Rosie said. 'Is it new? It fits so well it could have been made for you.'

Jane looked down at the wood, stroking the grain with her fingertip.

'I've had it for a little while.' She was telling the truth, in a way. She hadn't *just* bought it. But even with a shawl wrapped around her, she was certain people were staring. The dress was too clean. Too good. People would remember it. She needed to stop at a stall and buy something older. Clothes that no one would notice.

'We need to find them,' she said when Simon finished explaining what had happened at the Sheepscar house and Porter's visit.

'We will. We've made them panic and run. That's when people make mistakes.'

In the silence they could hear the soft tone of the tutor in the parlour, teaching grammar to Richard and Amos.

Jane stood. Sitting on the bench put a strain on her back. Walking might work it out.

'I'll start looking,' she said.

The dress was shapeless, whatever pattern it once had now washed until it had faded to a blur. Jane took it home. As soon as she put it on, she felt better. Drab, ordinary. She was anonymous again. She ran the word over her tongue, relishing the sound. A-non-y-mous. She could spell it, she knew the meaning. All of that from reading.

Happy, she folded the new dress in its brown paper, placed it back in the chest and left the house behind Green Dragon Yard.

Close to the parish church, Jane hesitated. Barely for a second, not long enough for anyone to observe. She drew in a breath, swallowed, and walked on to Timble Bridge. She stopped, staring over the parapet and down at the water. Her fingers pressed against the stone as it all came back into her mind. The pain, the way the Irishman hoisted her so easily and tossed her without a thought.

He could have crushed her in his grip, done it without effort. The next time they met, she couldn't allow him the chance to pull her close. She'd failed. She'd trusted to her senses and they'd let her down, their sharpness vanished. But she would see him again; she was going to make certain of that. She was going to pay him back for what he'd done.

The streets didn't scare her. Her new boots were comfortable, and in the old dress she knew no one would notice her. It was a warm day, so she only had a light shawl pulled over her hair as she walked up and down over the Bank, from the York Road down towards the river and back. Each step hurt, but the more she moved, the easier it became. She was invisible.

Jane had no reason to believe the body snatchers were around here. They could be anywhere in Leeds now. But the Irishman had made this area his home. Constantly shifting from place to place, but always close. It was somewhere to begin.

No sign of them. Not a whisper in the shops she visited. By afternoon her legs were aching. Her joints were sore and sharp pains jolted through her back. She could feel the bruises growing and throbbing. Still, Jane pushed herself, beyond the streets being built, out towards the countryside and the farmhouses. Few people walked this far; she needed to be careful.

By the time she turned back towards Leeds, she'd spotted two possibilities. Farms, although neither of them looked like they were still used for growing anything. The land lay untilled and filled with weeds. At one of them she noticed a handcart behind an outbuilding. Pushed from Sheepscar? Impossible to tell. She'd seen a few places where she could hide and watch.

Tomorrow, she thought. Today, her body had had enough. She limped home as the pain grew.

Jane rubbed more ointment into the bruises and cuts. It stung at first, then a gentle, soothing warmth spread across her body. Bread and cheese for her belly, a glass of one of Mrs Shields's cordials.

An evening of quiet talk between the two of them, about nothing in particular. The old woman rarely went anywhere these days, and she relished little pieces of idle gossip about the fashions and the way women wore their hair.

Finally Jane settled with her book, eager to know the fate of the Bennet sisters. A few short minutes and she was asleep.

'Simon!'

He turned at the sound of his name. Without thinking, his hand slid towards the knife in his belt, on his guard in case the shout was a warning. Only Barnabas Wade, pushing towards him through the crowd.

'There you are,' the man said as he neared. 'I've been looking for you.'

Not too hard, Simon thought. He was never difficult to find. 'I'm here now.'

'You wanted me to ask about Amanda Parker's money.'

'I hadn't forgotten.' So much had happened since then that it didn't seem as important as he'd originally thought. 'What have you managed to discover?'

'Well, she's definitely not as rich as we all believed.' Wade licked his lips and his eyes seemed to glow. 'Nowhere near.'

'How much does she have?'

'Only a few thousand. It's not exactly a grand fortune.'

Nowhere near as much as people claimed, but she wasn't likely to be begging on the streets, either. She could survive very comfortably on that. At the same time, she'd feel the loss of fifty pounds . . . He jerked his head up.

'I'm sorry, what did you say?'

'Her properties are all mortgaged. Her second husband was forced to do that. He lost a lot of money.'

Interesting. 'How many does she own?'

'She inherited a few. Four or five, I think. I wasn't keeping count. They're still in his name. Why do you want to know?'

'I'm just curious.' He gave Wade half a guinea and the man's face creased into a thankful grin. A bad week for selling dubious stocks, Simon thought. 'You did well.'

'I really was looking for you.'

It was a lie, of course. He'd waited until he was desperate for the money that Simon would pay. No matter; he had the information now.

The clerk at the Court House glanced at the pile of coins, then back up at Simon. A clink as he added two more, before the man swept them up off the desk and vanished into a back room. Five minutes later he returned with a list written in elaborate copperplate.

A nod of thanks, and Simon came out into the spring light, folding the paper.

A useful morning's work, he decided.

There was a heavy haze over Leeds, with its stink of smoke and oil and decay. A mail coach passed, the horses flecked with sweat, the driver shouting to warn people out of the way.

They'd come close, but the body snatchers had been cunning enough to stay a step ahead of them. Two steps, he thought ruefully; maybe even more. But things were moving. They were pushing; he'd meant what he'd said earlier. He and Jane had caught up to them once. They'd do it again, and this time they had more information.

The three men were still around; he had absolutely no doubt about that.

But in the middle of the hunt it was easy to become lost in the act and forget the reasons for doing things. *Why* all this was happening. Eight bodies, all dug up and sold to be dissected.

One of those corpses had been a young girl hardly older than his sons. Simon had looked her father in the eye. The family deserved justice, whatever way he could deliver it.

Morning. Simon looked out of the kitchen window. Overcast skies, with a hint of moisture in the air. The farmers would welcome that, he thought. April had been too dry; the young plants needed some rain to grow. He turned.

'I found two places they might be,' Jane said.

'Where?'

'Out past the houses they're building along the York Road. They both look like old farmhouses, and they're off by themselves.'

He nodded. It made sense. Somewhere quiet, but not too distant. Jane looked happier than she had yesterday. Her movements were a little easier, she wasn't holding herself quite so rigidly. But he knew it must still be bad; her back was probably a mass of bruises that would grow worse before they faded. She'd never admit to pain. That would be a weakness.

Simon brought out the paper, explaining what it was.

'The ones you saw aren't on this list. But Amanda Parker owned the place in Sheepscar. They might have gone to another property of hers.'

Five, dotted around town. Away from the crowds and the streets.

Rosie stabbed a finger at two of the addresses. 'These would be isolated enough for them.'

He nodded. 'I took a look yesterday. Very carefully,' he added. 'No one could have seen me.'

'What did you find?' Rosie asked.

'One's a proper working farm, so we can forget that.'

'What about the other?' Jane asked.

Simon chewed his lower lip for a few seconds before he answered. 'It looks empty. But there was something about the place. I can't explain. I didn't see a soul, but it felt as if there might be people there.'

'I'll go out there tonight,' Jane said. 'Look for lights.'

'I can take a walk with the boys and see one or two of the others this afternoon,' Rosie said. 'No one's likely to suspect a mother and sons.'

Simon grinned. 'That's an excellent idea.'

'Remember, the odds are against it being any of them,' she told him. 'Leeds is a big place.'

'It's a start, that's all.' A small shrug. 'Maybe we'll have some luck.'

'We could walk out to the houses off the York Road. You and me and the boys. They'd love the exercise. We'd just be a family strolling together. No one would think anything of it. If we're there around twilight they'll have lamps lit, we can see if anyone lives there.'

Jane knew the way without thinking. It seemed there was nowhere in Leeds that didn't flow in her blood. She'd passed this place many times before without noticing it was there. Just another building. Now she paid attention as she walked along, glancing across as she went by.

Her body hurt. Before she came out, Mrs Shields had rubbed ointment on her back, fussing at the bruises. Without looking, Jane knew how bad they must be; she could feel them whenever she moved. More pain ahead until they faded, too. But she could ignore that, put it away. She was alive, she'd have her retribution. Another new word she'd learned. As she walked she spelled it out in her head.

She saw the soft glow of an oil lamp in a window by the door. Two more at the back where the shutters didn't fit tightly in the frames. Simon's feeling had been right; someone was living there.

It wasn't full dark yet. Without stopping, she looked around and noticed two or three places to spy on the building without being seen. Tomorrow she'd arrive early. She was going to find the Irishman.

On her way back into town, she felt the prickle up her spine. Someone was behind her. Not close, not a danger. Not yet. But there and following her. At least her senses had not completely abandoned her. Was it someone from the house? Could they have recognized her somehow? It didn't seem possible, but . . .

In Leeds, her feet knew the way. This was her territory. She could easily hide and see who was following. For her own safety, she needed to know.

Jane ducked into a ginnel. Stretching, feeling sudden, tearing agony roar through her muscles, she forced herself to climb a blackened brick wall to reach a low roof then lay down and waited with tears of pain in her eyes. From here she could see everyone who passed along the street. She was safe; people never looked up, and she was hidden by the darkness.

The footsteps were light. She had to strain to pick them out. He was coming closer. She held her breath. Up in the sky, the clouds shifted and a shaft of moonlight caught his face.

Not one of the body snatchers. It was the coachman from Mrs Parker's house. Back once again. He held his right arm tight against his body, bandaged from the damage she'd done him. He was carrying a knife in his left hand. Every few paces he paused, a quick glance all around as if he expected someone to spring out at him.

She waited until he'd gone. Out of sight, not even the sound of him walking. Then she scrambled down and hurried home through the ginnels and lanes, moving like a ghost. She wasn't ready to confront anyone just yet.

Why had he returned? Had she sent him or was it his own idea? Was he hoping for a second chance to fight? The questions dogged her as she sat in front of the fire, not opening the book in her hands. The material of her old dress was stained with soot. Better something cheap than the one she'd had made, Jane thought, and smiled at herself. Vanity again. Tomorrow she and Simon would have to try and pick their way through this puzzle.

Simon and Rosie strolled arm in arm as the twins ran on ahead. Not as much traffic along the York Road as twilight arrived, but the passenger coaches still passed at speed, not stopping or slowing for anything. Twice he had to warn Richard and Amos to keep to the side of the road. The air was cleaner, here, clearer.

They passed one of the houses Jane had mentioned. Not a light to be seen, and no sense of life about the place.

'It looks neglected,' she said.

'It is,' Simon said. 'I doubt anyone's been inside in months. Maybe we'll have better luck at the other one.'

At least lamps glowed in two of the rooms. A handcart behind the house, just as Jane had said. That meant little; so many places had them. One to look at tomorrow, when it was light.

'What do you think?' she asked.

'Too early to tell.' Simon pushed his lips together and shook his head as he saw the boys heading into the distance. 'Come on,' he called. 'We're going home now.' He turned to Rosie. 'All we're doing is guessing and hoping out here.'

FIFTEEN

'He was after you again?' Simon asked in astonishment. He thought for a few seconds. 'I'll try to find out why.'

'But—' Jane began, then stopped and nodded. 'I can keep watch on that place you found.'

The spring sunshine was pleasant and soothing as she sat in the small hollow. Bees buzzed around and butterflies passed, swooping and dancing. Jane was out of sight, but still able to keep watch on the house.

She'd been here an hour, alert, her aches slowly easing in the warmth. The bruises were still blooming across her back and thighs, but Mrs Shields's ointment dulled the worst of the pain. Being out here in the light and fresh air helped.

Her mind was trying to make some sense of why the coachman had followed her again. The question had woken her three times during the night, but she couldn't puzzle out the answer. Yet another mystery involving Amanda Parker.

Jane glanced across at the house. So far there'd been no sign of anyone, although Simon said there had been lights in the windows last night. The only people who could afford to sleep late were crooks and the rich.

Another hour. Traffic passed a few yards from where she sat, but nobody spotted her. She picked out a pair of figures crossing the fields. Two men. She kept her eyes on them as they approached the farmhouse. They were joking, laughing together. One opened the back door of the building and they entered. A woman came back out with them and glanced up at the sky before returning to the house. Not the body snatchers. Just labourers, doing their work. This place was clean.

Jane rose stiffly and began the aching walk back to Leeds.

He still needed to talk to the coachman. First, though, home for his dinner. A rare luxury. But there was good reason. Rosie had walked out to take another look at the house on the York Road.

'I keep thinking about the parents of that girl,' she'd said.

'Gwendolyn Jordan.'

'Richard and Amos will be with their tutor. I'll have plenty of time. It's not far to go.'

'Would you recognize them?'

'Ackroyd has a heavy white moustache and his right arm in a sling. The Irishman has a dark stain down the left leg of his trousers, and he wears a battered top hat.' She paused. 'I can't remember anything about the other one. How did I do?'

He grinned. She'd done this work with him before. She was daring, and when she had to be, every bit as deadly as Jane.

'Just be careful.' He squeezed her hand. 'Please.'

'They're not living in the house,' she said after the boys had eaten and gone into the yard to play. A family is there.'

'Did you see them?'

'I knocked on the door and asked if they needed anybody to help them. The same thing I did in Sheepscar.'

The gown she was wearing wasn't her best, but it was still woven from good wool and cut to fit her body. 'In that?'

Rosie shook her head. 'I went out in old clothes. It was a woman who answered. I could hear a baby crying. She told me she and her husband have been living there for a year.'

'Now we know.'

'Richard and Amos are growing,' she said. 'I could start doing more. I miss it, Simon.'

In the years they worked together, she'd been good at the job. Rosie had a natural feel for intrigue and crime. She could put herself in a thief's mind. A third person would mean they'd be able to take on more business.

'Why not?' he told her.

The rain that had threatened for an hour never came. The roads were dusty. That meant plenty of polishing for a coachman. Maybe he'd be lucky and find the man hard at work.

Simon approached Burley House from the side, slipping through some woods and over the metal railings into the garden.

Yes, the man was rubbing the paint on the coach. Not working too hard, using his left hand with the right arm tight against his body. Simon waited until the coachman was hidden from the house and crept up quietly.

The man was in his shirtsleeves, his livery jacket tidily folded on the seat inside the vehicle. He was humming a song to himself, not even aware that anyone else was there until he felt the prick of a knife on the back of his neck. He stiffened.

'You've been following a young woman.' The coachman stood perfectly still as Simon hissed the words into his ear. 'She wounded you. That would be enough of a message for most men. Why are you still doing it?'

'I wanted her.' A lie. He'd hesitated just a beat too long before he answered. Now he drew in a sharp breath as the knife point pierced his skin and a tiny trickle of blood ran into the collar of his shirt.

'Try again,' Simon told him. 'I want the truth this time.'

'She told me to do it.' Very slowly, he turned his head towards the house. 'Not to kill her. Just hurt her.'

'Why?' He could feel the anger rising. All Mrs Parker's doing. He'd been right. She was deep in this.

'She doesn't tell me why. Just says what she wants me to do. Said the girl wouldn't dare kill me.'

'Don't be too certain of that.' Simon leaned a little closer. 'Even if she doesn't, I might. You'd be amazed how easily a body can vanish. No one would ever know what had happened to you. Not even Mrs Parker.' He turned the knife a little, hearing the man gasp. 'Do you understand me?'

'Yes.'

'The safest thing you can do is disappear. Pack your things and walk away this afternoon. If you don't, the next time could be the last.'

Simon was gone in an instant, before the coachman could recover. He'd tried to put the fear of death into him. Maybe it would work. No point in pressing him on anything Mrs Parker wanted or telling him to find out. She'd never explain herself to a servant; she'd be suspicious if he asked. At least now he was certain he was right about her, but he still needed to find out *why*.

'Amanda Parker.' Rosie spat out the name.

'We know now.'

'Proof,' she reminded him. 'We still need proof. Not just a servant's word.'

'Meanwhile, we're right back to the beginning,' Simon said after Jane told him what she'd seen as she observed the farmhouse.

Rosie shook her head. 'No, not quite. They must know we're searching for them.'

'They might have left Leeds,' Jane said.

'Where would they go?' Simon asked. 'They know people here. They have a system set up. They've been making good money. Probably more than they've ever had, by the sound of them.' He looked at the others. 'Do you think they'll be in a hurry to leave that?'

'Then how do we find them?' Rosie asked.

'We ask. Walk. Watch.'

Jane nodded. That was how she'd always worked. Rosie could help in the mornings while the boys were at their lessons. Between them all they should learn something soon.

Three days.

Nobody had seen the body snatchers. They'd gone to ground; either that or someone was hiding them. But they could still be out at night, digging and lifting. A hurried trip to the coaching office with a box, then the body was gone and they were left to count their money.

Jane asked the children who lived on the streets. Even they had nothing to report. She walked mile after mile around Leeds until the new boots were well worn in. Still comfortable and sturdy.

Her back was a painful mass of bruises, all turning from deep purple to blue and yellow. Her legs were sore every day. Her shoulders were stiff and slow. She couldn't cross Timble Bridge without being reminded of it all. The Irishman had defeated her. Humiliated her in front of the entire town. She'd allowed herself to grow lax. She ran her fingertips over the scars on her forearms. He'd displayed her failure. Yet even after that, Jane felt no urge to punish herself and cut her skin. The marks were old now, so faded that they seemed to come from another life. One she'd left behind.

Jane wandered the area either side of the York Road, down towards the river or up into Burmantofts. Circling, moving farther out. No reason, no knowledge. She simply *felt* they'd be here. It was a place the Irishman was drawn towards and he seemed to be the force behind the body snatchers.

Even though it was a warm day, she kept her shawl close around her head as she walked. Never dawdling, never hurrying. Observing everything and everyone. Stopping in the small shops and asking a question or two.

It was probably close to noon. She'd wandered out from Leeds, into the country. From the corner of her eye she caught a movement. A man disappearing over the brow of a hill. Someone big, she thought, and she'd caught a glimpse of something that could have been a battered top hat.

SIXTEEN

Jane hurried. Quick strides, as if she was walking with a purpose. Not running; people remembered that. The man had been at least two hundred yards ahead of her, she needed to make up the ground. Her heart thudded. All the pain had gone, and in its place, a mix: fear and anticipation.

She reached into the pocket of her dress and grasped the knife hilt. Her new blade, still waiting to be blooded. She'd worked it every evening, stroke after stroke across the whetstone.

By the time she reached the hilltop, her upper lip was damp with sweat. She wiped it with the back of her hand and blinked.

He'd gone.

She stood and stared, as if she had the power to conjure him out of the ground. Nobody was walking. A single cart pulled by a horse moved along the road, rumbling slowly towards her.

Had she imagined the Irishman? He'd been in her mind. Could she simply have wanted to see him?

She stood, looking and thinking. Tracks snaked away on either side of the road, vanishing into woods. Old trees with heavy trunks and thick foliage. A perfect place for the Irishman to hide.

The carter drew close, giving a nod of greeting.

'Did you see a man walking along here? Big, wearing a top hat.'

He scratched the back of his neck. 'I saw someone. Wasn't paying much attention, really. He went off down one of them tracks.' He turned on the wooden seat and pointed. 'That first one, over there, I think.'

'Thank you.'

The man grinned. 'Watch out for yourself, girl. He's probably not worth chasing.'

She smiled back at him as the cart moved away. He was wrong. This one was definitely worth the chase.

Jane walked along the road, glancing at the track. It curled through the woods and out of sight. It was hard to believe anything as isolated as this could exist no more than two miles from the middle of Leeds. Jane glanced over her shoulder at the smoke that hung over the town. She grimaced at the pain in her body.

The Irishman might have spotted her. He could be waiting, ready to finish the job he started on Timble Bridge. She drew the knife from her pocket, keeping it tight in her hand. It would only be right if he was the first to feel it.

She crouched, keeping low and feeling her body ready to scream. The trees offered some cover. Every three paces she stopped, listening and peering around. Ahead, she could see a clearing and a house. Standing, prepared to flee at the slightest sound, she looked.

An air of neglect hung about the building. But all the windows had their glass, no slates missing from the roof.

The man might have turned down the track to this place, the carter had told her. But there was no sign of anyone. No hint of someone moving inside.

Then . . . the slam of a door at the back of the building. Another minute and she heard the regular rhythm of something she couldn't identify.

Very carefully, Jane edged around. She drifted from tree to tree and waited for any shout, any indication she'd been seen.

A man sawing wood. Not the Irishman, definitely not Ackroyd. This one was younger, small. She waited until he raised his head. Kingsley. She'd seen him before, when he and Ackroyd collected the handcart. Somewhere in the branches above her a crow cawed, answered by the bright, angry chatter of magpies.

Kingsley paused, looking in her direction for the cause of the noise. Jane stiffened, pressing herself against the tree trunk, not daring to breathe. His eyes seemed to move over her.

She waited for him to call to the others. For something to happen. But he took a drink from a mug and returned to his work.

Her heart was beating fast. Nervous sweat trickled down her back. A full minute passed, maybe longer, before she allowed herself to ease back and fade into the undergrowth. Everything slow and smooth. Nothing jerky or sudden to draw his eye.

Her mouth was so dry she could hardly swallow. Jane forced herself not to rush. Safer to take her time, not give any cause for alarm.

Jane didn't feel at ease until she was back out on the road

with the sun warm on her face. She bent over, hands resting on her knees until her breathing seemed normal again, then slowly straightened and looked back.

The body snatchers had discovered the perfect place. Isolated. Not as close to Leeds as they'd been in Sheepscar, but no neighbours who might prove nosy. Yet at the same time, it would be easier to observe them. They'd have to use the track and the road to come and go. Plenty of spots for watching, and none so close that they were dangerous.

Jane smiled. For once, she'd had the kind of luck that a bag of money couldn't buy.

'Are you certain it was Kingsley?' Simon asked. He felt the words rush out, eager to know, to grasp at anything. 'Thin, looks like he's never had enough to eat. Dark hair and a sour face. Sharp features like a rat.'

'It's him,' Jane said. 'I'm positive it was the Irishman I saw, and that's the only place he could have gone. There was a hand-cart in the yard too.'

He paced up and down the kitchen, trying to put his thoughts in order. Could Jane have found them? It hardly seemed likely it could have happened so handily, but sometimes Dame Fortune smiled and he'd be a fool not to believe. Something Jane said clicked in his mind. 'Did you say he was sawing wood?'

'Yes.'

'Was he making a box?'

He could see her thinking, remembering, picturing the scene in her mind.

'He might have been. I don't know.' She shook her head. 'I didn't stay long enough to find out.'

'If he was, they might be planning to take another body soon. Possibly tonight.'

He wanted it to be true. But that didn't mean it was. He wasn't about to tell Porter until he was certain.

'Who owns this place?' Rosie asked. 'It's not on that list of properties that belong to Amanda Parker.'

'Something to find out tomorrow,' Simon said.

At home, Jane drank a cup of Mrs Shields's cordial. She drained the mug and poured another, sipping as she eased off her boots and stockings. The air felt good on her feet. She washed them in cold water, drying them carefully and finally smiling. For once she was happy with her luck.

'Have you finished for today?' the old woman asked.

She shook her head. 'Not yet. I have to go out again later.' They were going to watch the farmhouse in case the men planned to dig up another corpse in the darkness.

Catherine Shields frowned. 'You're nowhere near recovered yet. Don't push yourself too hard, child.' Her expression softened. 'Still, you have some time now. Why don't you show me how your reading has improved?'

They arrived a little before dusk, finding a hidden place along the trees, close to the road. Cushioned by tussocks and grass and ferns, they settled in to wait for a few hours.

'The body snatchers have to come out along that track.' Jane pointed. 'We'll be able to hear the wheels of the handcart as they approach.'

It wasn't a coaching road, and there was hardly any traffic as the day drew to a close. Three people on foot, another leading a packhorse. Then all that remained were the sounds of the birds and the scuffling of animals through the undergrowth as they came out for their night hunting.

Simon looked up. Away from the town it was a clear sky, so many stars on view. The moon had just passed full, shining clear and bright. Another hour, well into the night now, and still no one emerged along the track.

Jane rose.

'What are you doing?' He whispered the words. Sound could travel far in the empty night.

'Going closer. Maybe we can see a face.'

'I'll follow you.' She knew the ground.

Even with all her pain, she was sure-footed. But cautious, making sure she stayed out of sight of the house. He saw the knife in her hand; Simon tightened his fingers around his own blade. They approached from the side. He heard men talking, but it was lazy chatter, nothing more than conversation to pass the time. Not the sound of people making preparations, or in a rush to leave.

The handcart sat in the yard, a pile of cut boards leaning against it. Sawdust on the dirt. Simon eased up to a window with no shutter. It only took a moment to pick out the faces of Ackroyd and Kingsley. No doubt about it. This was the place.

Jane started to lead the way back to the road and he followed. After a few seconds she brought her lips next to his ear.

'Someone's walking.'

They crouched. He held the knife steady, watching and listening. The moon cast a strong light along the track. The sound of feet scuffling through the night grew louder.

He heard Jane draw a breath. Then he saw. The coachman. Just a few days since Simon had warned him to leave Leeds. He hurried along, looking over his shoulder to make certain no one had followed him. Seeing him here was a definite connection between Parker and the body snatchers.

For a moment Jane looked poised to run out and confront the man. Simon had his arm out, ready to stop her. But she didn't move until he was well past them.

'What are we going to do?' she asked.

'Nothing. We walk back to Leeds and think. They're not going anywhere tonight.'

'The coachman . . .' Jane began.

'We'll let him go for now,' Simon said. 'Wait and see what happens.' It went against the grain after he'd warned the man, but it was the right thing to do. He could see she wanted to speak, but he continued, 'I know what you want, but we'll let this play out. We're close. Very close. If we scare them again they'll vanish, and it'll be harder to find them next time. We might not have another piece of luck.'

It took a moment before she agreed.

'They're cutting boards, so they're going to take another body very soon,' Simon said. 'Probably tomorrow night. Why don't we spend the day trying to find out more about Amanda Parker? It might tell us how she's involved in all this.'

The ointment eased her pain. Mrs Shields had left her a tisane that tasted of mint and something she couldn't identify. Jane tried to read, but her mind refused to concentrate on the words. Instead she saw the coachman, then the empty face of the Irishman as he forced her over the bridge. Slowly they began to fade as she let tiredness overtake her.

*   *   *

It was light when Jane woke. A sky thick with the promise of rain to come. Her body ached, every muscle sore and painful when she moved. Before she dressed, she rubbed on the ointment again and examined herself. In the mirror, her back looked like someone had beaten her. Bruises across the flesh in a rainbow of colours. The black line of thread where Mrs Shields had stitched her skin together. A few minutes and she began to feel the warmth of the ointment. She walked around the house, eating bread and butter, pouring a cup of Mrs Shields's cordial and feeling her body start to ease.

A breeze was blowing as she opened the door; she took a heavy shawl, wrapping it around her shoulders and arranging it over her hair.

Simon wanted to know about Mrs Parker, but most of the people she spoke to scarcely knew her name; many more weren't aware of her reputation. The ones who were repeated the same, familiar tale of her life. At dinnertime, as a few lazy drops of water fell from the sky, she stopped to talk to Kate the pie-seller.

The woman glared for a moment. 'I have a bone to pick with you.'

The words shocked, like a slap on the face.

'Me?' Jane asked in disbelief. 'Why? What have I done?'

'I was worried about you.' Her expression softened. 'You never came to see me after what happened down on the bridge.'

'I was . . .' She let the words trail away. She knew Kate, but never imagined the woman thought much about her. 'I'm sorry.'

'You're working, so you must be mending.'

Jane shrugged. What else was she going to do? 'It still hurts.'

'Tell me. I want to know all about it.'

A short version as people came and bought pies, with Kate asking questions.

'Are you going to find this Irishman?'

'Yes,' Jane replied without hesitation. Her hand moved to the knife in her pocket, stroking the hilt. 'What do you know about Amanda Parker?'

'Probably nothing you won't hear from anyone else. I've never met her. Don't think I've ever seen her, unless she was in her carriage.' She thought for a moment. 'Do you know Mrs Dawlish? She's a widow, runs a small draper's shop over on St Peter's Square.'

'No.'

'She's been there since time began. They say the Parker woman grew up on Quarry Hill. If she really did, Mrs Dawlish would know her.'

'I'll talk to her.' Jane paid for two pies and added an extra threepence as an apology.

Kate smiled. 'Just look after yourself. Someone has to take care of that old woman you live with.'

Simon bustled around Leeds. He wanted to see people. Not the upright ones that Amanda Parker would have known through her husbands, but the men and women who lived in the shadows. People who might know about any darker things she'd done.

A few rumours about the way her husbands had died, that she might have carefully helped them on their way. Words were all, though; nobody could offer a shred of proof. Gossip wasn't going to convict in court.

Still, he'd learned that she had begun life on Quarry Hill, one of six children. Her father left not long after the youngest was born, and the family had no money. Amanda was pretty enough, and most of those he talked to claimed she really had been a whore. Simon didn't care. He knew – they all knew – that you did what was needed to survive.

Somehow she found a wealthy husband. By then her mother was dead. Amanda gave her brothers and sisters money, on condition they all left Leeds. She didn't want the strands of the past coming back to haunt her. The story was that they all accepted apart from one brother. A few nights later he was attacked. A robbery that went too far. He died. But who could be sure what had really happened?

She worked on the way she spoke, how she carried herself, until all trace of that Quarry Hill past was buried. But Simon knew all too well that you never completely lost your own history.

By the middle of the afternoon he had plenty to consider. Simon sat in George Mudie's printing shop, watching the man work as he explained his suspicions about Mrs Parker.

'You know, she's stuck in the middle,' Mudie said. 'She's supposed to be part of the *ton*, whatever that might be round here, and secretly they can't stand her.'

'The *ton*?' He'd never heard the word.

'The quality, Simon. Society.'

'Is that a guess or do you know?'

'I know. I used to run into Sir Walter Bertram, and he's right at the top of the tree. Tracing the family back for generations, all of that.'

'He pronounced judgement?'

'Very much. They all say that who she married doesn't matter. She's as common as you or me. From the bottom of the heap. You see her now . . .' He shook his head in admiration. 'She should have become an actress; she'd have been a sensation on the stage.'

The woman lived behind masks. She was ambitious, there was no doubt about that.

'Why are you so eager to know about her, anyway?'

'She hired us to find someone. Something about it didn't feel right, so a few days later I told her we were stopping.'

Mudie cocked his head. 'That's not like you.'

Simon hesitated before saying more. 'There are hints she's involved with the body snatchers.'

'What?' he began in astonishment. 'Come on, Simon, don't be ridiculous. Why would she do something like that?'

'That's the part I don't understand.'

'You'd better not start saying it in public or she'll have you up for slander.'

Simon chuckled. 'I'm not stupid.'

'Have you found any evidence?'

'Nothing definite. Nothing a lawyer couldn't tear apart.'

Mudie pursed his lips. 'She always had an evil streak about her. Do you want my advice?'

'I'm here, I've told you all this.'

'Watch her. You're doing the right thing, trying to find out about her past. I never paid much attention to the woman, but there's something about her.'

'I've noticed.'

Mudie tied string around a thick stack of handbills. With a grunt, he lifted them. 'I need to deliver these. I mean it, Simon, take care.'

SEVENTEEN

Jane read the names on the signs. From the goods in the window, there was no mistaking the draper's shop, but she revelled in the words, recognizing them and sounding them out in her head. A year ago, reading had seemed like magic, a mystery she didn't think she'd ever understand. She wasn't even sure she needed to learn. Now . . . Jane knew she had a long way to go, but she was proud of what she'd managed. Reading had come to seem like second nature. She looked up. *Mrs M Dawlish, Proprietor*. Just as Kate had said. The right place.

The woman was old, but she carried her years well, moving with a straight back and easy strides. Wiry grey hair that was mostly covered by a shawl, her face filled with lines and creases.

'Hello, dear. What can I do for you?'

Her voice had a welcoming, husky warmth. Jane glanced around the shop. Everything was organized, the wooden counters brightly polished. No lies here, she decided.

'Kate said I should come and see you.' As the woman frowned, she explained, 'The pie-seller.'

Mrs Dawlish smiled. 'You mean Katie Crawford. That was her name when she was a girl, anyway. You don't look as if you're looking for anything I sell.'

'Information,' Jane said.

'Oh?' Bemused, the woman cocked her head. 'I suppose you want to know about the old days. I can't imagine it would be anything else.'

'Amanda Parker.'

'Ah.' The woman studied her. 'I won't ask why. I don't think you'd tell me.'

Jane stayed silent. She didn't know how to respond.

'She was Amanda Lister back then. A beautiful child. A proper picture. The problem was that she knew it. She stayed that way when she grew.'

'People say she was a whore.'

Mrs Dawlish shrugged. 'It's true enough. Did you know it was her mother who encouraged her?'

'No. I don't know anything.'

'She was a good woman, really. Six children and her husband ran off, left her to look after them. Poor woman worked every hour she could stand up. The children went to the factories and the mills as soon as they could. But she saw the way men looked at Amanda. She had something . . . I don't know what you'd call it. They wanted her.'

'What did she do?' She was caught in the story, although she knew how it went on.

'A man talked to Amanda's mother. I don't know what happened. Maybe he showed her some money. Soon enough, Amanda had a string of men coming around and the family began to live a little better. You probably know most of the rest. A year or two and Amanda was gone from here. The tale that passed around was that a man was looking after her. Then she married her first husband.'

'Did she ever work on Briggate?'

Mrs Dawlish laughed. 'Oh Lord, I've no idea. It was a long time ago. If I ever knew, I've forgotten.' She was quiet for a moment, narrowing her eyes. 'Your name's Jane, isn't it?'

'How did you know?' She felt her heart suddenly beating fast. The woman knew her.

'Jane Truscott. Yes, that's you. You still look like you did when you were little. Did you know that until you were four, your family lived just around the corner from here?'

She shook her head; she had no memory of that. When she was small they seemed to move so often, from one dismal room to another.

'You work with Simon Westow, don't you?'

'I do,' Jane admitted.

'People talk about you, did you know that?' Mrs Dawlish asked.

'Me?' She didn't believe it. She didn't *want* it. An unknown life was much easier.

'Don't look so scared. It's just your name and what you do. Nobody knows your face. I'll tell you this, though, you haven't really changed from when you were a little one.' She paused. 'I heard what happened on Timble Bridge. From the sound of it, the Irishman, he's a nasty sort.'

'Do you know him?'

The woman shook her head. 'I don't want to, either. You need to look out for yourself.'

'I will.' She placed coins on the counter, not so sure it was the right thing to do. But Mrs Dawlish didn't refuse the money or change her expression.

'You live with Mrs Shields, isn't that right?'

'I do,' Jane replied. How much did people know about her? It made her uncomfortable. Wary.

'I hope she's well.'

'She's not as strong as she was, but fine.'

'Age.' The woman nodded her understanding. 'Tell her I said hello and wish her good health, will you?'

'You know her?'

'My shop used to be on Briggate. She bought things from me. Of course, Leeds was much smaller then. She might remember me.'

She couldn't escape her own past, Jane thought as she walked away. It lay all around her.

They sat in the kitchen at Simon's house, comparing what they'd learned as the twins ate. They'd pieced together most of Amanda Parker's early life, but it told them nothing of who she was now. No great secrets or shadows. It was largely as she told it herself.

Rosie beamed at them. 'I went to the Court House this morning. Dressed up like a lady to find out who owns the farmhouse where they're hiding.'

'Is it . . .?'

She shook her head. 'Someone called Youngman. It looks as if he's owned it for years.'

A pity, he thought. But things would have been too neat, too obvious, if it had somehow belonged to Mrs Parker.

'Thank you. I meant to go and ask, but . . .' Time had slipped away.

'You know I enjoy working.' True enough. A statement, but also a reminder, he thought: let her do more. Poor dead Gwendolyn Jordan had touched something in his wife.

Simon looked at Richard and Amos. The twins sat listening, rapt.

'Wash yourselves, you two. It'll soon be dark. Go upstairs and I'll come up and tell you a story.'

'Will the body snatchers work tonight?' Rosie asked.

'Probably,' Jane answered. 'It has to be soon.'

Lights glowed behind the windows in the farmhouse. Jane made her way through the woods until she could see the handcart standing behind the building. They hadn't gone to take any corpses yet.

She crept out again and settled next to Simon near the road. The promised rain had never happened, but with the darkness a thin wind had begun to blow. She was glad she'd decided to wear the old green cloak. Warmer for work like this, sitting and waiting for hours on end. In the undergrowth, she was absolutely invisible.

No talking; they both knew how sound could carry at night. She had plenty to occupy her mind. Words: weighing them, feeling them. Sometimes she believed she could almost taste them.

She went back over the last short lesson in numbers that Rosie had given her. Subtraction. Sub-trac-tion. She sounded it out. Taking one number away from another. On the table, as Rosie had demonstrated with pieces of Richard's jigsaw, it made perfect sense. She'd understood it immediately. Since then she'd been trying to fix it in her mind.

Jane was lost in thought when Simon prodded her arm. The first drops of rain were falling and the wind had grown stronger. He stood and she started to follow him back to town.

'They won't come out now,' he said. Even as he spoke, the rain grew heavier. 'No one's going to dig in this. We'll try again tomorrow.'

She glanced back over her shoulder. 'I wonder if the coachman is still there.'

'Something to discover in the morning. We're going to be soaked by the time we're home.'

Dawn came, bright and calm. For a short while the air smelled clean, as if it had been scrubbed by the rain. Blue skies above thin clouds. They disappeared soon enough and the pall of factory smoke over Leeds returned.

Jane had draped her wet dress and stockings near the fire while she slept. As she slipped them on, they held a little warmth. She talked to Mrs Shields. The old woman wanted to hear about Mrs Dawlish once again.

'We should go over and visit her. What do you think, child?'

They both knew it was a dream; Mrs Shields couldn't walk to Quarry Hill and back. But in a phaeton, perhaps, a small carriage. Jane had the money; perhaps she could hire one for an afternoon. Once all this was over.

'Yes,' she agreed. 'I think we should.'

Catherine Shields had another friend, a woman in Hunslet who owned a grocer's shop. They could make it an afternoon of visits. A surprise. A treat. Mrs Shields had done so much, taking her in, making her feel like she was family. That would be one small way to repay her for what she'd done.

There were places to watch Burley House. Out of sight, knife in her hand, Jane settled in a spot where she could see the coach house. She didn't have to wait long. Less than half an hour and the coachman appeared.

She stayed long enough to see the stiff way he moved his arm. Jane smiled; he'd had that coming, trying to attack her. She slipped away, no one aware she'd ever been there.

'They'll certainly be going for a body tonight,' Simon said.

'Yes.'

Clark Foundry seemed even louder than the last time they'd been here. A world of banging, the pained screech of ripping metal, voices shouting. But Joseph Clark and Harmony Jordan sat in the office as if it was nothing at all.

'We're sure they'll move soon,' Simon told them. 'Very soon.'

'What are you going to do?' Clark asked.

'We' – he gestured at Jane – 'have no authority to arrest them. We're going to follow. As soon as they reach the cemetery, I'll go and rouse Constable Porter. He and his men can wait at the farmhouse.'

'My Gwendolyn . . .' Jordan's voice was low and hesitant.

'The constable will question them. We know that one of the three was the man who sold the burial gown. That,' he reminded them, 'is a felony.'

Clark chewed on his lower lip. 'I know several of the magistrates. Would it help if I asked them to prepare the constable and his men for something?'

'As long as you don't tell them what's going to happen. I don't want anyone blundering in too soon. This is our best chance to catch them.'

'You won't receive any of the credit, Mr Westow,' Clark said.

'I don't care. I want them in prison for what they've done.' He could hear the cold fury in his voice. 'That's what matters.'

'I'll talk to the magistrate. Porter and his men will be ready.'

'I can't guarantee it. But if the weather holds . . .'

'Of course. I told you, I'll pay you for all your work once this has finished.'

They took Lady Bridge over Sheepscar Beck and the hard perfume of Leeds wrapped around them. Smoke, burning metal, the dampness of steam, the soot he could taste on his tongue; there was no mistaking the place.

'Are we going to do anything before dark?' Jane asked.

'Rest,' Simon answered. 'It's going to be a long night. We'll need to be sharp. Better to be out there before dusk. I'm not going to risk losing them again.'

'The coachman still worries me.'

He smiled at her. 'Today we'll take care of the body snatchers. The rest can wait.'

'What about Mrs Parker?'

Simon shook his head. 'I don't know. I truly don't. We'll have to see what she does after Porter makes his arrests.'

Mrs Shields was busy with her plants, snipping some with a pair of scissors, packing soil around others. The wisteria that climbed up the wall was ready to bloom in lilacs and whites.

Jane settled in a pool of soft warm sun with her book. The warmth eased the aches that filled her body. But the words refused to stay in her mind. They danced and shifted until she realized she'd read the same paragraph four times and couldn't remember any of it.

But sleep wouldn't come, either. Nothing. She pulled the shawl over her shoulders, kissed Mrs Shields on the cheek and vanished through the opening into Green Dragon Yard. When everything else failed, she could walk. Even if it hurt in every fibre of her body, it never let her down.

*   *   *

The first stirrings of dusk, the time when the light began to fade. Still too early for the body snatchers to be moving. Simon settled deep in the ferns, a good place to see anyone using the track to the farmhouse.

He watched Jane slide through the trees, soon hidden from sight. Five minutes and she returned.

'They're still inside. I can hear voices. I couldn't be certain, but it looks like there are things in the cart.'

'Tonight,' he said with a grim smile. 'We'll follow.' No knowing which graveyard they'd visit. 'You stay with them. As soon as we're close to Leeds I'll go for the constable and the magistrate and bring them out here. They can make the arrests.'

'I want the Irishman,' she told him.

'You'll have your chance. Just not tonight.' He heard the light rumble of wheels and they saw three men walking together, the biggest in the middle, pushing a handcart. 'Ready?' Simon whispered.

EIGHTEEN

The men moved slowly and steadily. No talking, only the creaking sound of the cart on the road. One of them glanced over his shoulder, but there was nobody on the road behind them.

Too easy to follow, Jane thought. She and Simon stayed among the trees and the shadows. All they had to do was keep silent.

The body snatchers continued through Leeds, staying on the quiet streets where lamps shone in the houses. Noise carried from Briggate, shouting, cursing, singing.

She kept the knife in her hand, grip firm on the hilt. The new weapon still hadn't been blooded. Perhaps tonight might change that.

The men walked through a small glow cast by a gas lamp on the road. She spotted Ackroyd, his arm cradled in the sling. Jane smiled to herself as she picked out the grubby bandage wound around the Irishman's head, covering the eye she'd cut when he hurled her into the beck. Some small satisfaction for the pain.

As they turned along Water Lane, she realized where they were going. The Quaker burying ground. Past the foundry and the heavy, menacing bulk of Marshall's mills, along the road to Holbeck village. She felt Simon touch her arm and gesture; he was leaving to meet the law.

The magistrate's name was Wilmott. He was in his forties, earnest-looking, starting to go bald, his hair thin enough to show a pale scalp. He stopped his anxious pacing when Simon arrived.

'Westow.'

Simon nodded to him and the others. Porter, along with three large men from the night watch.

'This had better be worthwhile.' The constable glared at him.

'You're going to arrest three body snatchers,' Simon told him. 'With a corpse they've just taken. One of them sold a burial gown they'd taken from a corpse. There's a witness. Is that worthwhile enough for you?'

'A felony is transportation. If the gown cost enough, maybe even the rope,' Wilmott said. His voice held a coiled eagerness. 'Where are they?'

'You'll need to follow me. We have to hurry and walk for a while. As soon as we're there, you hide and take them as they come home with the body.'

'Are you sure?' Wilmott asked.

'Yes,' Simon replied, and hoped he was right, that nothing happened to stop the men.

No light at the burial ground. Jane watched as the men left the cart out of view. For a moment, the moon shone as they brought out their tools: a spade with a broad blade, mattock, rope, and white sheet.

No buildings overlooked the cemetery, but they were cautious. One of them lit an oil lamp, trimming the wick so low that it became no more than a suggestion of light. She was far enough away, caught so deep in the night that they'd never see her. Yet even at this distance she was scared to breathe, wary of moving in case she made a noise.

They must have had information; they knew exactly where to go. In the lamp's dim glow, she caught the unfolding of a dirty sheet beside the grave. Another minute and she heard the sound of the spade breaking through the earth. Muted, though. Not the hard, sharp sound of metal. Something different. Wood.

It only took a few seconds for the digger to establish a crisp, steady rhythm, down and push, tipping the soil on to the sheet. The Irishman, big and strong enough to do that. With a fresh burial, the ground wouldn't have had time to settle; the work would be easier.

He kept going without any break or pause. Jane raised her head above the low stone wall. But they were little more than darker shapes against the night. She was on the other side of the graveyard, invisible to them.

They were experienced, used to working in silence. It looked as if one of the men was raising the lamp. But the light was so dim that it didn't help her. The digging slowed and she heard the dull thump of wood against wood.

The Irishman had reached the coffin.

A moment and she heard the crunch of the mattock breaking

through the lid. Short, sharp sounds that carried in the night. Tearing the wood away. Three minutes of muffled noises. A grunt. The flutter of a sheet, its hint of paleness against the dark.

Then the Irishman was steadily shovelling the dirt back into the hole as the other two lifted the corpse in its sheet and carried it back towards the cart. Jane ducked down again, even though they were nowhere close. No risks, she thought. Not tonight. Porter and the watch would deal with the body snatchers.

Finally, she heard the sound of the Irishman stamping the sod back into place, so it would look as if nothing had ever happened here. Half a minute later she heard the cart wheels on the road.

No need for her to follow; she knew exactly where they were going. Instead, she ducked around, taking the footpaths, slipping through the new streets, hurrying to be ahead of them.

'It's down here,' Simon said as he led them along the track to the farmhouse.

'Isolated,' Porter said. The men from the night watch straggled behind him.

'How long before they arrive?' Wilmott asked.

'I don't know.'

'Are you certain they'll have a body with them?' That had been the man's constant worry. His third time with the exact same question.

'I am.' If they'd turned back, lights would already be burning in the farmhouse, but everything was dark.

They followed Simon into the yard.

'They'll come here with the cart. If you look around, there's probably a box, ready for the corpse, so they can take it into town and send it off tomorrow.'

'It's over here,' one of the watch said as he stumbled against something.

'What do you suggest?' Wilmott asked Simon. 'You found them.'

'Everyone needs to spread out. Make sure no one can see you. Keep quiet until they're right here. One of them was wounded recently. He probably won't be able to give you much trouble.'

'Wounded?' the magistrate asked with a sharp look.

'His arm.' Easier to deflect the question. 'The big one is the danger. Everyone seems to call him the Irishman. One of his eyes is bandaged but he'll fight.'

'He won't get the better of my men,' Porter said.

'Maybe not. I hope you're right. But be careful, he's brutal.'

'Is he the one who tossed that girl of yours off the bridge?' one of the men said.

'Yes.' Simon didn't allow anything to show in his voice.

'I heard he picked her up like she was nothing.'

He let the comment go by. 'She cut his left eye. You'd do well to tackle him from that side.'

'What about you?' Wilmott wanted to know. 'Where will you be, Westow?'

'I'll be nearby. You have the men; you'll be able to surprise them.'

'You wouldn't warn these body snatchers, would you, Westow?' Porter asked.

Simon took a step towards him and the constable shuffled back. 'Don't be stupid.'

He stalked off. If they used their brains, they'd be able to make clean arrests. The law could take the glory for it. Porter would be happy, and Wilmott would enjoy having his reputation burnished. He was eager to be known.

Simon settled back in the ferns on the far side of the main road. Less than two hours since he'd left here. It felt much, much longer.

He must have drifted off. Simon heard the shuffling in the undergrowth and reached for his knife in a sudden panic. Then Jane sat beside him.

'They're on their way.' A whisper, close to his ear. 'They worked very quickly.'

Of course, Simon thought; they were professionals. They were good at what they did. How many bodies was this? Nine now? Ten? More?

'How far ahead of them are you?'

'Probably a quarter of an hour.'

They waited in silence. Simon thought about the Jordans and the other families who believed their relatives were buried and safe under the ground. People bereaved twice. He was aware of Jane turning her head.

'I can hear the cart.'

Kingsley was in the lead, constantly turning his head, listening for anything. Then the Irishman, with the dirty bandage under his top hat. He was pushing the cart. No effort at all; it could have been empty, not weighted down with a body and tools. Ackroyd at the rear, keeping watch for anyone following.

They passed, then turned down the track to the farmhouse. Any moment now, Simon thought.

NINETEEN

The sound of the cart faded. Simon strained to hear, but there were only the noises of the night. A hunting owl after his prey, animals padding through the undergrowth.

Then the shouts erupted. Voices tangled and climbing over each other. The dull noise of blows. A scream that didn't stop.

He rose. He couldn't help himself. Someone had been stabbed. A figure appeared, running hard towards town.

Simon dashed through the grass, then along the track. He took one knife from his belt and pulled a second from its sheath up his sleeve. Jane wasn't with him. He thought no more about it as he turned the corner into the farmyard.

It was all over. Men looking dazed, nursing their wounds. He felt as if he'd stumbled into the aftermath of a battle, too late to do anything.

The cart had been toppled on to its side. Something long and large had tumbled out of it, lying in the dirt.

Someone had lit a lamp. Bright light shone around.

Ackroyd stood, motionless, silent, as one of the watch guarded him, sword drawn. From the man's face, all he wanted was the smallest excuse to run him through.

Porter was kneeling beside the screaming man on the ground. Blood had soaked into the dirt, leaving a dark stain.

Wilmott the magistrate walked around, dazed. He had a broad red mark on his cheekbone that would soon become a bruise.

'What happened?' Simon asked. As he gazed around, he saw no sign of Kingsley or the Irishman. Two of the watch had vanished. 'Where are the others?'

'We surprised them, right enough,' Wilmott told him in a dull, empty voice. 'Started to line them up against the back wall of the house.' A long hesitation. 'The watch were supposed to have disarmed them and be keeping an eye on them. Cameron must have glanced away from the Irishman for a second. He had a knife concealed somewhere and stabbed him in the belly.'

Cameron's screams had become long, awful moans.

'The Irishman ran?'

The magistrate nodded. 'Porter and I were looking in the cart. He tipped it over, trying to trap us underneath it. Hit me and hared off into the trees before we knew what was happening.'

'What about Kingsley? The third one?'

'He slipped off in all the confusion. One of the men has gone after him. I sent the other to warn the infirmary.'

Five minutes and the corpse was in the house, one of the men left to guard it. They'd lifted Cameron on to the cart, hurrying across the night to Leeds. Simon followed with Ackroyd. He'd found a piece of rope and tied it around the man's neck. Not a shadow of a doubt that he'd sold the burial gown; he fitted the description right down to the missing little finger on his right hand.

'I should have done for you in Goulden's Yard.'

'You didn't,' Simon told him. 'You were the one who ended up wounded. Now you're going to Van Diemen's Land, unless the judge decides to hang you.'

Ackroyd snorted. 'Trying to scare me? They don't do that for taking bodies.'

'They do for stealing a burial gown and selling it.' He shoved the man in the middle of his back, making him stumble. 'Move.'

Jane watched Simon vanish. The screaming continued; she tried to push it to the edge of her mind.

The Irishman had escaped. She knew it the way she could sense her own heartbeat. Slowly, she stood, feeling every ache and bruise, cherishing them, then moving until she was lost among the trees. Leeds was the only place he could go. Somewhere big enough to hide him, people who could help, whether they liked it or not.

She spotted him.

She wouldn't let him get away. Jane was going to collect on the debt he owed her.

He kept a quick, steady pace. With her shawl over her hair, staying out of sight, she slipped through the darkness like a ghost. Listening, watching.

Maybe he believed no one could hear him. But he was loud. His footsteps kicked up dust and snapped twigs that echoed like sharp cracks in the night.

Jane trailed behind, too far away for him to see. She wanted him, but on her terms, when the time was right. Tonight, she was content to follow and see where he went.

He seemed happier with buildings around him. At ease among solid brick and the smell of soot. He moved with more confidence, as if he knew exactly where he was going. Down through the maze of streets off the York Road. His territory.

She followed the Irishman to Spinner Street. He stopped, staring around, then knocked on a door. Jane pressed herself against the wall at the corner, only her eyes showing. Someone lit a lamp and the Irishman vanished inside.

Stay? Go? She weighed the choices. She'd remain until the house went dark again. That way she'd know exactly where to find him.

He didn't stay long. Five minutes, maybe less, and he appeared.

The Irishman set off down the hill. She kept back, far enough that he was just barely in view. He walked without a care, not trying to hide himself. Maybe he believed he was king here, untouchable. She'd prove him wrong.

They were drawing closer to Timble Bridge. He kept marching. As they approached it, a prickle of fear rose up her spine. Was he leading her back there to finish what he'd begun?

The questions stopped as soon as he turned into Goulden's Yard. Now she understood. The empty house was the perfect place. Thomas Rawlings's corpse had been removed; his remains ought to be close to the sea by now, damaged far beyond any hope of recognition. No one was likely to search here.

Clever.

A few more minutes, then she drifted away. Back to the house behind Green Dragon Yard, and sleep.

The gossip was already in full flow by the time Simon reached the coffee cart outside the Bull and Mouth. Clouds had rolled in during the night, bringing a light, misting drizzle to damp down the dust on the streets.

'Did you hear that the constable took a gang of body snatchers? They were fresh from the grave, had a corpse there with them.'

'A right battle. That's what they're saying, at least. One of the watch was badly wounded. Not sure if he'll live.'

As he moved around, there was more of it. The only topic of

conversation, details exaggerated beyond anything he remembered. No one mentioned him, though. Good. It was better if his name stayed out of this. Made it easier for him to hunt Kingsley and the Irishman. His job wasn't finished yet.

Simon wandered up Briggate and turned the corner. A small group had gathered across from the gaol, angry men who had nothing better to do with their time. Constable Porter was outside, talking to someone who carried himself with a swagger. He turned his head and Simon recognized him; one of the town councillors. A minute and he'd gone.

'Receiving congratulations?'

The constable snorted. 'He seems to think two of them getting away and one of mine badly wounded is a victory.' His expression soured. 'If things had gone right, it would have been worthwhile. What do you want, Westow?'

'How's your man?'

Porter drew in a deep breath. 'The surgeon says he'll survive unless something goes wrong. Won't be able to work on the watch again, though. Might not be able to do much at all. We're searching for the pair who vanished.' He cocked his head. 'Do you know where they went?'

'No. But my client will prosecute the one you have in the cell.'

'Good luck to him. I've been trying to find out a few things from him. About the only thing he knows is how to keep his mouth shut.'

'I'd like to talk to him.'

Porter shrugged. 'Be my guest. He isn't going anywhere.'

The cell was cool, damp. Ackroyd sat on the bench, gazing down at the flagstone floor. He looked up as the heavy key turned in the door and Simon entered.

'What?'

'You already know you're in trouble. Accused of a felony. I told you that you're going to court. You understand what that means.'

Ackroyd spat.

'He might be willing to let it go if you give him some information.'

It was a lie; Clark would never allow things to drop. But Ackroyd didn't know that. He'd need an incentive to give up any useful pieces.

'What do you want to know?'

'How many bodies have you taken?'

He shook his head. 'Never kept count.'

'Where did you send them?'

'No idea. Kingsley handled that. I don't know what he did.' He glanced up. 'I don't. I left it to him.'

'You sold a burial gown.'

He snorted. 'I've sold a few of them. Good little extra.'

'From the girl you lifted in Headingley.'

'Aye, I remember that,' he said after a long moment.

'Where did you send her?' Simon asked. Maybe there was *something* he could tell Harmony Jordan. Some thread he and Clark could begin to tug. 'Who bought the body?'

'I said: Kingsley never told me. My job was to help and make the body fit the box.'

'You didn't see the address when you left the box at the coaching office?'

'Wouldn't make a blind bit of difference,' Ackroyd told him. 'I can't read.'

Simon was walking on Lady Lane when he heard the footsteps behind him. He turned, knife already in his hand. Jane, purposeful and deliberate.

'I'm on my way to see Clark again,' he said. 'At least the constable arrested Ackroyd.'

'I followed the Irishman back to Leeds,' Jane told him.

Simon nodded; he thought she'd vanished to go after him. 'Where did he end up?'

'Stopped at a place, then he went to Goulden's Yard.'

'Cunning,' Simon admitted. The Irishman already knew that nobody would come looking there. He believed he was safe. 'We should tell the constable.'

'I want him for myself.'

If the man's corpse was discovered, Porter probably wouldn't ask too many questions. Very likely he'd be relieved that he hadn't had to battle the man again. Simon stared at Jane. The bruising on her face. There would be much more of it all over her body. She'd earned her revenge. This time he'd be there to help her.

'All right.'

As they strolled along Mabgate, Simon told her the little he'd learned from Ackroyd.

'We need to find Kingsley,' he said. 'He's the one with the knowledge.'

She stayed silent for a long time. Around them, Leeds was a town of steam and smoke and the clatter of machinery. Making goods. Making money.

'They won't stop,' Jane said finally. 'They've been doing too well. Kingsley and the Irishman will find each other and start again.'

'If we watch Goulden's Yard, Kingsley will appear sooner or later. They're going to have to replace Ackroyd, but that should be easy enough,' he said. 'They'll need to find another new place, too.'

TWENTY

Clark stood behind his desk, head bowed. He'd given up his chair to Jordan. The two of them listened without interrupting as Simon told them about the farmhouse and Ackroyd's arrest. He watched their expressions, but it was impossible to judge what they were thinking.

'This . . . man . . . really doesn't know where Gwendolyn was sent?' Jordan asked when he'd finished. He kept wiping at his damp eyes.

'That's what he claims. For what it's worth, I believe him. One of the others organized things. A man named Kingsley.'

'Can you find him?' Clark asked.

Simon glanced across at Jane. Her face was as empty as ever.

'We can look.'

'I'm willing to put up a reward.'

'No.' Simon shook his head. 'If you do that, he'll probably run. Vanish from Leeds. I told you: as the law stands, if he's caught, he only faces a short time in prison. Let's give it a few days and see what happens.'

'Very well,' Clark agreed. 'Remember, we want to know where they've sent the bodies they've taken.'

Simon watched Jane go, following the streets into Quarry Hill and Marsh Lane to watch Goulden's Yard, then he crossed Lady Bridge and walked up the Head Row.

George Mudie was turning the handles on his printing press, keeping a careful eye on the sheets as they appeared. For a moment, Simon watched him through the window before he entered the shop.

'I heard what happened last night,' Mudie said. 'Two of them escaped?'

'Two out of three.'

'The council's claiming it was a great success.'

'Porter isn't. He's not that stupid. You noticed he hasn't

mentioned how he learned where to find them and when they'd
have a body?'

'Ah . . .' His eyes widened. 'I should have guessed he couldn't
have managed all that by himself. They should hang the one they
caught. Make an example of him.'

'You know the law—'

'More's the pity.'

'He sold a burial gown from a child's body. It's Van Diemen's
Land or the noose for him, anyway.'

'I'm not going to shed a tear. Is that what you came to tell
me, Simon?'

'No,' he replied. 'I have a question. I asked you about Amanda
Parker the other day.'

'I remember.'

'I told you there might be a connection between her and the
body snatchers.'

'I remember that, too. All air and whispers, from what I
gathered.'

'Not enough to stand up in court.'

The room seemed to fill with silence. Mudie paced in a
circle, rubbing at his chin.

'You're really serious? You honestly believe she might be
involved?'

'I don't know.' He wasn't sure what he thought any more.
'There's no evidence I can touch. But plenty of things keep
hinting at her . . . and part of me wants to believe it.'

'I'll give you the same advice as before: unless you have
something it's impossible for her to deny, keep your mouth shut,'
Mudie told him. 'She's probably had half the men on the council
as lovers at one time or another.' He snorted. 'Not that they'd
ever admit it. I warned you, Simon; in a quiet way she carries a
lot of power in this town. Be careful.'

'But can you *imagine* her involved?'

'Why?' he asked. 'What's in it for her? It won't make her
a lot of money. She doesn't need it. She's rich.'

'Nowhere near as wealthy as people believe. That's what I've
been told.'

Mudie shrugged. 'Doesn't matter. It's still going to be more
than the likes of you or me will ever know.'

He couldn't deny that. Amanda Parker still had plenty, even with much of her fortune gone.

'For the excitement?' Simon asked. 'The thrill.'

'How would I know? I've never met the woman. People say she's wild, but like that? I couldn't begin to guess.' He frowned. 'I'm going to say it one last time, as your friend. Don't go repeating any of this to other people. That would be a good way to find yourself in court.'

There was only one member of the watch at the gaol.

'I want to talk to Ackroyd again. The one you brought in last night.'

'Has Constable Porter said you can?' He looked doubtful. 'He never told me.'

'He has.' A complete lie, but Simon didn't care. 'You wouldn't have him if it wasn't for me.'

With a sigh, the man picked a ring of keys from the desk and led the way through to the cells.

Ackroyd was slumped on the bench. Wearily, he looked up. 'What do you want now? I told you everything last time.'

'I didn't ask it all then. Someone visited you at the farmhouse.'

For a few seconds, Ackroyd's eyes were blank. Then he smiled. 'You must have been spying on us. You saw Frank.'

'Who is he?'

'A friend of Kingsley's. He was bringing some food.'

Simon reached down, grabbed Ackroyd's shirt and dragged him up to his feet. 'You're going to tell me everything you know about him.'

'That's it. That's all.'

'The girl you took in Headingley was just ten years old.'

The man shrugged. 'Was she? We've taken younger than that. Smaller. I like them. They're easier to move, and pack.'

It was too much. Simon's fury boiled over. He bunched his fist and hit Ackroyd's wounded arm. Once, twice, three times. Putting every ounce of his fury into each blow until the man slumped over, screeching with pain.

'Ten years old,' Simon repeated. He was panting, feeling the sweat on his forehead. 'Where did you send her?'

'I told you, I don't know.'

Simon raised his fist again and Ackroyd rushed to speak.

'I don't. It was Kingsley who looked after all that. It's the truth.'

He looked so desperate that it couldn't be a lie. The man was no actor. Ackroyd didn't have anything more to give. He'd been honest when he said he knew nothing.

Jane stood all day. People came and went from Goulden's Yard. On foot, in carts. She didn't recognize any of the faces. No Kingsley, no coachman.

She read the advertisements pasted to the brick walls. All of them. The newer ones at first, then the ones that had been stuck there for weeks and months, ink fading, smeared with soot. It filled a little time.

The Irishman might have moved on from the house. It could have been somewhere to pass a single night. Impossible to know. She settled, shifting her weight from foot to foot to try and ease the pain that filled her body. Soon enough the bruises would fade. But the memory of how they happened would always remain.

Simon arrived a little after noon, carrying a pair of warm pies. She took the chance to walk and ease her stiffness.

Jane strolled up Marsh Lane, letting her mind drift. She cut through Marton Row to York Street and back towards town, all the way past the burying ground. Suddenly, close to the small St James's church, she felt the familiar ripple up her spine that meant someone was behind her.

But she knew these streets too well. Every twist and turn of the courts and the ginnels. Less than five minutes and she'd turned things around. She'd led him deep into a web of tiny paths and courts. Herding him, even if he didn't know it.

He was lost, caught in the confusion and tiny ways and paths. Unless he turned around and managed to retrace his steps, there was only one way out. It led to her, standing still, holding her knife.

She watched him start to glance over his shoulder as soon as he saw her. Weighing his chances. He was ready to run but he already understood how pointless that would be.

'What do you want?' Jane asked, and the coachman glared at her.

*　　*　　*

Simon wondered where Kingsley might hide. Of the three men, he was the mystery. The Irishman was muscle and anger, the strength. Ackroyd had been the carthorse, just sly enough to try to make a little extra for himself, and in custody now. But Kingsley? The only thing Simon knew with certainty was that the man had no skill at cards.

He seemed to be the one in charge of the body snatchers. He was organized. He must have had contacts at churches and grave-yards. Somehow he knew surgeons around the country who'd pay for the cadavers.

How?

He'd learned next to nothing when he'd asked about the man before. Time to start digging again, and make sure he discovered the truth this time.

Two hours passed and Jane hadn't returned. The afternoon turned overcast, with a light, misting sprinkle of rain, so fine it was hardly noticeable. Where was she?

The coachman was dressed in ordinary clothes, a black jacket with a broad stain and old trousers.

'Answer,' Jane told him. 'What do you want?'

'Maybe I want you.'

He took a pace forward, eyes shifting around, searching for a way past her. But she'd chosen this place deliberately. There was no escape. No sliding away.

'Did she send you?'

'Who?'

'Mrs Parker.'

'I don't know anyone called Parker.'

Jane shook her head. 'You tried that before. I don't believe you.'

He shuffled his feet, edging closer. The coachman had a vicious gaze. From nowhere, his left hand snaked forward to grab at her breast.

The same thing the constable's man had done to her at the gaol. She'd been powerless to stop that. Not this time. He wasn't fast enough. Now she drove the knife forward with all her strength. Right through his hand.

She pulled the blade back. First blood for the new weapon.

He was in shock, staring at the wound. She hooked her boot around his ankle. A quick push and he fell backwards.

Jane knelt on his chest, holding the edge of the knife against his throat.

'You'd better understand this.' Her voice was a low, angry hiss. 'The next time I see you, I'll kill you. Remember that, it's a promise.'

Before he could react, she'd gone.

'The coachman,' Jane said as she returned to Simon.

No injuries; nothing he could see. But he felt a pang of worry. 'What did he do?'

Two short sentences were enough. She moved into place to continue watching over Goulden's Yard. For a moment, Simon thought about saying more, then decided to keep his silence. He'd be wasting his time; she'd built her wall around it all.

Instead, he'd find out more about Peter Kingsley.

It took three hours of questions before he had a stroke of luck. The barman at the Talbot thought he remembered the name. He stood with a tot of rum, frowning as he tried to place the man.

'Kingsley.' He ran the name over his tongue and squinted. 'Does he have dark hair, thin?' the man asked eventually.

'That's him.'

'I can see him now.' The voice grew more confident. 'It must have been a year or two ago. He used to come in here with some others. They were all young men.'

'What were they?' Simon asked. 'Clerks?'

'No, it wasn't that. They came in during the day.' He raised his head and smiled, eyes suddenly bright. 'I remember now. Students. Medicine. Once when they appeared, two of them had blood all over their clothes. None of the other customers would sit near them.' The barman nodded. 'That's it.'

Simon placed a few small coins in front of him. If it was true, the man had earned them.

He should have guessed. Of course. A medical student would know who wanted bodies for dissection, the best type of corpse to take. Was he still a student? Dr Thackrah might know.

*   *   *

'Peter Kingsley,' Thackrah said. 'Yes, he was one of my pupils for a while. He left about a year ago. I don't remember exactly when.'

He was standing outside the infirmary, smoking a cigar, wearing an old jacket heavily stained with blood.

Found him, Simon thought with satisfaction.

'Did he show any talent for it?'

'Not for medicine or surgery. He seemed to prefer games of chance and cards.' The man sighed. 'Unfortunately, he had no real aptitude for those, either. Why are you interested in him, Westow?'

'He's part of something.' He wasn't sure he trusted the doctor enough to tell him the truth. The man had claimed he never bought any bodies. Maybe.

Thackrah smiled and studied the glowing tip of his cigar. 'Something to do with these resurrection men, perhaps?'

Simon ignored the question. 'Why did he leave?'

'There were two excellent reasons.' He raised a finger. 'One, he simply wasn't good enough. The more important factor was that he no longer had the money to pay for his studies. We came to a . . . shall we call it an amicable parting of the ways?'

Everything fitted into place now. It explained why Kingsley came to be in charge of the body snatchers. Some education, the names of surgeons around the country, and an urgent need for money.

'Who were his friends?'

'One of them is right over there.' He pointed his cigar towards a pale man leaning against a wall and studying a book, concentrating fiercely as if he was trying to memorize every word. 'He's called Archer. Can't remember his Christian name. He used to know Kingsley. Maybe he can help you.' He threw the rest of the cigar to the ground and strode off.

'Mr Archer.'

The man raised his head. He had a worried, hunted look, like a rabbit sensing a fox. He couldn't be more than his middle twenties, but he looked as if the years were pressing down on him. Sunken eyes and deep shadows, a man who'd forgotten what enough sleep might be.

'Who are you?' A wary voice.

'My name's Simon Westow.' He smiled, trying to put the man at ease. 'Dr Thackrah pointed you out. You're one of his pupils?'

Archer's head bobbed up and down. 'He's a good teacher.'

'He told me that you knew another man he was teaching. Someone called Kingsley.'

'Peter, yes. But he ran out of money.'

'Were you good friends?'

He considered the question for a curiously long time. 'Four of us used to go drinking sometimes. We were all Dr Thackrah's students. There are only two of us left now. Peter was a little older than the rest of us. I think he'd tried a few things before medicine. He didn't do well in his studies and finally his family cut his money off. But no, I can't say we were ever friends.'

'No idea what happened to him?'

He shook his head. 'None. I keep busy enough here. I know he liked to play cards. I do remember that.' Archer gave a fleeting, nervous smile.

'Did he have any other friends you know about?'

'There was one. Another of the students. Robert Morgan.'

'Where can I find him?'

'He's dead,' Archer said. 'It must be, what, nine months ago?' He frowned. 'It might even be a year, I'm not sure.'

A small tingle of alarm. 'What happened?'

Archer shook his head. 'It was terrible. He must have been attacked on his way home one night. They found his body the next morning. His purse had been stolen.'

'Did the constable find his murderer?'

'No. But he was Peter's friend.'

There was nothing to gain by asking more questions about that.

'What do you know about body snatching? The resurrection men?'

He looked shocked by the idea. 'I've read about it, but that's all. Dr Thackrah would never . . .'

'Was Peter Kingsley interested in it?'

Archer cocked his head, remembering. 'We talked about it, the idea of having bodies we could dissect to learn anatomy. I'm sure you can understand. It would help our studies.'

'Yes, of course.'

'I suppose he was curious. Both him and Robert, really. They were often talking, but I don't think it was anything more than that. Why?' he asked, then his eyes widened with the realization. 'That body snatcher who was arrested. Peter was involved, wasn't he?'

'He was.' Simon had nothing to lose by admitting it. He might even find something to help. 'But he escaped. Do you have any idea where he might go?'

'No. His family is from somewhere in Lincolnshire, I think. But I doubt he'd want anything to do with them after they cut off his money.'

'I'd like to give you three names. Did Kingsley ever mention them, or do you know if he had a connection with them?'

'All right.' He'd closed his book, thumb marking the page.

'Mrs Parker.'

'No.' Archer shook his head.

'Someone called the Irishman. He's very big, vicious.'

'Definitely not.'

'Thomas Rawlings.'

No hesitation. 'Yes, Peter knew him. I don't think they met that often. He introduced us all once, when we were out together. They were cousins, I believe. Why, is he part of this?'

'I don't know,' Simon told him. 'He disappeared a little while ago.'

The shock on Archer's face was genuine. He couldn't have faked that.

'But . . . do you think Peter had something to do with that?'

'I don't know.'

'He liked Tom. He seemed to, at least. I . . . no, I can't believe that.'

'Please don't mention any of this,' Simon told him.

'Who would I tell?' Archer asked. 'Nobody would believe me.'

'Then it's easier to keep it to yourself. Thank you. I appreciate your help.'

More for the web of connections. Rawlings to Mrs Parker. Rawlings to Betsy and the Irishman. Rawlings to Kingsley. The coachman to the body snatchers. The coachman to Mrs Parker. Link after link after link.

Amanda Parker was involved. He knew it in his bones, even if he couldn't prove it yet.

How? *Why?*

What was she doing when she tried to tangle them in all this? What did she want to achieve? He knew he should have walked away instead of taking her job. But he'd thought he was cleverer than her, and he wanted to discover what she was trying to do. He'd managed to slip out of the arrangement quickly, but had it been fast enough? She'd still tried to bring the constable down on Jane. It hadn't worked, but he wasn't certain they were out of her clutches yet. The woman might be keeping something back for later.

Jane picked out the familiar footsteps before she could see him; Simon had a particular way of walking, the right leg coming down a little more heavily than the left. It was late in the afternoon, a slight chill just beginning to creep through the spring air. A quiet time of day, before the shift ended and the workers marched off to their homes.

A moment and then he was there.

'Anyone?' Simon asked, turning his head towards Goulden's Yard.

'Plenty of people, but no sign of the Irishman. I haven't seen Kingsley either.'

'I've been hearing a few interesting things about Mr Kingsley.'

As he told her, her face hardened. 'He's the one we really need.'

Simon nodded. 'Kingsley certainly seems to be the one with the brains. He'll be the most cautious. That means he'll be the hardest to find.'

'He'll come here to look for the Irishman.' Her gaze drifted. 'I wonder how badly I cut his eye.'

'We'll find out when we take him. But we can't spend every hour of the day here, waiting and watching.'

'The Irishman could go somewhere else,' she said.

'He *could*, but I'm not so sure,' Simon said. 'He knows he has a good spot. His size means people will notice him when he's walking. He'd be a fool to move.'

A coach dashed by, the driver whipping the horses to urge them on. A moment and it had passed, nothing more than a blur and a rush of sound.

'If Kingsley's going to come, it will probably be after dark,' she said.

'He'll have to do it soon,' Simon said. 'They're going to need to decide what they do next. It'll be dark soon. I'll watch tonight. You might as well go home.'

She left, her head tangled with questions. By the time she reached the cottage hidden behind Green Dragon Yard, she'd found no path through them. Tonight she'd let it all go and return to *Pride and Prejudice* and the world of the Bennets, although she didn't understand why anyone would want a husband, rich or poor. Never mind; she relished being part of their lives for a few hours. All too soon she'd finish the book, though, and she'd have to say goodbye to these people who seemed so real. What would she do then?

'After that you read another book, child,' Mrs Shields told her with a broad smile when she asked. A small pile of them stood on top of a chest of drawers. 'Any of them. You might not like them all, but there will be a few you'll enjoy.'

'It won't be the same, though.'

The gentle laugh. 'No, of course it won't. Would you want it to be?'

'I—' she began, then stopped. Would she? 'I'm not sure.'

'You'll visit different places in other books. When you're ready, you can always go back and read this again. Whenever you want, you can visit Elizabeth Bennet.'

That felt like a comfort, as if Miss Bennet was a living, breathing friend. She could leave her card and go over for tea.

For a moment she considered sitting with a whetstone and sharpening her knife. Grinding off the coachman's blood. Instead, she settled into bed, pulling up the blanket and adjusting the lantern. No more body snatchers or Mrs Parker tonight. She was going into a cleaner, genteel world.

TWENTY-ONE

Simon waited until long after darkness had fallen. The workers had left the businesses in Goulden's Yard and the parade of carts rumbling along Marsh Lane had dwindled to nothing. Another coach passed, the driver pushing his horses to make good time on the road to York. The sound faded into the distance, and he was surrounded by the night.

A few people walked by, but they never saw him. Kingsley didn't appear. Simon edged into the yard, staying hidden by the shadows. No light glowing in the house.

Was the Irishman still there? All Simon could do was hope and trust the man remained inside. Too dangerous to enter. There was no reason for him to move anywhere else. Not until they had a new place where they could work.

Maybe Kingsley was searching for one.

There was nothing Simon could do for now. Leaving was a gamble, but no more than staying; he could be wasting hours standing here and see nothing worthwhile. He'd take the chance, go home and sleep. Tomorrow might bring some answers.

'Maybe Kingsley decided to leave Leeds before he could be arrested.' Rosie said. It was late, the twins asleep upstairs, snuffling and snorting in their dreams. The pair of them sat at the kitchen table, trying to make sense of everything.

'It's possible.' But he knew she could see the doubt on his face.

'If it's not that, what do you think?'

'All they had when they ran from that house were the clothes they were wearing,' he said. 'Kingsley would need money to start over in another town. Money to get there, too, unless he was willing to walk.'

'They'll need money to rent somewhere here, too, and buy tools,' Rosie told him.

'They know people here.' Simon paused. 'At least one of their friends has money and power, and properties.'

They were silent for a minute. Finally Rosie said, 'My mind keeps going back to Gwendolyn Jordan. I never knew her, but it caught me. Just ten years old . . .'

He placed his hand over hers, deciding whether to tell her what he'd learned. She was his wife. He knew how she felt about all this. She deserved to know.

'Ackroyd said she wasn't the youngest.'

She stared at the table. 'We have to find every single one of them involved in this, Simon. They have to pay.' Rosie raised her eyes and a tear ran down her cheek. 'Every single one.'

'We will.'

Sunday morning at the coffee cart on Briggate. One more week and it would be May Day. A new month with all the hope and joy of spring.

The gossip about the body snatchers had withered away. Nothing more had followed the arrest; it had turned into stale news.

Simon wandered off. Up Briggate, then along the Head Row and down the long hill towards Burley House. Everything quiet on the Sabbath. Hardly any carts, only two coaches charging out of the town. A few couples strolling to church.

All too easy to find somewhere out of sight and watch the house for an hour or two. He had no real reason, nothing more than a wild idea that Kingsley might appear. He was hoping against hope, and he knew it. But what else was there to do? He had no clue where the man might be, and he was certain Mrs Parker was involved. If he appeared, that would be the evidence he needed. But nothing he could take to court.

Simon watched as the coachman slowly polished the paint on the carriage. Frank, that was the name Ackroyd had given him. But the young man who'd believed he was the cock o' the walk had been replaced by someone who moved as if every step was fragile, his left hand wrapped in a thick bandage where Jane had stabbed him.

The last time they met, Simon had given him a warning: leave, or face the consequences. The coachman was still here. Simon weighed the idea of pressing him, terrifying him into talking. So much depended on the kind of hold Mrs Parker had over him. If they hadn't found Kingsley by tomorrow, perhaps he'd come back and scare Frank.

Two hours. He saw a man and his wife arrive at the main house, then leave a while later. Simon was about to go himself when he caught something from the corner of his eye. Not so much a movement as a sudden shift in the light. He concentrated, and it was there again. More substantial this time: a figure moving away from the coach house. A man, sliding slowly and stealthily through the bushes around the courtyard towards the kitchen door.

Simon held his breath, following each cautious step. The man stepped into the light for a moment and Simon saw his face before it vanished into the shadow once more. Kingsley.

So the man had run here for shelter. But was it to the coachman or Mrs Parker? Or both? Whatever it was, catching a glimpse of him had been sheer good fortune. Lady Luck smiling down.

His heart was thumping. Kingsley was close. He could take him as he came out of the house. He just needed to be in the right spot . . .

Before he could move, Kingsley reappeared, carrying a small satchel. One hasty glance and he darted off into the bushes.

There was no simple way to follow. Simon had to plunge into the undergrowth, a thicket filled with brambles. Thorns clawed at his cheeks and hands; he felt the thin, warm trickle of blood.

By the time he reached the spot where Kingsley had been, the man had disappeared along a spindly footpath. Simon ran all the way to a low wall that led to the road. But he'd gone, not even a speck in the distance.

Simon rested his hands on the stone. So close . . . so damned close. Lady Luck's smile had been nothing more than a tease.

A moment's thought, then he clambered over the wall and hurried back towards Leeds. Maybe, just maybe . . .

Perhaps Simon was right, and Kingsley wouldn't come during the day. But Jane didn't know where else to look for the man, so she stayed out of sight, watching Goulden's Yard.

It was quiet, all the businesses closed for Sunday. No carts to deliver or collect goods. The music of everyday life was hushed until tomorrow.

She'd read every notice and advertisement on the walls so many times she thought she'd be able to recite them in her sleep. The time passed so slowly she could feel it crawl along.

Then she picked out a figure in the distance, hurrying up Marsh Lane. Simon. He was walking quickly towards her. Once he was close, she could see faint smears of blood on his face. She reached for her knife and stared beyond him. Nobody was following.

'What happened to you?' she asked.

'Kingsley.' He was out of breath, panting hard.

She didn't understand. 'What about him?' His face was only scratched, nothing bad. No real wounds. 'Did he try to attack you?'

He shook his head. 'I saw him.'

'What?' She could hardly believe it. 'Where?'

'Has he been here?'

'No. Why? Is he coming?'

'I thought he must be on his way to see the Irishman.' He pressed his lips together. A moment longer and he told her what had happened.

'He went into the main house. When he came out, he was carrying a satchel. It could have been food. I thought I might catch him.'

'I haven't seen the Irishman at all.'

'Maybe he's being cautious.' He glanced down at the cuts on his hands and nodded at the horse trough a few yards up the road. 'I'll wash this off.'

An hour passed, and they heard the parish church bell toll the time. Kingsley didn't arrive, the Irishman didn't leave. At least it was another grey, cool day, with no sun to leave them sweating.

'He has somewhere else.' Simon slapped the wall in frustration and sighed. 'I hoped . . .'

Jane said nothing. What could she add? From all Simon had said, Kingsley didn't know anyone was trying to follow him.

'I'll stay a little longer,' she said. 'Maybe he'll appear.'

They both knew that he wouldn't, but the idea offered some salvation.

'No.' Simon shook his head. 'You've been standing long enough. You go.' He hesitated. 'We'll meet here as soon as it's dark.'

'What do you want to do?'

'If there's no sign of them, we'll go into the house and see if the Irishman is still there.'

Jane felt the fear crawl through her and she forced it back

down. He might be close, no more than a few yards away. She was going to face him. After the last time at Timble Bridge . . . She needed to beat him, to take her revenge. 'Yes,' she agreed.

'Are you sure?'

A sharp nod and then she strode away. She felt as if the world was washing against her, drowning her, and she needed to try to breathe.

Simon watched her go. He'd seen the way her expression shifted when he suggested going into the house. It was simple to understand, displayed on her face. The bruises on her body were only just beginning to fade. The ones in her mind would linger much longer. She was terrified.

They had to do something. They didn't even know if the Irishman was still in there, but something was better than nothing at all.

Another hour and he didn't see either of the men he was seeking. He'd be back later. For now, it was time to stir things up.

Simon watched her come out of the twilight. Jane had the shawl raised over her hair, hand reaching into the pocket of her dress to clutch the hilt of her knife. She looked around warily.

'I went to see the constable,' he said and watched her frown. 'He and his men will be here very soon. We'll let them go in and take the Irishman.'

'I thought . . .' she began, then gave a quick shake of her head.

'They're paid to risk their necks. Remember, he wounded one of theirs out at the farmhouse. They want him too.'

'He might have gone already.'

'Then they can be the ones to find out. When I went and told Porter this afternoon, he rubbed his hands with glee. He was eager to come straight round here. I persuaded him it would be better to wait.'

'If they're doing everything, why did we bother coming?'

He grinned. 'Don't you want to see what happens?'

'No,' Jane answered. 'I want the Irishman.' There was no lightness in her voice.

He cocked his head. 'You hear them?'

The constable arrived with four of his men. Stocky figures,

marching awkwardly as scabbards banged against their thighs. Their faces were a mix of fear and eagerness. Two of them looked very young, the others worn and dulled by drink.

'Which one is it?' Porter asked.

'Over in the corner.' Simon pointed.

'Any back way out?'

'No.'

The constable narrowed his eyes. 'How do you know? Have you been inside?'

'I've been around the buildings.' Not quite a lie; just not the entire truth.

'Is the door locked?'

'I haven't tried it,' Simon told him.

Porter shook his head. 'Doesn't matter. We can batter it down.'

'If you do that, anyone inside is going to have the advantage.'

But the watchmen were already moving like they'd been unleashed, loud and baying in the darkness. If the Irishman was in the house, he had plenty of warning. Shoulders hammered against the door until the wood finally splintered and gave way.

Simon glanced at Jane. She was staring at the house, eyes on fire with hatred.

Grunts and shouts from inside. A scream that started, only to end before it could properly begin. He tensed at the noise. Finally, there was just the constable's voice, bellowing out his orders.

They had to work at it, but they dragged out the Irishman. His wrists had been bound behind him; the men forced him along with kicks and blows.

Porter was the last one out. He looked haggard, as if the last few minutes had aged him by ten years. 'My man Griffin's dead.' His voice was empty as he looked up. 'Tell me, is it worth the cost, Westow?'

'I can't answer that.'

'He was married to my wife's sister. How am I going to tell her?'

'Arrange a pension. It's not much consolation, but . . .'

The constable nodded. 'I know. It's something.'

'You can hang the Irishman now.'

'I'd as soon save the trouble of a trial.' He gave a long, weary sigh. 'So would the men. Griffin had been with them for five years.'

He trudged away, following the others, stooped as if the weight of the world was pressing down on his shoulders.

'It could easily have been one of us dead in there,' Simon said once they were alone.

'Or the Irishman.' Jane's voice was flint. He knew what she was thinking: she'd been cheated out of her revenge. Now the Irishman would dance at the end of a rope, not on the tip of her blade. But the man was huge, shot through with violence. He was a killer, he'd already proved that a few times, and there was one more body tonight to add to his list. He might easily have beaten them.

Sometimes the wise choice was to pick your battles. This way they were alive, they could keep hunting for Kingsley. He was still out there. There was another question to settle, too: Amanda Parker and her coachman.

TWENTY-TWO

The coffee cart rippled with talk. Nothing like death and violence to put some meat into the start of their week. One or two had known Griffin, the dead watchman. Others tried to imagine what had happened, how they'd taken down the Irishman.

'Were you there?' someone asked Simon. When he shook his head, the man chuckled. 'Bet you wish you had been. Must have been a real scrap.'

He moved around, listening. After a few minutes he drifted away. None of them had anything new to add. Nothing he hadn't seen last night from the entrance to Goulden's Yard.

More people outside the gaol today, ten of them across the street. Another four or five came to join them as he looked. They were restless, bristling with anger. All the makings of a mob.

Two of the watch stood outside the gaol, swords through their belts, looking nervous as they stood guard. One reached out a hand to stop Simon as he tried to enter.

'Don't,' he said, pushing past. 'If it wasn't for me, you wouldn't have either Ackroyd or the Irishman.'

Constable Porter sat behind the desk. He glanced up. 'Why are you here, Westow?'

'To take a look at the new prisoner. I've never seen him properly.' He paused. 'I'm sorry about your man.'

'So am I. He was experienced, too.' The constable sat back in his chair and shook his head. 'Did you hear that Mr Clark from Clark Foundry is going to prosecute Ackroyd for taking that burial gown?'

'He said he would.'

'That's your client, is it?'

It was hardly a secret now. 'Yes.'

'Ackroyd will be going to trial for that and the body snatching. We have the Irishman for murder. That will hang him. No doubt about it.'

'Have you found out his name yet?'

Porter shook his head. 'He won't say a word.'

'He's through there,' the constable said. 'Go and take a look. We're sending the pair of them to York tonight for next week's assizes.'

'Be careful, then. There's a crowd outside.'

The constable nodded. 'I know. Probably half of them would gladly storm in here and hang the body snatchers. I'm tempted to let them.' He rubbed his hands down his face. 'But we'll be taking them out the back way, through the yard. Do all we can to see they arrive safely and get their time in court.'

The Irishman was in the closest cell. He seemed to fill the small room, a stinking hulk of a man. Battered now, bruised, wrists and ankles shackled with heavy chains. He grinned when he saw someone watching him. Some of his teeth were broken, most of the others gone. A grimy, stained bandage covered his left eye, something yellow weeping from under it and down his cheek.

Dirty trousers, thick twine holding his shoes together. He was an ugly man, but intimidating. Powerful. He oozed danger, the sense that the smallest thing might start him off.

There was a heavy, barred door between them, but Simon still took a step back. He'd made the right decision the night before. The Irishman could have killed him and Jane without pausing to catch his breath. They'd have been powerless to stop him.

'What's your name?'

The Irishman looked at him and spat. The phlegm caught on the bars of the door and dripped slowly down.

'You'll need him well guarded for the journey,' Simon said when he returned to the main room.

'He will be,' Porter said. 'If either of them tries to escape, we'll kill them, and they know it. They won't be a loss.'

That was true, he thought as he left. No one would miss that pair. Outside, the air was heavy with soot; he could taste it as he breathed. The haze sat thick over Leeds, all the smoke from the factories and mills. Very slowly, it was choking them all.

Jane moved around the town, seeking out the groups of children. They were harder to find during the day, scattered all over Leeds. Seeking food, picking pockets, doing whatever they could to survive. She knew; she'd been one of them.

Only one claimed to have seen Kingsley. Close to the new houses they were building in the Leylands, out past Moore Street. She gave the girl a coin and began to walk.

Two new streets were going up, the labourers shouting and laughing as they worked. Carpenters, bricklayers, men mixing up the mortar. Kingsley wouldn't be here while all this was going on. He'd come later, once all the people had gone.

Some of the houses had roofs. A few even had windows. Shelter from the night and rain. It was easy to imagine him here. She'd return after dark. Before then, she'd hone her knife. Maybe she couldn't have the Irishman, but she'd be ready for this one.

The carriage was gone from Burley Hall; Mrs Parker must be off visiting. It was easy work to pick the lock on the coach house. Inside, Simon stopped, eyes moving around.

The coachman's quarters were upstairs. He took each step carefully, holding his breath as he let his weight fall on the wood. No squeaks or groans. Another lock at the top: no barrier at all.

It was a sparse room, lazily kept. A bed, a small chest for clothes. He rummaged through, but there was nothing worthwhile. A pair of bandages, washed out and drying, still stained with blood.

Simon spotted some scraps of paper, wadded up and pushed aside on the corner of a table. He crammed them in his pocket. It was safer not to spend too long here.

He'd barely finished closing the lock on the coach house when he heard hooves and the jangle of a harness at the bottom of the drive. Quickly, he slipped off into the bushes. They'd never know he'd been here.

No sign of Kingsley, but perhaps the papers he'd taken would tell him something. Perhaps . . .

Simon walked down Briggate; none of his thoughts went anywhere. He glanced down Kirkgate and saw people gathered around the gaol. Maybe thirty of them now. Mostly men, two or three women among them.

Still only two members of the watch standing guard by the door. At least the constable had given them rifles to go with their swords. But they looked uncomfortable with the weapons, nervous as the crowd clustered. Porter stood to address the mob, coat drawn back to show a pistol.

'I know what they've done,' he said. 'I know it better than you do. I lost one of my men because of them, and there's another that won't be back on this job.' He looked as if he wanted to call down the wrath of God on the body snatchers. 'But these men still have a right to a trial. That's why I'm sending them to York tonight. If you want to shout, go ahead. But if you try anything more, the mayor will read the Riot Act and I'll call the cavalry down from the barracks.'

'Bring them out,' a man called.

'We'll hang them for you.' A woman's voice, shrill and angry. 'Save the courts the trouble.'

Simon could smell alcohol; he saw a bottle of gin circulating. At the moment, the violence was still an undercurrent. But the tension was rippling through the air. One tiny thing could bring it to the surface. He didn't want to be here for that. He turned on his heel and walked away.

Mrs Shields dozed, woke, dozed again for a little longer. Jane sat in the corner, slowly sliding a whetstone along the knife blade. Towards dusk she put the weapon away in her pocket and moved around the kitchen, making supper for the old woman. Nothing special, toasting a crumpet by the fire and smothering it with butter and jam. Simple, warm and satisfying.

That and a tisane would see Mrs Shields through the evening. By the time she carried the tray through, the woman was awake again with a book perched on her lap.

'Thank you.' She guided it down with her pale, spindly arms. 'Are you going out tonight?'

'Very soon,' Jane answered. 'It's work.'

Mrs Shields reached up and stroked Jane's face. 'Your bruises are going. Everything will be back the way it was. Will you be careful? Please?'

'Yes,' she said, and smiled. 'I promise.'

It was one thing to agree, she thought as she walked up the Head Row, and another to truly take care. In her work the two didn't mix. She had to take chances. Sometimes she lost. But more often she won. The way to survive was to be deadlier than your opponent.

The new streets were quiet. Far enough from the centre of town to be clear of the noise and bustle, hushed in the darkness. Not long ago there had been trees here. A copse where a row of houses now stood. She'd been here six months earlier and only seen field and wood. All a memory. The air smelled of dirt and fresh-cut timbers. Jane crept around, listening, staying out of sight in the deep shadows. She spotted a group of children at one end of a row, gathered around a fire of lumber scraps the builders had left.

She moved among them, whispering her questions, giving out a coin or two for an answer. By the time she'd finished, she'd learned that Kingsley was close. There were three possible houses where he could feel safe, all with roofs and windows.

She stood and looked at them. Which one? None of them had doors yet. She could walk in and look. But Kingsley would be alert for danger. He could be watching her now. She eased away, through a ginnel to the next road then up and around, to drift down from North Street.

Taking a breath, she entered the first house. Coming this way, he couldn't have seen her; she'd kept out of sight.

She paused, cocking her head to listen. No creak of the floorboards, not a single sound inside the building. Jane held the knife tight in her hand. Suddenly, a soft scratching from somewhere upstairs. She froze, breath caught in her chest. A few seconds and it came again. Leave? Go and look? Was he waiting up there? Jane turned her head towards the steps. Then, a hurried scrabbling, claws hurrying across wood. She exhaled, feeling her body ease. Just a rat. She was on edge; it shouldn't have bothered her at all.

He wasn't here. Two more places to try. She stood for a minute, waiting until her heart calmed again.

Her palms were slick with sweat; Jane wiped them against her dress as she started to move. Outside, the night felt chilly, dangerous. She swallowed hard before she entered the second house, her body tight, ready for him to spring out.

Nothing. But he'd been here. She knew it; she had a sense of him. His smell was still in the air. Thick, strong with sweat and fear and movement. She could almost taste him on her tongue. He'd been gone a few minutes at most.

So close. Had he seen her and made his escape? Or had he simply decided to find somewhere safer?

She went to the third house, but even before she set foot inside, Jane knew she was wasting her time. Kingsley had vanished, still one step ahead of her.

Walking home, lost in her thoughts, Jane thought she heard voices. A crowd of people. Baying, yelling. But it was far off in the distance. If it was important, the news would be all around Leeds in the morning.

The banging on the door pulled him out of sleep. Simon blinked. A faint grey light coming through the shutters. Still early, but the knocking was insistent.

He'd slept later than usual. By now he should be at the coffee cart, but he and Rosie had stayed at the kitchen table long after the boys were asleep, trying to make sense of the scraps of paper he'd stolen from the coach house.

George Mudie was on the step, wild-eyed, his face alive with excitement. 'Did you hear?'

'Hear what?'

Mudie pushed past, striding through to the kitchen.

Simon had no choice but to follow. 'What is it? What's happened?'

'You're interested in these body snatchers, aren't you?'

'You know I am.' For a moment he thought the mob must have broken into the gaol. A riot.

'Last night the constable shipped those two prisoners he had to York, ready for the assizes. The body snatchers.'

'Porter told me what he was going to do. There'd been a crowd around the gaol all day.'

Mudie nodded, eager to press on. 'They stopped the coach a little way along the York Road.'

Simon felt a shudder of fear. 'For the love of God. How many of them?'

'Close to fifty, I heard. They all had kerchiefs pulled up like highwaymen.'

Fifty. More than he'd seen on Kirkgate. Word must have spread as soon as the coach arrived to transport the men.

'Go on.'

'There's not too much more. I was told they dragged the pair of them out. Hung the smaller one from a tree before anyone could stop them.'

'Ackroyd,' Simon said. 'What about the Irishman? The last time I saw him, he was shackled.'

'He still was, wrists and feet. They tried to put a noose on him, too, but they couldn't get close. He kept swinging his chains around. Do you know how much those things weigh, Simon?'

'Enough, I'm sure.'

'He took a sword from one of his attackers and wounded a couple of them, then he ran off.'

'Ran?'

Mudie shrugged. 'I only know what I heard. After that all the people melted away before the constable and the rest of his men arrived.'

'Wasn't the coach guarded?'

'Two men. They decided it wasn't worth going against a crowd. Not for a pair of body snatchers. You can hardly blame them. They're not paid enough for that.'

True; they were used to taking drunks to the cells, not trying to defend men who pulled corpses from the earth. The Irishman had killed one of the constable's men and wounded another. They weren't likely to help him. But it seemed as if he'd saved himself.

Ackroyd? Simon wouldn't shed any tears for the man. His life might have ended on the gallows, anyway. Still, not that way. Nobody should die at the hands of a mob.

'What has Porter said?' Simon asked.

'He's insisting they'll find the Irishman. All the usual words.' A quick snort of derision. 'You know it means nothing, and he's not likely to hunt down the men who stopped the coach. It wouldn't be popular and everyone would lie.' He glanced at the clock. 'I need to go and open up the shop. Maybe someone will have a broadside about last night that needs printing.' He rubbed his hands together and gave a ghoulish smile. 'All money in the purse.'

There were waves of chatter as Simon marched through town. Some were happy, their blood lust satisfied. Others looked ashamed, horrified at what they'd done, who they'd become as they were caught in a few minutes of madness. He considered going to the gaol, but there was nothing for him there. All he'd see was the constable desperately trying to make it seem better than it had been, while the mayor and the councillors raged at what had happened.

Instead, he cut through the smaller streets to Vicar Lane, down to Lady Beck and crossed the bridge to Mabgate, thinking about the wadded notes he'd found in the coachman's room. They were terse, scribbled sentences: *We'll need somewhere new.* Another: *Do you have somewhere? You know the type of place.* A third: *We'll need money. It's all gone.*

A man's hurried scrawl. Who was meant to read them? The coachman? Mrs Parker? If it was her, had she sent replies? Taken one way, they were damning. But any lawyer worth his salt could argue they meant nothing at all.

'It's her,' Rosie had said when he showed them to her. Her face was set, cheeks burning with anger. 'You know it is.'

'Very likely,' he agreed. 'But it's still not proof. We still haven't managed to find a single thing that's absolute. Not enough for a court, and definitely not against someone like her.'

'It's . . .' She shook her head and let her clenched fist fall on the table with a dull slap. 'She's going to get away with it.'

'Maybe she won't,' he told her.

But they both knew the truth: Amanda Parker would probably stay free, he thought as he walked into the metal din of Clark Foundry. She still had money, and that meant power. It always had.

TWENTY-THREE

Clark's face was drawn. He looked much older than thirty this morning. Beside him, Harmony Jordan still wore his loss on his face.

'I heard,' Clark said. 'I suppose all of Leeds knows by now.'

'Word travels quickly,' Simon agreed.

'Especially about something like that.'

'The one the mob hung, is he the man who sold Gwendolyn's burial gown?' Jordan asked.

'Yes.'

'Then our business is done.' Clark pursed his lips. 'It's not the way I wanted it to end, but it's over.'

'Not quite.'

'No,' Jordan said. His voice was dry, cracked. 'We don't know where her body is.'

'We may never find out,' Simon said. 'But Kingsley, the man who knows, he's still out there.'

Clark gazed out of a grimy window. 'Do you think you can catch him?'

'He's been elusive so far. But yes, sooner or later we'll find him.'

The man drew in a breath. 'I'll make it worth your while, whether he has the information or not.'

'All right.' Simon hadn't expected that, he hadn't come to ask for it. 'We'll do what we can.'

'I'll pay you for everything so far,' Clark said. 'You've already earned that.' He placed a hand on Jordan's shoulder. 'But Harmony and his family deserve the truth.'

'If it can still be found.'

'Of course.' He extended his hand. 'Thank you, Mr Westow.'

'I was close to him last night,' Jane said. She was sitting at the table in Simon's kitchen, facing Rosie. Simon stood, listening and rubbing the bristles on his chin.

'How close?'

She thought for a second, remembering the feel of the middle house, the way the smell of the man remained in the air. 'Probably no more than five minutes behind him.'

'When we catch Kingsley, we need to keep him alive. I want to find out where he sent the bodies.'

'Much more than that.' Rosie's voice was sharp and bitter. 'We need to know how Mrs Parker was involved.'

'*If* she was,' Simon told her.

'We both know the truth of that.' She looked at Jane. 'Did Simon tell you he found notes in the coach house?'

'None of them were from her,' he said.

'It doesn't matter. She's in this.'

Rosie was certain, Jane thought. Completely convinced by whatever she'd learned. That was enough.

'I want the Irishman.' Jane rubbed the bruise around her eye. The skin was still tender.

'He could kill you.'

But she could kill him. She had the need, the fire. She had speed. He had strength, but he was half-blind now. A one-eyed giant, roaring and wild.

'Are you sure?' Simon watched her face.

'I'm certain.'

A nod. 'Then you hunt him. I'm going after Kingsley. But if you find the Irishman, come and get me. We'll tackle him together.'

Jane opened her mouth. Her expression made it clear: she was about to say no. Instead, she kept silent. Maybe he was right; the two of them probably would stand a better chance against someone like that. As long as she had the satisfaction of the final blow . . .

She left. Simon heard the front door close.

'You know what she's like,' Rosie said. 'It doesn't matter what she says. If she finds him, she won't wait for you.'

Oh yes, he knew that; it was what scared him. However good she was, on her own she stood no chance against the Irishman.

Jane believed Kingsley had sheltered in the new houses off North Street. Somewhere to begin, Simon thought.

Men were working, a foreman bellowing instructions to the labourers. They climbed ladders, hods full of bricks balanced on their shoulders. Others erected scaffolding, hammering wood or digging, observed by the engineers, who were careful to keep dirt from their good suits and neatly buckled shoes.

When Simon described Kingsley, they shook their heads. They'd rousted one or two sleepers when they arrived that morning, but he hadn't been among them.

Of course not; the man was too clever for that.

Even before the clock at the parish church struck noon, he could feel the day starting to trickle through his fingers. A moment's thought and he turned, striding fast down the Head Row towards Burley House.

Through the woods, watching the coach house. The doors were open, the carriage on display. Could Kingsley have come back here? Very possibly. If he was sleeping in unfinished houses, he had nothing. He'd been here before; it was as likely as anywhere else. Mrs Parker had money, if she was prepared to give him any of it. The notes Simon had taken made it clear he was desperate. Perhaps he'd returned to beg once again.

A long hour of standing, feet aching, before he gave up. Maybe Kingsley was hidden away in the coach house, but Simon had no chance to search. Tonight he'd go out again. Kingsley loved to gamble; he knew that. If he'd persuaded Amanda Parker to stake him a few pounds, he'd probably try to increase it at the card table.

The Irishman would go back to the streets he knew; to Jane, that was obvious. He had people he trusted there. One or two who'd take him in, feed him and give him a place to sleep.

He'd been chained when he escaped. The first thing he'd want would be to lose those. Too heavy to keep hauling around; they'd restrict him. She needed to find the blacksmiths and the farriers.

The man was shoeing a horse, the hoof up as the owner held the animal's bridle and spoke soothing words to it. A final nail, some quick strokes with the rasp he pulled from his leather apron, and the work was done. A couple of coins, then the owner led his beast away. The farrier turned to her.

'You don't look like you own a horse.' His eyes were brown and warm. He had a hint of kindness in his voice.

'No.'

'What are you after? If it's directions to somewhere, I'll help you if I can.'

'There was a man who escaped from the watch last night—'

He nodded. 'You mean the one they call the Irishman?'

'Yes. How—'

'He went to see Sam Barrett the smith. I heard about it first thing this morning.' He studied her. 'What are you going to do if you find him? If Sam's right, about three of you can fit into the Irishman.'

'I'll beat him.'

She felt his eyes on her, then the slow approval. 'Maybe you really can give him a run for his money. Why don't you go and talk to Sam? Top of the hill, turn right and after about twenty yards you'll start to feel the warmth of the furnace. Tell him I sent you. My name's by the gate.' He narrowed his gaze. 'You can read, can't you?'

'Of course I can.' She bristled, as if the question had been an insult, that all women like her could read. Inside, though, she felt a burst of pleasure at being able to say it.

'All right then. Good luck to you.'

The smith was stripped to the waist, chest covered by a heavy leather apron. His skin was slick with sweat from the heat, and he wiped an arm across his forehead.

'Over there,' he said. He pointed and she saw the chains coiled up, a pile of dull iron.

'What did he do?'

Barrett spat into the dirt, grimaced, and took a swig of beer from a mug.

'I was just locking up for the night, about to put the padlock on the gate. My wife and my little girl were here, they'd stopped by to surprise me. He came out of nowhere, hauling those chains like they were nothing, when I know they weigh a good twenty-five pounds. Picked up an old sword that I had by the anvil and grabbed my daughter. Said he'd kill her if I didn't cut through the bolts.'

'What did you do?'

He spat again. 'What do you mean, what did I do? Are you stupid or something?' The bitterness and impotence shone in his eyes. 'I did exactly what he wanted and I prayed he wouldn't hurt her. What would you have done, for the love of Christ?'

'What about when you finished?'

'He let go of her and walked away.'

'He didn't say anything?'

'Not a word.'

'Is your daughter all right?' Jane asked. 'He didn't hurt her?'

'No, he didn't, but she was terrified,' he replied. 'She was shaking all night. We sat with her. As soon as she began to settle, she was awake again.' His face turned hard. 'Why do you want to know? Who are you?'

'I work with Simon Westow, the thief-taker. We're looking for him.'

'Are you the one he threw off Timble Bridge?'

All of Leeds knew, she thought. The anger roiled through her as she felt a wave of pain whip across her back. 'Yes.'

'Going to arrest him, are you? I'll tell you this, if I find him on his own, I'll kill him,' Barrett told her.

'You might not have to. Which way did he go?'

'Back down the hill, whistling like he didn't have a care in the world. You wouldn't think he was an escaped prisoner.'

Now she knew what to expect. The Irishman was unchained and armed, and he was somewhere around here.

Shortly after Simon arrived home, Rosie vanished upstairs. He could hear her moving around as he ate. Frustration had left him hungry, and he hacked at bread and cheese and gulped down some beer from the jug.

When she reappeared, Rosie was dressed in her best gown, a silk dress in a shade of deep plum that set off her complexion. A simple gold necklace around her neck, hair pulled up as she pinned a hat into place.

'What do you think?' she asked.

'Do we have an important invitation I forgot about?'

'More of an idea,' she said. 'You'll have to look after the boys for the afternoon.'

That was a pleasure, and she knew it. Time with Richard and Amos always felt precious. Taking them out to run and play. Walking along the river, up to where the water was still clean, cutting switches and knotting lines on them to catch fish.

'Where are you going?'

'Have you ever heard of a fund to help the poor bereaved?' she asked.

'Never.' Simon frowned. 'Why?'

'I'm one of the wives who represents it,' she told him.

'I see. Who are you visiting?' It was one of her tricks. A smile played across his lips. He could guess who she intended to see.

'I thought Mrs Parker might like to contribute. She might even grace us and become a patron.' She produced a card. Heavy white stock, the words *Mrs Rose Westow* printed in crisp, flowing copperplate. 'George Mudie made some for me yesterday. He'll be sending you the bill.'

He handed it back to her. 'What do you think you'll achieve?'

'Maybe nothing. But I've never met her. Everything I know about Amanda Parker comes from what I've heard. This way I'll have a proper sense of her.' Before he could object, she continued, 'Don't try and stop me, Simon. I'm certain she's involved with the body snatchers. You're right about one thing: we don't know how. But if I talk to her—'

'She's not likely to admit it to you.'

Rosie shook her head. 'Of course she won't. I don't think she's that stupid. But she might drop something. To show off, maybe. It has to be worth trying.'

'It's always possible that she doesn't have anything to do with it,' he said.

'Do you honestly believe that?' She put a hand on his chest, over his heart. 'In there, do you?'

'No,' Simon admitted. He lifted her hand and kissed the palm. 'She's guilty, I can feel it.'

'Then let me see if I can do something to prove it.'

'Be careful of that coachman.'

Even as she smiled at him, a knife appeared in her hand. 'Don't you worry.'

He laughed. 'A visiting card and a knife. Just what every lady needs. Keep your eyes and ears open in case Kingsley's there.'

A quick hug and a kiss on his cheek and she was gone, just the hint of her scent left on the air.

For once, he couldn't lose himself in the twins' pleasure. He laughed with them, he chased them, but all the time Simon felt as if he was standing apart and watching someone else play his part. He worried about Rosie. He couldn't see the sense in what she was doing. It took her inside the house and gave her a chance to meet the woman and look around. That was all. Mrs Parker wasn't likely to support any charity. She'd know exactly whose wife Rosie was, and she'd be suspicious.

It seemed like a lot of risk for so little gain. Still, Rosie never did things on a whim. She must have her reasons. More than the hatred for Amanda Parker that seemed to burn through her. He could understand that; he was certain she was right. But he still needed proof to convict the woman, real proof.

Finally, once Richard and Amos had run until their cheeks were bright red, he took them home, hoping she'd already be back. But the house was empty. He cut thick slices of bread for the twins and smeared the slices with dripping.

They were still eating when Rosie returned. He heard the front door close, then her feet hurrying up the stairs. Then . . . silence.

Simon waited a minute. She didn't appear.

'Eat,' he told the twins. 'Play when you're done.'

TWENTY-FOUR

Rosie was sitting on the bed, still in the grand gown, wiping at something on the sleeve with a small handkerchief. Her face was set hard, her mouth a thin, straight line.

'Did you see her?' he asked.

'Oh yes.' She raised her eyes to him. 'I saw her. Gave the maid my calling card and spent five minutes in the drawing room before she graced me with her company.'

'What did she have to say?'

'She raged about you.' Rosie worked to keep her voice even. 'Call you faithless, lazy, a cheat . . . that was just a part of it. She had even more to say about Jane.'

'I can't say I'm surprised. It makes me glad we walked away.'

'Oh, you did the right thing, I've no doubt about that.' Rosie bit down on her lip before she spoke again. 'I swear she has a touch of madness. You should have seen her, Simon. When she was worked up she had little flecks of spittle around her mouth.' She looked up at him. 'She scares me.'

Strong words; very little usually disturbed his wife.

'What did she think to your proposition?'

'She looked at me and laughed. There was . . . an edge to her. Like mania. Then she spat at me.' She rubbed the sleeve again.

'She did what?' At first he thought he must have misheard. Spat? 'She—?'

'It's the truth. She spat. I didn't know what to do.' Slowly, she shook her head. 'There's something wrong with her, Simon. There has to be. People don't *do* that.'

'No,' he agreed. 'They don't.'

'The way she was, I kept my hand in my pocket, holding on to my knife. I thought she might attack me.'

Simon thought of the woman he'd met. Amanda Parker had a temper, no doubt about that. He'd seen it when he told her he wasn't continuing with the search for Thomas Rawlings. But nothing like this. She sounded like someone careening out of control.

'What do you think now? Is she really mad? Is she involved with the body snatchers?' he asked.

'I'm positive she's in with them,' Rosie answered without hesitation. She exhaled. 'I needed to walk after I'd talked to her. I had to think about what she'd done. I don't know; maybe she is mad. I've never seen a woman do anything like that before. It . . .' She shook her head, still filled with disbelief. 'I looked around and someone was following me. I'd seen him at her house, polishing the carriage. He had a bandage wrapped around his left hand.'

'That's her coachman.'

She nodded. 'She must have sent him. God knows why.'

'What did you do?'

She gave a dark, satisfied grin. 'I walked towards him and started to take out my knife so he could see it. He ran off.'

The image of Frank the coachman turning tail made him smile for a moment.

'Maybe she thought he'd frighten me.'

If the woman really believed that, she didn't understand Rosie at all, Simon thought.

'Amanda Parker is part of this,' she continued grimly. 'I saw it right there in her eyes.'

'Why, though?' He could see no reason, no matter how he looked at it.

'Maybe it appeals to the mad streak in her. Maybe she likes the risk. The power of raising the dead. If I ever had any doubts, they've gone.' She started to unbutton her dress. 'I want this off.'

He helped with the buttons, hearing the soft sound as her gown puddled on the floor.

'I needed to see her for myself,' Rosie went on. 'What kind of person she was. She's dangerous, Simon. She still hates you. Be careful with her.'

'She tried revenge once, remember? She had the constable arrest Jane. It didn't go anywhere.'

'I just have a feeling she isn't done yet.'

Everyone called him Curly. Maybe Martin Gerrard had deserved it once; more likely it was a joke at the expense of a man who'd gone bald when he was young. Only a few straggling tufts of hair remained under a low-crowned hat with a feather in the band.

Simon watched him strut along Briggate with his confident swagger. He was a sporting man, a gambler at the tables, the fights, the racecourse. More than that, he had a habit of winning. If he cheated, no one had ever found him out.

In the overcast evening, he was wearing a bright blue jacket, an embroidered waistcoat with a crisp white linen shirt and stock. Pale fawn trousers that stretched too tight across fleshy thighs, and black shoes polished until they reflected like a mirror. With his ebony walking stick, he was every inch a jaybird.

'Simon Westow.' Gerrard had a carrion's smile. 'Going for a game of cards tonight?'

'Maybe for a little while,' Simon said as they shook hands. 'What about you? You're looking very grand.'

He preened. 'It's a new jacket. Do you like it? I just came from the tailor and wanted to show it off.'

Gaudy, Simon thought, but Curly Gerrard loved to be at the centre of attention.

'Actually, I'm looking for someone. He likes to play. You might know him.'

'Who's that?'

'A man called Peter Kingsley.'

A shadow crossed Curly's face. There and gone again in a moment.

'We've met. I hear he's in trouble, though.' A tight smile. 'He must be, if you're after him.'

'I've seen him in the Yorkshire Grey,' Simon said. 'Where else does he like to go?

A list of places, six or seven of them.

'I heard he had something to do with those body snatchers,' Gerrard said.

'He does. But he didn't kill anyone.'

Curly shook his head. 'Doesn't matter. If he has any sense, he'll be keeping out of sight.'

'Someone said he needs money.'

Gerrard snorted. 'I've never known him when he didn't. But if he's looking, you should definitely try the Yorkshire Grey. There's going to be a big game there tonight. I was thinking I'd look in, but if there's likely to be trouble . . .'

'No trouble,' Simon told him. 'I'll make sure of that. Not in there, anyway.'

'He has no chance of winning, I can tell you that right now. At best, he's average at cards and he'll be up against some very good players.'

'I appreciate the advice. Don't tell him I'm after him, though.'

'I won't.'

'That new jacket suits you.' It was a lie, but the words made Curly Gerrard smile with pleasure. It seemed the least Simon could do for the information.

The Yorkshire Grey was a fug of smoke from pipes and cheroots, all mingled with the smell of beer. Simon waited outside until two men entered, then eased his way in behind them, head down, studying the ground and trying not to show his face.

He found a spot on a bench at the far side of the inglenook, and ordered beer from the potboy. Two tables were filled with card players, but it was easy to pick out the serious ones. They were men with empty expressions, intent on the cards. They all looked prosperous, apart from one.

Peter Kingsley had found himself a place. Mrs Parker must have let him have some money; he had a small stack of coins on the table, the metal glinting in the light. Now he was picking up the cards as they were dealt and studying them with deep concentration.

It would be easy to take him now. Drag him out or send word to Constable Porter for him to do the job. There was more than enough evidence to arrest him; he'd been at the farmhouse when Porter and his men raided.

But if he waited, then followed Kingsley, the man might lead him to the Irishman. Stealing bodies was their trade; they needed each other to do it. Hold off until they were together, then call in the watch to take them both. No mistakes this time, no chance of escape.

Simon sat and studied the man. He seemed to ooze desperation, so nervous that he might jump out of his seat at the smallest noise.

He tried to keep the picture of Harmony Jordan's face in his mind. The reason for doing all this. A man whose world had shattered into so many fragments they could never be put back together. It wasn't only him. All the other families who didn't know bodies had been stolen. They all deserved justice. They deserved to know.

Simon considered everything Rosie had told him about her visit to Amanda Parker. Had it helped? Probably not. But the woman had shown a different side of herself. Spitting. Maybe Rosie had unnerved her, and she was feeling the pressure, the squeeze, just like the body snatchers.

His eyes moved back to the table. The men playing cards spoke only to bet. The pile of coins by Kingsley's arm was growing smaller with each hand. He had a thin sheen of sweat across his forehead.

Curly Gerrard entered, parading around to flaunt his new coat, studying the table and offering a few greetings before retreating to the bar. He never glanced over at Simon.

An hour passed. Money ebbed and flowed among the players. Kingsley was definitely down. He signalled the potboy for another glass of rum and drank it in a single gulp when it arrived. A very worried man. If he didn't make a big win in the next two hands he'd need to leave before he lost everything. But from the way he'd been playing, the chances of turning his night around were slight.

The cards were dealt. Bets made and the play began to flow. Simon kept his eyes on Kingsley. The man's body was tight, as rigid as steel. He hesitated before adding another coin to the pile in the centre of the table.

Men drew cards, discarded others. Bet more. Kingsley paused, then shook his head. Sticking with what he had. Waiting out the hand until the others finished.

A minute passed, close to two, before they were done. Turning over the cards. Kingsley was the last. All the others had turned to face him. He let his cards flutter down from his hands to the wood. His shoulders slumped. He'd lost again.

Then he began to straighten. He was poised to do something. Simon half-rose from his chair, ready to move, picking out a path across the room.

Kingsley leaned forward, gathered up two large handfuls of coins and pulled them close to his body. Some scattered on the floor. He moved fast, shoving the money into his pockets as he kicked his seat back. He started to run.

It happened too fast for the others to stop him. Two of them reached out, but by then he was halfway to the door.

Simon's feet pounded across the floorboards. Kingsley was

already down the street as Simon came out on to Kirkgate. He glimpsed him, close to the parish church. Heard the ring of boots on the pavement.

Simon could run, but Kingsley was faster. He stayed behind him, trying to keep pace, his lungs on fire. Kingsley was spurred by fear. He risked a glance over his shoulder, then added a quick burst of speed.

Over Timble Bridge, along Marsh Lane. Past Goulden's Yard. Turning on to Mill Street. Simon was still chasing, refusing to give up. The ground was flat. Soon enough it would rise steeply. That should slow him, Simon thought.

Drawing each breath was painful. He tried to ignore it. His legs pumped like an engine. Every stroke hurt. He pushed down harder, trying to make each stride longer.

It worked. He made up a little ground. Kingsley was having to work more, to force himself up the hill. Suddenly he disappeared. Slipped off to the right, along Muck Lane. The slap of his soles echoed off the houses and up into the night.

Another sharp turn, back downhill on Hill House Bank. If he didn't swerve again, Kingsley would come out by Fearn's Island, next to the river. From there he could turn back into town or out along Far Bank by the water.

Dear God, the man had to be tiring. No matter how good a runner he was, this was a killing pace. Surely it was impossible to keep it up much longer.

But Kingsley never paused. At the bottom of the hill he darted along the path by Nether Mills, out on to the Island. What was he doing? He had to know he was trapped there. There was only one way on or off. He'd had plenty of choices and taken this one. Why?

Simon slowed to a walk, hands on his hips, his heart still racing. No need to rush now. The man had nowhere else to go. He could feel the sweat, slick on his neck and his back. His shirt was sticking to his chest. He tried to let his breathing slow. Took one knife from his belt, another from his boot. Before he came out he'd spent a few minutes sharpening them.

Just a few yards away, water was rushing over the weir in a torrent of noise.

Except for the mills, there was nowhere to hide. Kingsley was crashing through the undergrowth, not even trying to be quiet.

He was there, caught in the moonlight, silhouetted against the sky. He looked back at Simon and smiled. Then . . . no hesitation. He dived into the river.

For the love of Christ . . .

TWENTY-FIVE

Simon couldn't follow. He couldn't swim; he'd have drowned if he'd tried. Even weighted down with coins, Kingsley pulled himself easily through the water. The small waves in his wake seemed to glow in the darkness.

He'd picked his spot well, down where the island bulged and just upstream from the low weir that separated river and canal. He only needed to cover forty yards to reach Leeds lock. All Simon could do was watch, helpless, as the man hauled himself up on to land, walked back and over the lock gates. Kingsley brought his hand to his forehead in a mocking salute and strode off into the night.

Gone.

Clever. Kingsley had the brains to change his plans once he realized he couldn't lose his pursuer. Daring, too. Simon would never have thought of that.

Defeated, he ambled home. Was there anything at all he could have done to stop the man?

'Very good. We know what happened to the Irishman,' Simon said as he rested his elbows on the kitchen table. 'But he's still out there and he's armed.'

'The farrier said he didn't seem worried,' Jane told him. 'He wasn't hurrying away or looking over his shoulder.' That had nagged at her. Not frightened meant he had somewhere he could go, people who'd hide him. Who, though? Why protect someone like that?

'I've been thinking about Kingsley swimming the river.' Rosie rolled a mug between her palms. They could hear the voice of the tutor in the front room, then Richard and Amos repeating their lessons. 'It takes some courage.'

'Yes.' Jane nodded. She couldn't swim, would never dive into water of her own will. Being thrown into the beck by the Irishman had been enough for a lifetime. She shuddered and felt a chill pass through her body.

'But we'll find him.'

'We will,' Simon agreed.

'What are we going to do about Mrs Parker?' Rosie asked.

'Nothing,' he replied. 'Certainly not for now.'

'She has that . . . evil in her.' He knew the thought had been preying on her mind.

'It wouldn't mean anything in court, would it?' His voice was gentle.

Jane watched him reach out and squeeze his wife's hand, and for a moment she wondered what it would be like to have someone like that, a man who cared for her. But it passed. She was better alone. Safer that way. She had Mrs Shields; she didn't need anyone else. A man would only hurt her in the end.

'You're miles away.' Simon's voice pulled her back to the room. She felt the warmth rise in her cheeks, suddenly embarrassed and guilty. 'I asked what you were going to do today.'

'Try to find people who can lead me to the Irishman.'

'I'll keep on looking for Kingsley.' He narrowed his eyes. 'I don't think they have a new place yet.'

'Don't be so certain,' Rosie told him. 'Kingsley has a little money now.'

'Not enough. He wouldn't have snatched the pot from the table last night if he did. That was asking for trouble. Things must be tight. He certainly wasn't expecting me to come after him. He'll be feeling squeezed.'

Rosie rested her chin on the back of her hand and narrowed her eyes. 'We have that note he sent to her. She gave him money, she might have been more generous and let them use a property she owns, too. I'll have another look at the places we know about while the boys are with their tutor. I'm going to prove she's guilty.'

While they talked, Jane slipped quietly away. On her own, there were no discussions, no arguments.

The day was bright, a tiny flutter of a breeze that rippled the shawl over her hair. She clasped it tight at the neck. As she approached Timble Bridge, her free hand reached for the knife in her pocket. Fear prickled along her arms as she remembered the feeling of tumbling through the air. She wouldn't give him another chance.

After an hour she found a small knot of people who knew him, members of the Irish families starting to move into the area. A woman gave her his name, patiently leading her as her tongue slipped around the words: Pádraig Colm O'Coughlan.

Names had power. She'd always understood that. It was why she only allowed a few to know her surname. But she had him. With his name, she could catch him off-guard and then strike.

Now to find him.

She walked. It was the only way she knew. Walked, and talked to the children and the beggars. A couple of boys had spotted the Irishman just a few minutes before, striding along, hands deep in his pockets, down towards the river.

With her shawl tight over her hair, Jane followed. Plenty of places to turn, but she could feel him. He'd kept going down the hill. At the bottom she halted. Turning right would lead her back towards town. She weighed the possibility, then went left, moving along downstream with the water and sniffing the air as if she might catch his scent.

Her hand was wrapped around the hilt of her knife. When she met him, she'd be ready. She wasn't going to give him a chance.

A pair of fishermen sat on the bank, scrawny, ancient men with weather-beaten faces who looked as if they spent every day here. They were dressed alike in old jackets and hats; they even looked alike, with sunken cheeks where their teeth had been pulled.

Jane saw them studying her from the corner of their eyes as she approached. A nod of greeting once she was close.

'Caught anything?'

'Not yet,' one replied with a grin. 'Plenty of time.'

'We've got all day,' the other said.

'Have there been many along here this morning?'

The men looked at each other. 'One or two, why?'

'Was one of them big? A lot taller than me, broad? Pale trousers, stained?'

'He was here, right enough,' the second man told her with a nod. 'Not a word of hello, even when we spoke to him.'

She'd made the right choice. 'Did you see where he went?'

The man shrugged. 'Didn't pay much attention once he'd gone past. There are a few spots, I suppose . . .' He looked at his companion. 'What do you think?'

'You ought to ask at the ferry. Arthur always keeps a good watch, doesn't he?'

'Always,' the first man agreed.

Another half mile, round the bend in the river. The ferry was a small boat, its paint long since peeled away, tied to a wooden jetty and bobbing lightly on the water.

'Going across?' The ferryman tilted his head towards the other shore. All countryside and a track leading down to the Wakefield Road.

'I don't know yet.' She took out a few coins. 'Have you taken anyone over there today?'

'One or two,' he said. 'Why?'

She described the Irishman and placed three pennies in his palm; the skin was as hard as the soles of her boots.

'I had him on board.'

She smiled. 'Then you can take me, too.'

It was a strange way to travel. She gripped the wood, scared and exposed on the river, hoping the vessel wouldn't sink. The ferryman didn't seem worried, pulling easily on the oars. He was grizzled, with a windburned face and ropes of muscles along his arms. Just two minutes before they landed and he helped her up on the bank, but it seemed to last a year.

'Did he go down the lane?' Jane asked.

The ferryman frowned at her. 'No other way to go, is there?'

The track was wide enough for a cart. Her feet kicked up dust as she walked, and the sun warmed her skin. There was little around. A few farms, but they all looked tended. This was too far out for body snatchers. Too dangerous: they'd be walking for miles with a corpse.

The track ended at the Wakefield Road and Jane turned back towards Leeds, walking through Hunslet. It was still wild out here, but the houses and the mills were beginning to push outwards from town.

Kingsley had ended up south of the river last night, swimming over to Hunslet. Now the Irishman had taken a careful, roundabout route, one that should have shaken off anyone following. She'd been lucky, but now she'd lost him.

She stood, looking around. They'd found a place over here, she felt sure of it. Where?

*   *   *

Simon crossed Leeds Bridge, smelling the stink of the River Aire. Another dry, cloudy day, with the haze making it seem as if the sun was shining through gauze. Tiny flecks of soot caught the light and landed on his suit.

He strode out along Dock Street until he reached Leeds lock. A barge was passing through, avoiding the weir in the river. He looked across the stretch of water. The river had a strong current; Kingsley's crossing was a powerful feat of swimming.

Simon turned, gazing at the land stretching into the distance. Houses hadn't reached too far yet. He could see them in the distance, the scaffolding and faint shouts of the builders. A few months and people would be living here. Beyond that it was still smallholdings.

A good place to hide. A fine place for body snatchers.

Rosie was waiting at the house, feeding the boys after their lessons. She looked over their heads and shook her head.

'I went round all those properties Amanda Parker owns. No body snatchers,' she told him.

It had been worth checking, but Simon had never expected much. They were almost back where they'd begun. Not quite, though; Kingsley and the Irishman knew that people were searching for them. They'd be constantly looking over their shoulders.

He was still thinking when Jane arrived and told him where she'd been.

'That's where they are,' Simon said. 'Somewhere in Hunslet.'

'Mrs Parker doesn't have any properties over there,' Rosie said.

'They've found somewhere to hide. They're going to need to work soon. If Kingsley's stealing the pot from a card game, they're desperate for money.'

'The coachman,' Jane said. 'He's taken them things before.'

Simon nodded. That was very possible.

'Do you want to watch him?' She turned to leave and he added, 'If he goes anywhere, just follow. Don't hurt him.'

'Do you think he'll lead us there?' Rosie asked once Jane had gone.

He let out a deep sigh. 'What else do we have? We can hardly knock on every door and ask about them.'

* * *

She almost missed the coachman as he slipped out of the kitchen door and into the dusk. Jane caught a flash of movement, then she was moving, quiet and cautious. She'd been lost in thoughts of what to read now she'd finished *Pride and Prejudice*. The ending had pleased her, with everybody happy, the sisters in love and married. She'd been part of their lives, seen everything unfold. She could feel their joy. Now, though, she wondered how real it could be. Did anyone have a life like that?

She needed something different. Mrs Shields had books, a dozen or more, enough to keep her busy for a year. Maybe something by Mrs Burney . . .

Jane stayed twenty yards behind the coachman. He wasn't wearing his livery, and a bulging leather satchel was slung over his shoulder. He kept to the main streets, happy in the throng of people, as if the crowds might keep him hidden.

But following people was her skill. She kept her distance. He'd never suspect she was there, but she wouldn't lose him.

He moved down Briggate, glancing around as he approached Leeds Bridge to cross the river. She smiled. There was only one place he would be going.

He kept a brisk pace, hurrying along. Moving silently behind him, she kept saying the Irishman's name silently in her mind, letting it give a rhythm to her strides. Burning it into her head to nestle alongside the hatred.

By the time he left the streets behind, the darkness was complete. A few clouds, stars scattered, enough moon for her to make out the road, a ribbon ahead of her, blackness to the sides.

The coachman never hesitated; he kept moving. He knew exactly where he was going, Jane thought; he must have been out here before.

They were surrounded by night noises. Suddenly, something felt different. His footsteps were veering off to her right. He'd turned down a lane, just wide enough for a horse and cart. Fifty yards away, a lamp gave out a dim glow in a window.

This was it. She could sense O'Coughlan. The Irishman. Her hand caressed the handle of her blade. Soon. Very soon.

She hung back, waiting until the coachman had to be inside, then she eased her way closer to the house. It seemed small, only a tiny yard behind the building. An old handcart stood, the wheels at an angle as if the whole thing might fall apart at any second.

She crept back to the road and stood, gazing around for some landmark. Impossible to discover anything in this blackness. Scuffling around, she gathered stones, piling them into a small cairn close to the track. Enough for her to know the place again.

TWENTY-SIX

'**Y**ou found them,' Rosie said and turned to Simon. 'Are you going to tell Porter and let him finish things?'

He'd been thinking as Jane talked. The nub of an idea that might work, something that would satisfy the constable and Jane.

'Are there places we can watch this house of theirs?'

'I couldn't tell,' Jane answered. 'It was too dark to see much.'

'We need to find out. We know that Kingsley is the one who finds out about burials and arranges the sale of the bodies. He'll have to go out to do all that.'

'Catch him alone?'

'It's better than facing two of them together. He doesn't have a hope of beating us. I want to ask him a few questions, and after that we can give him to Porter.'

'What about the Irishman?' Jane asked.

'Once Kingsley's safe in gaol, we can tackle him.' He saw her face harden. 'He's yours. Don't worry about that. I'll be there just in case you need me.'

She nodded.

Jane led the way over the bridge and down the road into Hunslet. Not even ten minutes and they'd left the clamour of the town behind. Simon breathed deep. The air tasted sweeter and clearer.

She stopped, looking around for a moment, then moved on. They hadn't gone too far before she pointed to a small heap of stones.

'It's there. Up that track.'

He could make out a small house set back among a stand of young, scrubby trees.

'We should keep on walking,' he said. 'One of them might be watching the road.'

Another mile, then they turned around, moving back towards town. Not together this time. She walked four hundred yards ahead, head down, hurrying. Simon took his time, glancing around, trying to find somewhere hidden enough to watch the house.

A coach went galloping by. The horses were straining, the outside passengers white-faced, holding on to straps, to luggage, to anything at all. He looked up at them and grinned.

Jane was by Leeds Bridge, ducking between a coalman's cart and a gig driven by a gentleman in his frock coat and shiny top hat. She ignored them to squat and talk with a beggar, this one missing his left arm. She seemed to know all the wounded birds around town, Simon thought wryly.

She stood as he approached, taking some coins from her pocket and placing them in the beggar's hands.

'He knows the Irishman by sight. He says he passed here an hour ago, going into Leeds. He was on his own.' She wore her hunter's smile.

'Kingsley might be at the house alone, or it could be empty.'

'Yes.'

'We'd better hurry.'

It was a chance, he thought, as they turned and strode back along the road, as good a one as they were going to be given.

Crouching low, they crossed the field at a run, slowly circling round and trying to use the spindly tree trunks for cover until they reached the back of the building. The door was closed. No lock; nothing more than a simple latch.

The old cart in the yard kept them hidden from sight. He looked at her. She nodded.

Simon took out his knife and dashed. Lifted the latch and he was inside.

A single room, everything dim with the shutters closed. Jane stood, letting her eyes adjust. The pulse in her wrist was beating fast and hard. But there was no danger here right now. No sign of Kingsley, not a corner or a nook where he could hide. Two piles of straw for beds, food standing on a small table that looked as old as the building. A heavy wooden spade and a mattock leaned against the wall. The tools of their trade.

They hadn't tried to start a fire in the hearth. The chimney was probably blocked, anyway, she thought. Smoke would attract attention to a place that was supposed to be empty.

She saw Simon quickly leaf through a notebook then set it back down. He shook his head and they left, careful to leave things as they'd found them. A quiet snick of the latch as it fell and they were gone.

Jane realized she'd been holding her breath and gulped in the air. They were back at the road before she spoke.

'Did you find anything?'

'Nothing useful. But they're living here, no doubt about that.' He glanced back over his shoulder. 'You know, the last farmhouse was a long way down from the place in Sheepscar. That seemed like a home. This . . .' he shook his head, '. . . it's nothing more than a hovel.'

'They're still free,' she said.

'Not for long. They know we're breathing down their necks.'

Maybe they did, she thought. But they were still walking around. The Irishman was still alive.

Another hundred yards and she cocked her head. 'How about over there?' She gestured towards a dip in the ground behind an oak tree. 'We won't be able to see the house, but they'll have to come past on their way to and from town.' Jane scrambled across a field, feeling him behind her.

He slid down and looked around. 'Yes,' he said with a smile. 'I'll stay here for a few hours. Why don't you come back near dusk?'

She was happy to leave him there. Her heart was pulling her into Leeds. The Irishman was there. Pádraig Colm O'Coughlan. She spoke it under her breath as she marched, reciting the words like a child's rhyme. The sooner she found him, the quicker all this would end. He wouldn't fill her mind any longer. She'd finally be able to rid herself of the pain of the bridge, the sense of flying. Spill his blood and send him into history.

By the end of the day, frustration rasped at her. Nobody had seen the Irishman; he might as well have vanished into the air.

Kate had a fresh tray of pies to sell, shouting her wares on the corner of Briggate and Boar Lane. All beef, she claimed, still hot from the oven. Maybe it really was beef, Jane thought as she bit into one. Maybe not. It didn't matter as long as it warmed her and filled her belly.

She was hungry, wolfing down two of them as Kate looked on in approval.

'I've always said you were too thin,' Kate said. 'These will put a bit of weight on you. You're going to need that as you get older.'

She was a big woman, hefty arms and a bark of a voice. The type to scare people. Yet under the size and the bluster she was warm, even timid. Jane knew that her husband beat her if she didn't bring enough money home each day. She'd never fought back or walked away.

'Those bruises are beginning to fade,' Kate said. 'Won't be too long until they're all gone.'

Maybe the colours and the ache and the tenderness would become nothing, Jane thought. But she knew this would be a piece of her past she'd never be able to forget. That was why it burned in her, why she needed her revenge.

'People will remember. Every time they see me . . .'

'They won't.' Kate shook her head. 'Half of them will have forgotten what happened today by the time they wake up tomorrow morning. They won't care about you.'

Perhaps, Jane thought as she strolled off. She'd prefer them to forget, not to notice her at all.

Sometimes Simon felt as if he'd spent too much of his life waiting and trying to disappear from sight. Days of it, probably even months if he ever tried to tally it all up. He was no better at it now than when he'd begun. He liked things to happen. Once they began to move, they'd soon be over.

They'd been after the body snatchers for more than three weeks. It felt like an age. Most jobs lasted a few hours, very rarely longer than a day or two. Here, nestled in a hollow behind an oak tree watching people and carts move along the road, it was easy to forget the reason he was here.

It wasn't only for the fee. Not this time. It was for Gwendolyn Jordan. The other bodies. The undercurrent of rage in his wife. The need to find answers to the rest of his questions. To discover the truth.

Jane arrived before dusk, bringing one of Kate's pies. Very welcome after a day with nothing to eat.

'I haven't seen any sign of Kingsley or the Irishman,' he said. The darkness was growing around them.

'I'll slip down to the house and check.'

Before he could say anything, she was gone.

*   *   *

The air felt soft as she moved, velvet against her skin. Jane picked her way through the undergrowth, one hand on the knife in her pocket. She moved her head from side to side, eyes flickering, ears alert for the smallest sound.

Nothing human, and no light shining in the house. She circled the building and made her way back.

'Not there.' She stretched, palms pressing against the small of her back to ease the strain on her muscles. 'The cart is still in the yard.'

'We might as well go home.'

'Why?'

'They're not likely to come back and go out again tonight. They need a third man, anyway. Someone to replace Ackroyd.'

Jane stared at him. 'They already have one.'

'What?' She saw him thinking. 'Who?'

'The coachman,' she answered, as if it was obvious.

'But—' Simon began and stopped. 'Maybe you're right. They know him, they seem to trust him.' He'd still have his duties for Mrs Parker, but she'd let him go when they needed an extra man. If it was true, it would forge more links between her and the body snatchers.

They started to walk back to Leeds along the road. Simon guided them away, following a faint game trail through the fields.

'This will take us longer,' she said.

'I know, but they could be on their way home. This is better than blundering into them in the dark. We've waited this long and seen them get away twice. Just a little more patience.'

She knew he was right. But she itched for it to be over.

Frank the coachman, Simon thought as he lay in bed. Rosie was sleeping calmly beside him. If he listened carefully, he could pick out the boys' breathing. A light, gentle snore for Amos, while Richard always seemed to fight the night, as if he resented the hours lost in sleep.

The more he considered the idea, the more obvious it seemed. But so, so dangerous. Amanda Parker was juggling fire by allowing it. Perhaps that was what she wanted, to see how far she could go without being burned.

Why, though? What did she have to gain from it? That was

the part he couldn't understand. Maybe Rosie was right and the woman had a wide streak of madness in her.

Time for all that tomorrow. Now he needed sleep.

The light was just beginning to grow when Jane settled behind the oak. Still chilly in the darkness; she was wearing her old green cloak for warmth. She'd already been to the house. There was nothing to see or hear in the darkness. She'd needed to see it, to be certain the handcart was still in the yard.

Jane crept away, invisible. She was still stiff when she started to walk, but each morning it grew easier and easier. Last night she'd studied herself in the mirror. Kate was right, the bruises were fading.

'Another fortnight and they'll be no more than a memory,' Mrs Shields said as she rubbed in the ointment. She'd removed the stitches from Jane's back a few days before. The flesh had knitted together well, just one more scar on a body filled with them. 'You can hardly see them now.'

But Jane still flinched as the woman's fingers moved across the middle of her back.

'Does it still hurt there?'

'A little.'

'The bruising must be deep inside,' Mrs Shields told her. 'We can't see it. Don't worry, child, it will go away in time.'

'How long?'

'By the time those other bruises are gone, you'll probably barely feel it any more.'

Now, with her back against the root of the oak tree, the ache seemed to cut through her body. Whatever way she shifted, it was still there, and she had hours left out here.

It was the middle of the morning before the Irishman left, strolling down the road, whistling a broken tune. The bandage still covered his wounded eye.

Good.

Jane let him go by, feeling a tingle of fear as she gripped her knife. A picture came from nowhere, the day she'd seen Betsy the whore stroll off along the Calls with him. The woman couldn't have suspected he was about to kill her and toss her body in the river. All because she'd become an inconvenience. Somewhere the woman would have had a family who would never know what happened to her.

Jane owed him a debt for her, too. She'd have her chance against him. Not just now, though.

Half an hour went by before Kingsley passed. He was in a hurry, taking long strides and pulling a watch from his waistcoat pocket to check on the time before speeding up again.

It was simple to keep him in sight where the road was quiet. She could keep a long distance. Once they were in Leeds, though, she had to stay close, easing between people.

Outside the coaching office by the Bull and Mouth on Briggate, Kingsley shook hands with a thick-set man who wore long, curling side whiskers.

Jane stood by Kate the pie-seller, hearing gossip as she watched. The men talked for five minutes. Twice, Kingsley held his arms apart, as if he was indicating the size of something, and the other man nodded. Finally they were done. Kingsley very carefully counted out a few coins from his pocket.

He strode away, not noticing her as he hurried down Briggate towards Leeds Bridge.

On the river, barges were lined up by the wharves, two and three abreast, to load and unload. A procession of men carried sacks on their backs, bent over under the weight as they deftly kept their balance.

Jane quickened her pace after Kingsley turned on to Dock Street. He entered an ironmonger's shop and came back out a minute later, hands empty, then on to a sawmill.

Not even ten minutes until he was out again, hefting some cut wooden boards over his shoulder. They were fastened together with rope, but still an awkward weight. He seemed to sag under the strain.

Why hadn't he brought the Irishman? He'd have been able to carry them with no effort. At the end of the street, Kingsley leaned his load against the wall, rubbing his shoulder as he looked around.

He hadn't come far, Jane thought, only struggled a couple of hundred yards. If he kept that up, it would be dark before he reached the house.

Kingsley waited. In the space beyond a rotting boathouse, she stood in the shadows.

Ten minutes passed before the Irishman arrived. Kingsley paced and paused, paced and paused. She watched the Irishman hoist the load and start to walk as if it weighed nothing at all.

She had no need to trail behind them. They were going back to their house. Instead, she drifted up Briggate, glancing through the window of the coaching office. The man she'd seen earlier was there, behind his desk.

Outside, she studied the board. It was Friday today; she needed to know what coaches were leaving tomorrow. York, Manchester, Gloucester. At quarter past ten, the flyer to Edinburgh. Scotland.

Jane leaned forward on the bench.

'Tonight,' she told Rosie. 'Tell him they'll be going digging tonight.'

They sat opposite each other in the kitchen. No sign of Simon, no idea where he'd gone. She described everything she'd seen during the morning.

'You're right,' Rosie agreed. 'We can take them.'

'There's a coach leaving for Edinburgh tomorrow. Didn't Simon say the surgeons there buy bodies?' Suddenly it struck her that she'd read the list of destinations and never given it a second thought; the act had seemed completely natural.

'Yes.' Rosie gave a grim, eager smile. 'It would be a good place to end things, wouldn't it? They wouldn't dare do much in the middle of Briggate, and if they have a body with them, they can hardly deny it all. After that we can see about Mrs Parker.'

'How?' Jane asked. 'I thought we didn't have any proof.'

She paused and ran her tongue around her lips in anticipation. 'I have an idea. Just you and me . . .'

Simon sat in George Mudie's printing shop, watching the man inspect sheets as they emerged from the press.

'If you had a scrap of sense, you'd tell the constable where they are and let him deal with it, Simon.'

'He's had two chances. What do we have for it? One man from the watch dead and another badly wounded. A body snatcher hung by the mob and the other escaped. It's not exactly glorious, is it?'

'You need to make sure you do better.'

'We will,' he said. All he needed was the right opportunity. That would come very soon, he knew it.

Rosie sent the boys outside to play. A shower that ended a little while before had left puddles for them to stamp in all across the yard. She and Simon sat next to each other in the kitchen, Jane on the other side of the table.

'I still want to follow them tonight,' he said. 'We can see where they go and whose body they take. That way it can be returned later.'

'I can go after them,' Jane said.

He shook his head. 'No, it should be both of us. They'll be very careful. We're not going to do anything to worry or scare them, we'll let it happen. But if there's any trouble, we'll stand a better chance together. No constable this time.'

He saw her considering the idea, then nodding her agreement.

'I've asked Mrs Fisher on Alfred Street to look after Richard and Amos tomorrow morning,' Rosie said. It was her way of announcing she intended to take part. 'They enjoy playing with her son.'

Another person would be useful. She didn't look it, but his wife could be deadly. She'd killed before, and she could again.

'We're settled, then.' He turned to Jane. 'Meet before dusk out by the oak tree.'

Things were moving. Soon this would be over.

TWENTY-SEVEN

Walking home, Jane felt the tingle up her spine. She began to reach for her knife, then stopped. Nothing to scare or worry them, Simon had said. No confrontations. It was simpler to disappear, to skitter away through the courts and ginnels where no one else was likely to follow her.

Two minutes and she knew she was on her own. Home was close, the cottage behind Green Dragon Yard. Once she was through the wall, Jane felt safe, letting the world drop away. She and Catherine Shields were here. That was enough.

She washed and prepared food for the two of them. After they'd eaten, pots and dishes scoured, she looked at the books once again. Not Mrs Burney, she decided. Maybe *Sense and Sensibility*. There was a balance in the words of the title that pleased her. She picked it up and read the first page. The style, the characters, reminded her of *Pride and Prejudice*. Just like the other book, the author was anonymous, listed only as *A Lady*.

'Is it the same person?' she asked Mrs Shields.

'It is, child.'

Soon enough, Jane was caught in the bright, clean world of the Dashwood sisters. She knew they'd become her very good friends, just like the Bennets.

The book was a perfect escape. When she raised her head, she was surprised to discover she was still in Leeds. Jane set it aside. Work was waiting, dirty and ugly.

'I shouldn't be too late,' she told the old woman.

'Be careful.' The same thing she always said.

'I will.' A kiss to the cheek and she was gone, clutching the cloak around her. Still light, but she could already feel the first hint of an evening chill in the air as she hurried over Leeds Bridge.

Simon was already there, waiting in the shelter of the oak tree.

'In case they decided to move early,' he said.

Instead, it was another long, dead hour before they heard the squeak of the wheels along the track. The Irishman was pushing the cart, the tools and a sheet inside. Kingsley walked beside him, gaze roving around, face nervous.

They were safe here, Simon knew, as he ducked down, away from sight. He didn't raise his head until he could barely hear them in the distance.

'Only the two of them.'

'Where's the coachman?' Jane asked as they began to follow.

The answer was waiting at the bottom of Kirkgate. Frank the coachman stood, nervously shifting from foot to foot, then falling in beside the others.

Not too far to go. Church Lane, Somerset Street, over to Mill Garth, then up to Ebenezer Chapel. This wasn't a churchyard set off by itself. The graveyard here was a thin stretch of land in the middle of town. It was surrounded by buildings, houses close by. The body snatchers were either daring or desperate if they were digging in this place, Simon thought, and he doubted they were that daring.

A whisper, then Jane was lost in the darkness. Gone to the other side of the burying ground. Maybe the light was a little better over there. All Simon could see were a few glimpses from the shielded lantern.

He guessed the coachman was holding it while the others did the work; the glow jumped around. The man was very likely terrified of the watch appearing. It didn't stop the Irishman. Even with a wooden shovel, the rhythm of digging began to echo off all the walls. A pause.

The coachman raised the lantern higher. In the glow he saw Kingsley and the Irishman, heads together as they talked. The digging started again, faster. Hurried now, more urgent. They had to know it would only be a matter of minutes before someone came looking.

Soon enough, there was silence. A soft grunt carried through the air as one of them eased down into the hole. A sharp crack, bringing the mattock down to open up the coffin.

They needed a brighter light now, shining down so they could put the rope around the corpse and haul it out of the coffin. It had to be Kingsley in the ground, bending, threading, with the Irishman to do the brute lifting.

The coachman seemed to dance around, too scared to stay in one spot.

A few seconds and the body was up. Resurrected to the air and the night. The Irishman was hastily shovelling dirt back into the hole, then standing on it to push it down as Kingsley swiftly wrapped the body and lifted it on to the cart. They replaced the sod they'd cut, stamping so no edges would show.

The coachman scurried ahead to light the path for them. Simon heard the protest of the cartwheels as they moved away. He stayed behind them, watching until they moved into a pool of light from a lamp outside a tavern. Just two of them again, Kingsley and the Irishman. The coachman had disappeared. Back to Burley House, at a guess.

The pair didn't talk. No need. They were professionals, this was another night at their trade. Simon brought out his watch. A little shy of twenty minutes since they'd entered the graveyard and they were already on their way home.

'Are we going to follow them?'

Jane was standing next to him, staring at the figures disappearing into the distance.

He shook his head. 'No need.'

'What about tomorrow?'

Simon thought for a moment. 'We'll meet early at the oak.'

'When do you want to take them?' Her voice was eager.

'When they drop off the box at the coaching office. They'll think it's all done by then.'

'What are we going to do about the coachman?'

'Let's worry about him once we've finished with Kingsley and the Irishman,' Simon told her. 'Go and sleep. We'll have plenty to do in the morning.'

Jane kept a hand around her knife hilt as she walked home. Friday night and Leeds was loud. Not even the end of the working week, but men were out, drinking, singing, looking for a fight, looking for a woman.

She moved quietly, purposefully, not looking around, not appearing worried. Men sensed fear. Some of them loved to prey on it. She'd learned to hide hers many years before. It was a way to survive when you lived on the street.

She thought about the body snatchers. She'd hardly been able to see a thing, just a constantly bobbing pinprick of light and the sound of the wooden spade. It seemed to go on forever, lasting so long that she felt sure they must be caught. Then it was over in an instant, and they were marching away with the body. Who had they taken? Would the family discover it?

The truth would come out when Kingsley and the Irishman were arrested.

She and Simon would have Rosie with them. The two body snatchers wouldn't expect her. They'd take her for a lady; they'd underestimate. But they'd learn soon enough.

Tomorrow Jane would settle accounts with the Irishman. She'd speak his name. She'd coo it and screech it, take away his power with it. Then . . .

As she walked, the day drained away from her. All the aches in her body rose to the surface. She began to feel the hurt and bruises. Her shoulders and legs, the pain in her back, deep under the flesh. She needed to rest.

In the cottage, hearing the old woman's soft, even breathing as she slept, Jane lit the oil lamp and trimmed the wick low. Enough light to read. She opened *Sense and Sensibility*. Within a few lines she was back in the genteel world of gowns and dances and handsome young men with fortunes. Tomorrow she'd fight. Tonight she'd flirt and dance.

Rosie was awake, sitting at the table, her knife and whetstone in front of her.

'All ready?' Simon asked.

'Completely,' she told him.

She'd clung fiercely to him in the bed, finally drifting away into sleep with a hand across his chest. He closed his eyes, trying to imagine all the things that could go wrong in the morning. Too many. Far too many.

Jane woke early, thinking she'd heard a noise. She listened, but nothing. Quietly, she slid from the bed, picked up her knife and walked around the house. Everything was ordinary. Her imagination, maybe, or the fading tendrils of a dream.

She rubbed some of Mrs Shields's ointment into her bruises. The soothing warmth spread through her body. Dressed, she put an edge on her knife as she ate.

'You're off with the fairies,' the old woman said.

'Not that far,' she answered with a smile.

'There's going to be violence today, isn't there, child?'

'Maybe. Not if we can avoid it.' A lie. Catherine Shields could probably see it on her face. But the words satisfied them both.

A gentle hug before she left. A bright day outside. Jane took a deep breath and ducked through the gap in the wall to Green Dragon Yard and out into Leeds.

Simon was up and ready before the boys were awake. No lessons for them this morning, a day of play with Mrs Fisher's son instead. They were old enough to know that something was happening, even if they didn't understand exactly what.

He took the pistol from the secret drawer in the stairs and loaded it, feeling the weight in his hand. Better to have the weapon and not need it.

'Are they that dangerous?'

He turned as Rosie entered the kitchen. She was dressed in the plain gown that she wore every day, a white apron, a cap covering her hair. No fancy bonnets or gowns. Nothing to draw the eye. Like this, she looked ordinary. He knew she was anything but that.

'They've escaped from the constable. The Irishman did it twice. I'm not taking any chances.' He slid the gun into the large pocket of his jacket and checked his knives for the final time. All three of them in place. 'Time,' he said.

'Be careful,' Rosie told him. 'I'll be near the coaching office from nine o'clock.'

'They'll want to be in ample time to make sure their box has a good spot on board.'

'It's not a box, Simon. It's a body.'

'Yes.' It was. He needed to remember that, to keep the flame roaring under his anger. For Gwendolyn Jordan and all the rest. Today he could bring them some small measure of justice.

Jane was sitting by the oak. She twisted the gold ring on her finger, the one Mrs Shields had given her to keep her safe. She'd need it against the Irishman, but she would beat him. She couldn't let herself believe anything else.

'Have they stirred yet?' Simon crouched beside her, looking up the road at the track that led to their small house.

'I've heard some hammering. It stopped about ten minutes ago.'

The body was packed. Probably the label was already pasted on the lid.

'They'll go soon. Once they've passed, we'll take the back way and beat them into town. I want us to be waiting by the coaching office so we can take them by surprise.'

It was a little after half past eight by his pocket watch when Kingsley and the Irishman appeared. The wood of the box was bright and new as it lay in the cart. It looked too small to hold a human body, not even three feet long. How had they managed to cram anyone into that? Simon pressed his body back against the tree, not glancing again until they'd passed.

The men were in no hurry, walking at a slow, steady pace, exchanging a few words of conversation. He watched how they moved, to see if they favoured one leg. Nothing unusual he could notice.

The Irishman's eye was still bandaged. He'd be blind on his left side. They'd need every kind of advantage against him. Simon reached into his pocket and caressed the polished stock of the pistol. If he had to shoot, he'd need to be close to do any real damage.

Finally, he exhaled. 'Now,' he said, and began to walk.

Jane twisted the gold ring again, looking all around. She kept the shawl around her head, feet moving quickly, right hand on the hilt of her knife.

She could smell Leeds, taste it in her mouth, soot and dirt on her tongue. She swallowed. Simon was keeping a quick pace. His jaw was set, lost in his own thoughts. She stayed beside him, eyes always wary.

Feet echoed on the cobbled street. Men were busy, loading and unloading carts. Nobody gave the pair of them a glance.

They hurried over the bridge, dodging the carts and crossing to the other side of Briggate from the coaching office. Simon ambled up the pavement until he had a clear view of the place.

No need to be quiet, but he still brought his mouth close to her ear. 'I'll stay here. It's far enough down the street that they're not likely to spot me. Can you cross over and find somewhere?'

Jane glanced, then nodded. She didn't even need to look. Every inch of this town was in her brain. 'Where will Rosie be?'

'Farther up, closer to Boar Lane. They don't know her, so she doesn't have to be hidden. She'll be ready if they try to run that way.'

Rosie was good, but she'd never be able to stop the Irishman; Jane knew that. He'd run right through her and leave her for dead.

'When do we go for them?'

'As soon as they've handed over the box. While they're doing that, we'll start walking up. Kingsley will take in the forms. As soon as he comes outside, we'll be there. No running, we don't want to do anything that might warn them.'

'All right.'

Briggate was busy. A passenger coach was trapped between carts, the driver shouting and cursing. A gaggle of servants gazed into shop windows at things they'd never be able to afford. A street-singer raised his voice in one of the old ballads. There were a few coins in the hat by his feet. She added another one as she passed.

This wasn't a good place for a battle, Jane thought. Too many innocent people around who could end up hurt. The Irishman certainly wouldn't care. He had nothing to lose. If he was arrested, he'd hang for killing the constable's man. Kingsley might be more cautious. The worst sentence he would face was six months for digging up the dead.

Nobody noticed her. Their eyes passed over her face and immediately forgot her. That was how she wanted it. Invisible.

No sign of the body snatchers yet. Jane couldn't see the coachman. She turned her head to look at Simon. He was staring intently at the coaching office, breaking off as a man he seemed to know approached him.

'Westow! What are you doing out here?' Dr Thackrah asked.

Sweet God, Simon thought, this was the last thing he needed. His mind raced for an excuse, then he remembered that Kingsley had been one of the doctor's pupils. If Thackrah saw him and called out his name, it could ruin everything. He needed to hurry the man away.

'Working.' He smiled politely.

'Am I interrupting?' He stared up and down the street, searching for something criminal.

'Please don't take this the wrong way, but yes. Something's going to happen here. Very soon. You'll be much safer somewhere else.'

It was enough to make the man turn pale.

'I see. Will you tell me about it the next time I see you?'

'Gladly.'

Thackrah bustled off like a frightened rabbit, down towards the bridge. Simon took a deep breath and looked across at Jane.

He brought out his watch again. They should be coming very shortly. He was willing them to arrive, to end the waiting. He'd be calm as soon as things began to happen. Before they did, he was always uneasy, letting himself imagine the worst.

This would go calmly. He'd take Kingsley and march him to the gaol. The Irishman? Jane had made it clear. She wanted him. She needed that. He'd help if he could, but he'd never take the fight away from her.

Jane watched Simon talking, then the man left, walking quickly. Her fingers touched the ring once more, then her hand checked her knife for the hundredth time.

The Irishman might kill her. He had the strength and the size. He was an ogre, a giant. But this time she might beat him. Perhaps she'd fail, but she had to try. She *had* to. Not just for pride, but for who she was. She searched the words she knew, but couldn't find any that described it. Once she'd learned more, she decided.

Her body stiffened. They were there, the cart stopping outside the coaching office.

It was time.

TWENTY-EIGHT

Simon watched as Kingsley took papers from the pocket of his old jacket. He sorted through them, plucking out the ones he needed. The Irishman hefted the box on to his shoulder. It was so small, surely too small to hold a corpse . . .

They entered the office. Simon began to walk, never taking his eyes off the doorway. A few seconds and the Irishman emerged. He brought out a pipe and tinder box. Soon he was leaning against the cart, puffing, content as he stared up Briggate.

Keep looking in that direction, Simon thought.

A very quick glance across the street. Jane was there, chafing at having to move slowly. But the timing was important.

He paused, shuffled his feet. Stood. Kingsley should have been back outside by now. Had something gone wrong. Had the coach clerk discovered what was in the box?

Then Kingsley appeared, beaming, clapping the Irishman on the shoulder.

Simon exhaled and began to walk again. On the other side of the street, Jane was moving. Glancing up Briggate, he picked out Rosie in her plain fustian edging towards the body snatchers.

They weren't aware of anything. The Irishman jammed the clay pipe in his mouth and picked up the handles of the cart. Kingsley was talking to him.

All around, people were going about their business.

Now.

Simon crossed the road, coming up close to the men. No more than two yards away. He had his hands down by his side, each one holding a knife.

'Mr Kingsley. Peter Kingsley, isn't it?'

The man heard his name. He turned, face falling as he recognized Simon. Kingsley began to run.

Simon was right on his heels. He was prepared for this. Kingsley was fast; he'd learned that. But this time he had the edge.

Two steps behind, that was all. Just a little closer and he could take him.

People were stopping. Staring. Drawing back. From the corner of his eye he saw a man put his arms around a woman's shoulder. Someone screamed. A voice bellowed for the watch.

Somewhere at the edge of his mind, Simon was aware of it all. But the only thing he could see was Kingsley.

The man dodged to the side as something blocked his path. Rosie, trying to act as if it had been an accident.

Kingsley started to go around her. Before she could do anything, he was behind her. One hand around her neck, the other holding up his knife.

'If you try to take me, she's going to die.'

Simon watched him. Careful not to glance at Rosie. He knew she had her own plan. She'd prepared for this. He'd already caught the look in her eye.

'What do you want?'

As Kingsley began to run, the Irishman moved, ready to start after him. Jane twisted the gold ring, then took a breath.

'Pádraig Colm O'Coughlan.'

Her shout rang above the screams and the shouting and the fear on Briggate. Jane yelled the words, once, then again, until he turned.

'Pádraig Colm O'Coughlan.' She faced him as she said it for a third time. 'I know who you are now. I've stolen your power.'

He started towards her, drawing his knife. Waving it.

She felt completely calm. All her fear of him had vanished. She shifted to his left. His blind side. He had to turn his head to watch her.

'Pádraig Colm O'Coughlan.' It was a taunt now. She wanted to goad him. To force him into a sudden move. But he wasn't going to be pressed that easily. He kept his distance, too far for her to lunge.

She stayed on his left, taking advantage of his bandaged, blind eye. People were watching. She heard men making bets, putting money on the Irishman to kill her. She wasn't going to let him.

Jane danced off further, then made a quick feint forward. He brought his right arm around, slicing through the air with his knife to stop her. To hurt her. She'd already moved away, then darted forward. Quick enough to swipe across his forehead with the blade then back again, out of reach.

She needed to stay clear until the blood began to flow. If he caught her, if he could grip her, the Irishman would squeeze the life out of her.

'Pádraig Colm O'Coughlan.' Singing it like a children's rhyme as the blood began to trickle down his forehead. He tried to wipe it away with the back of his left hand. But not a sound from him. Not a roar, not a cry. Not a word.

He had to keep blinking his right eye to see anything. Blood trickled down his cheek and neck. He was wounded, but still powerful.

Moving forward, trying to force her back against the wall. If she let him, he'd win. She slipped around behind him, her blade slitting the back of his neck before he could face her.

The Irishman drew himself up, towering over her. He stood completely still for a moment, then shook his head like an animal and ran towards her.

He had speed. Faster than Jane expected. She stepped to the side, ducking her head. His left arm was flailing. It caught her on top of the head. Hard. Solid. Strong enough to send her sprawling on to the cobbles. Sharp, sudden pain jolted through her body.

She rolled, springing back to her feet, knife still in her hand. He came again. She began to move, but he hit her once more, his open hand catching her in the face. She felt the crunch of bone, blood streaming from her nose.

She must have passed out. Just for a second. Jane was on her back, trying to focus. Her face was on fire. Eyes full of tears. She tried to spit the blood from her mouth. Jane knew she had to stand or he'd kill her.

Stand. At first her body wouldn't obey. All it felt was the pain in her head.

Stand.

Jane lurched to her feet. She tried to steady herself but her legs had no strength. She had to be ready for his third charge. When he came, she never had a chance. His fist landed like a hammer in her belly, forcing the air out of her. She went crashing back down to the ground.

Another moment and he'd be on her. She gripped the knife. Her only chance.

*   *   *

'I said, what do you want?' Simon repeated.

'You let me go free.' It was the first time he'd really heard Kingsley's voice. Thin, reedy, shot through with fear that he tried to cover. He was still waving his knife in the air, not against Rosie's throat.

Never draw a weapon unless you're willing to use it. An old fighter had taught Simon that years before, and he'd learned it was true. Kingsley had trained as a surgeon; he should know how to handle a blade. But he'd probably never done it in anger or desperation.

'If that's what you want, you'd better take your hand off the woman.'

The man's arm was still around her neck. 'She's coming with me until I'm sure you're not following.'

'If you hurt her—'

'*I warned you*: if you try to stop me, I'll kill her.' He was shouting, eyes bulging.

Simon was suddenly aware of all the people standing and watching, as if they were putting on a spectacle. He risked a glance at Rosie. She was waiting for the right moment to strike.

'You're not a fighter—' Simon began, but a man's voice from the crowd rode over his.

'Let her go.'

Kingsley jerked his head to try and see who'd spoken. That was all the opportunity Rosie needed. She plunged her knife into his side. He screamed. Before Kingsley could do anything, she squirmed out of his grip.

Blood was starting to seep from the wound. Kingsley tried to stop it with his hand, but it oozed between his fingers, down over his trousers.

Simon and Rosie faced him. Her eyes glittered with the lust of violence.

'Put your knife down,' Simon said. 'It's over. You're done.'

He let it fall from his fingers. Simon picked it up and searched him as Rosie stood guard. As simple as that. Another of the resurrection men caught.

Simon leaned close to the man. 'We're going to the gaol. Don't resist or I'll tell everyone here that you're a body snatcher. You know what they did to Harry Ackroyd.'

A hurried nod of agreement. Simon began to march him up the street. The crowd parted, moving away from them in a wave.

'Do you want to reach the gaol alive?'

'What do you mean?' His voice cracked. 'What?'

'You took a girl; she was just ten years old. I want to know where you sent her. If you don't tell me, I'll let all those people know what's in that box you took to the coaching office. Who bought her body?'

'Which one was she?' He lifted his fingers. They were shiny with blood. 'I'm going to need a physician. I'm bleeding badly.'

Simon tightened the grip on his knife. The man didn't care. He didn't know names, ages. They weren't the dead. They were goods to sell. He had to stop himself from slamming Kingsley against the wall.

Instead, he swallowed, tried to speak calmly. 'You dug up her body in Headingley. You have until I count to three.'

The man didn't wait. He'd seen Simon's face. He knew his life depended on it. 'That one. She went to Edinburgh. Dr Adams.'

'And the rest? How many of them?'

'Nine.' Kingsley tried to think. 'No, it was ten.'

Ten. For the love of God . . .

It was so tempting to turn around. To state his crime and leave him to the mercy of the crowd. He didn't deserve any more than that.

So tempting.

Instead, he kept on walking, taking Kingsley to the gaol. He had his information; Kingsley would have his trial.

He saw the senior watchman turn the corner from Kirkgate to Briggate, two men behind him, looking as though they were trying to hurry. They'd taken their time covering a few yards.

'Bringing him to us, Westow? What's he done?'

'He worked with Ackroyd. You should know him. He escaped from the raid on the farmhouse.'

The inspector smiled. 'Did he now? Then he'll be able to tell us all about it.'

'Take him.' Simon began to turn away. Jane was facing off against the Irishman. She'd need help.

'You're coming, too. The constable's going to want to hear what you've been up to today.'

He hesitated. The shouting from farther down Briggate grew louder. The watchman drew his knife.

'I wasn't giving you a choice.'

Simon looked at Rosie and nodded. She began to run.

Jane was braced for his weight. Blade ready to stab him in the belly. Over and over, before he could crush her. She tried to breathe. All she could manage were small gasps of air. She could feel the agony of the broken bone in her nose. Taste the blood in her mouth. Jane coughed and tried to spit it out.

She was ready.

Seconds passed. She turned her head. A stab of pain.

He wasn't there.

The Irishman had gone. Why? He could have finished her.

Jane put out her arms. Tried to push herself up and struggle to her feet. On her knees, she closed her eyes, ready to topple over. A moment or two, catching her breath and she forced herself up.

She was standing, but she knew her legs wouldn't last. Jane reached towards the wall, then Rosie was there, holding on to her. She could see people staring at them.

Jane started to struggle. She needed to go after him. Rosie wrapped her close.

'Not yet,' she said. 'You're hurt.'

She sent someone for a bowl of water, another to fetch cotton rags from the draper. Rosie washed the blood away, cleaned her face. Gently, with soft fingertips, she traced the shape of the nose. Jane flinched at the touch.

'It's definitely broken,' Rosie told her. 'I'm going to straighten it. For a moment it's going to hurt worse than anything you've ever known, then it'll start feeling better.' A gentle look. 'Don't worry, I've had to do it for Simon before.'

She screamed. It was bad, exactly as Rosie had promised. But not the worst pain she'd endured; that was locked away in memories she didn't want to unearth. It was over almost before it began. Rosie rolled up small pieces of the cotton.

'Put those in your nostrils,' she said. 'Do you think you can stand on your own?'

A nod. Jane felt little stronger now. Her head was clearing.

She tried to shout the question, but the words came out as a croak, 'Where did he go?'

'Down there.' A man pointed towards the bottom of Briggate and Leeds Bridge.

Jane felt panic rising inside. He could be anywhere by now. She took a wobbling step.

'Not yet.' Rosie stopped her. 'You wouldn't last long enough to find him. You need to rest first.'

Simon saw them at the table in the kitchen. Jane's nose was red, swollen to more than twice its normal size. The bruises were already coming in around her eyes. He knew how much a broken nose hurt, like being stabbed with shards of glass.

He'd heard the story on the way home, half a dozen different versions of it. How she'd almost murdered the Irishman. The way he'd come close to killing her. Now he saw the truth. Ugly, but not deadly.

'How are you?' he asked. Rosie had put food in front of her; it didn't look as if she'd taken a bite.

Jane's voice was thick. 'He got away.'

'We'll find him.' He wanted this done, over. He'd already put out the word, the promise of a reward that was large enough to make people talk. 'The constable's sent men out to the house they had. If he ran there, they'll find him.'

'I cut him,' she said.

'I heard. You did well.'

Jane shook her head and winced. 'No, I didn't. Not well enough.'

The silence began to rise. He didn't know what to say. She'd done all she could.

'What happened with Kingsley?' Rosie said. He was grateful for something, anything to change the topic.

'He's in the cells.' Simon stroked her cheek. 'Are you sure he didn't hurt you?'

'He never even came close. He was too frightened to do anything.' A grin. 'Did you tell him who I was?'

'I said my wife always carries a knife. You should have seen his face once he understood what I meant.' He turned to Jane. 'We need to hunt later. Are you going to be well enough?'

'I'll be ready.'

'All of us,' Rosie told him.

'What about the boys?' In the safety of darkness, the Irishman would kill.

'I talked to Mrs Fisher. Richard and Amos are going to spend the night at her house. They think it's one of the best things that's ever happened.'

No doubt they did. But he'd rather they were here and his wife home with them. He wanted her safe.

'What did Kingsley tell you?'

'Enough.'

He'd had time with the man before Porter arrived at the gaol.

'How was the coachman involved?'

'Who?'

'Frank. The one who held the lantern for you last night.'

'You followed us? I never knew anyone was there.' Sly, Simon thought. He was trying to ease away from the question.

'The coachman.'

'He wanted some money and we needed another person now Harry Ackroyd's dead.'

'He works for Mrs Parker.'

'Who's she?' Kingsley asked. 'I've never heard of her.'

His answer was too quick, too smooth.

'You haven't? That's strange. You've sent her notes. I have them.'

A flicker of worry crossed the man's face.

'How do you know her?' Simon asked.

'Through Tom Rawlings. He worked with us sometimes, when he was short of cash and she wouldn't let him have any.'

'Who killed him?'

Kingsley raised his eyebrows. 'Is he dead? I heard he disappeared.'

'His body was in the house at Goulden's Yard until you sent him down the river.'

'You found him?' He pursed his lips. 'Why didn't you say anything? Maybe the constable would like to know.'

A fair share of bravado.

'What are you going to tell him?' Simon asked. 'There's no evidence. His body's gone. Which of you murdered him?'

A small sigh. 'The Irishman. They had an argument over that whore. Betsy.'

Maybe it was true; maybe not. It didn't matter now.

'Rawlings introduced you to Amanda Parker. Are you her lover?'

'Am I?' The smirk on his face told the truth.

Simon asked his questions until Porter barged through for a look at the prisoner, but Kingsley had little more to say. Nothing about Amanda Parker's involvement. He had just enough chivalry to try to protect her.

TWENTY-NINE

Jane's face was a mass of pain. At the smallest touch it screamed through her body, bile rising from her belly. She had to close her eyes and sit quietly until the wave passed. The blood had stopped gushing; that was a start. She tipped her head back as she eased the cotton from her nose. It felt like she was drawing out her insides; she forced herself to do it quickly. Better than prolonging the agony. At least she could almost breathe properly once again.

The bruises that the Irishman had given her on Timble Bridge still covered her body. Now he'd given her others to join them.

Rosie helped her upstairs and settled her in the big bed Richard and Amos shared.

Simon had gone out. She'd wanted to stand, to leave with him, but her legs wouldn't let her. A few halting steps and she had to lean against the wall.

'Rest,' Rosie ordered. For once, she didn't refuse. She lay on her back, the covers pulled up to her neck, letting the warmth soak through her skin, all the way to her bones.

She shouldn't be here while the Irishman was still loose. But if she found him now, she wouldn't last ten seconds.

Jane closed her eyes and exhaled slowly.

Simon moved among the people he knew. Not a single one of them had seen the Irishman. The constable had led a party to the house, but he hadn't returned there.

Hurrying all over town, going from one place to another wasn't going to help. The money he was offering was enough to make people talk if they saw O'Coughlan. A quick word, a tip, anything at all.

'I just looked in on her,' Rosie said. 'Sleeping.'

Simon cut himself some meat and bread. He realized it was the first thing he'd eaten that day; he'd had no appetite when he

woke. Now he felt the hunger, washing the food down with a
swig of beer.

'People are looking for the Irishman,' he said.

'Jane wants him for herself. Now more than ever.'

'He's beaten her twice now.'

No need to say more. Not yet. He tried to settle, to read the
Leeds Mercury and the *Intelligencer*, but after a few minutes
the words became a blur. Instead, he paced from room to room
until Rosie finally sent him out of the house.

Close to Mill Hill, a man caught his eye. A thick coating of
stubble across his cheeks, dark eyebrows that almost met at the
bridge of his nose. Gaze constantly shifting as if he expected
the world to betray him.

'You're looking for someone.'

'Who are you?' Simon asked.

The man ignored the question. 'Prepared to pay?'

'Not for any lie someone wants to make up.'

The man grinned. Stained teeth, brown and rotted. 'How much?'

'It depends on the information. If I find him.' He glanced at
the man again. He wasn't a fraud. He knew where the Irishman
was. Simon felt his heart begin to beat faster. This was what he
wanted. 'Where is he?'

A long silence, then the man shrugged. 'Right now? No idea.'
Simon swallowed his disappointment. But the man hadn't
finished. 'He'll be at the night market as soon as it opens. He's
going to collect some money he's owed before he leaves Leeds.'

'How do you know this?'

'It's a friend of mine he's meeting. He lives out near Horsforth.
The Irishman told me to pass on the message. To make sure my
friend was there.'

Simon gave him a silver sixpence.

The man looked at the coin disdainfully. 'Is that all?'

'If he shows up, come and see me tomorrow and I'll have
more for you. Who is your friend?'

'He sells old cutlery. Buys it, cleans it, polishes and sharpens it.'

'What's his name?'

'Henry. The Irishman said he'd be there as soon as the market
opens, before it's too busy. He wants to be away tonight.'

Simon handed him a second sixpence. 'I told you, more if
he's there.'

'It's cheap to talk.'

'Even cheaper to lie,' Simon told him. 'I make sure liars never prosper.'

Jane rose slowly. Cautiously. As soon as she'd woken, the pain in her nose had returned. Sharp, stabbing all the way through her skull. She stood, lifting a hand for a nervous touch to her face. The skin was tender, burning as her fingertips brushed against it. No need to look at herself in the mirror. She could guess how bad it would be; she didn't want to see it. All because of the Irishman. Every muscle, each joint; they all ached as she moved.

She hadn't been good enough. He'd escaped. She'd had her opportunity, taken him on and he'd beaten her again. A hard, bitter truth. He could have killed her if he'd wanted. When they found him again she had to be better.

She hurt, but she made herself put it aside, to ignore it. She dressed and walked carefully downstairs, treading gently on the steps and steadying herself with a hand against the wall. Each time her foot touched the ground the shock jarred through her.

Jane ground her teeth together. She was alive. This would fade.

Simon and Rosie were in the kitchen, heads turning to watch her as she entered.

'How . . .' Rosie began, but Jane shook her head as an answer. She could walk. She could use her knife. She was able to go looking for him.

'He's going to be at the night market.'

'Why?'

'Collecting some money that he's owed,' Simon told her. 'He's probably going all around town right now, doing that. Every penny. Once he has it, he's leaving Leeds.'

'Tonight,' Jane said.

He nodded. 'All three of us are going. We can take him together—'

'I want him.'

'He's yours.'

'Is he?' She stared at him, accusing, seeing doubt flicker in Simon's eyes. Whether she'd be strong enough for it.

'Yes,' he answered eventually.

She wanted to believe him. Needed to.

'How do you want us to do it?' Rosie broke the tension. She was toying with her knife, spinning it on the table.

'We'll go early. He may well decide to come before it opens and slip away in the crowd.' Simon glanced at the longclock. 'We still have a few hours before we need to go.'

Jane took out her whetstone and began to run it along the knife blade.

The last of the light was still clinging as Simon locked the door behind them. Saturday night and the factories had stopped, the machines fallen silent until Monday morning. But their smoke and the haze remained. The taste of soot that never quite disappeared.

He moved his hand, checking all the knives were in place. Couldn't be too careful. Rosie walked beside him, Jane a pace or two behind, alert for anything.

Only four weeks since he and Rosie had brought the twins to the market. His first visit in years and now he was here again. With a purpose this time. Posters pasted to brick walls announced a circus arriving at the end of May. All the acts and the spectacle. Maybe they could take Richard and Amos to that.

His mind was drifting. Snap out of it. He couldn't afford that.

'You know how many people come here,' Simon told them. 'Trying to take him in the middle of a crowd is going to be dangerous.'

'There were plenty of people on Briggate,' Jane said.

He nodded. 'On the street they can run. They'll all be packed together at the market.'

'Where do you want us?' Rosie asked. They were standing on the edge of the site. People were beginning to set up trestles and light the lanterns. Only a few; most would lay a sheet on the ground to display their items.

'I'll stay over here,' Simon answered after looking around. 'Can you move towards the back, over where they're roasting the meat?' He turned to Jane. 'If you stand at the far side, across from me, we can start to push him towards Boar Lane.'

The watch would be waiting on the street. During the afternoon, Simon had gone over to the gaol. No sign of Porter, so he'd talked to the man on duty. He had listened and simply said, 'We'll be there.'

Jane wanted the Irishman. But he'd hurt her. He'd been brutal with her. Twice he'd come close to murdering her. He was a deadly ogre of a man. Simon wasn't certain that all three of them together could manage to bring him down and stay alive. It wasn't a price he was prepared to pay. Let Jane rage with fury; in time she might understand.

'It sounds simple,' Rosie said.

Jane nodded.

From where he stood, Simon could see them both. More people kept arriving to prepare their wares. He remembered a few faces from his last visit. The girl crying out her walnuts. A man with a barrel of oysters. The street singer.

It was growing dark. He checked his knives once again. All of them in place. The pistol sat primed and ready in his pocket.

His eyes searched for a man selling old cutlery.

A lantern glinted on polished metal. Jane watched the man placing the knives and forks on a blanket. She edged closer, until she could see bone handles turned yellow with age. He kept glancing around, as if he expected to see someone. This was him. This was the one the Irishman was coming to see.

In an instant, she felt the mood shift. The first customers surged across the ground, pausing to examine this and that. She kept her gaze higher, watching the tops of their heads. The Irishman was tall; with his old top hat, he'd be easy to spot. There was enough of a crowd to hide her.

She glanced towards Simon. Too many people pushing along to pick him out. Jane turned her head the other way, searching for Rosie. The same thing. They were each on their own.

Then the Irishman was there, lumbering through the crowd. Shouldering people aside. He still had the dirty bandage over the left eye. But he'd added a rag tied around his head; it was crusted with dried blood where she'd sliced his brow open.

A fearsome sight. He must know it. Very likely he didn't care. He seemed intent on one thing.

He spotted the cutlery seller and forced his way through to stand in front of him. More people were pouring into the market every minute. A wave of them. She couldn't allow him the chance to hurt any of them.

The two men were talking. The cutlery seller brought a purse from his pocket. Bulging, hefty, yet it seemed so small when the Irishman closed his fist around it.

Jane twisted the gold ring on her finger. Pain from her nose stabbed through her body as someone barged against her.

None of it mattered. Tonight she'd have him.

The Irishman began to move. She shadowed him, edging closer. Too many people about for him to notice and more arriving all the time. Where were Simon and Rosie? Impossible to see them.

There was no need to push O'Coughlan towards Boar Lane; he was already heading that way. She stayed on his left, his blind side. People were swirling around, edging away as soon as they saw his face. Each one gave her the opportunity to move a little nearer to him.

Jane gripped her knife handle tight, holding the blade down against her leg.

The Irishman shouldered people aside as he hurried along. She was near enough to smell his stink and see the vivid line on the back of his neck where she'd cut him.

Her dress snagged against a trestle. She had to stop and drag it free. The Irishman turned his head and saw her. His eyes narrowed.

She couldn't fight him in here. Instead, she darted among the people, out towards the street. He'd follow.

Jane was small. She could weave and slide between people. As she passed she felt the heat of their bodies, heard the anticipation in their voices. A hurried glance over her shoulder. The Irishman was shoving people away as he came after her, not caring when they shouted and screamed.

A final dart past a family and she broke through to Boar Lane. She took a moment to breathe without a press of people all around. The air felt cooler against her face. But she could see him coming towards her. Jane moved back, raising her knife.

The Irishman hesitated for a second, looking around. Just long enough for her to slip close and slide the knife into his belly. All the way to the hilt. She twisted it and heard him grunt.

As she drew back, Jane felt the warm rush of his blood over her hand. The Irishman took a pace forward. He was still coming, slicing wildly down with his blade. All he caught was air.

Every scrap of pain in her body had gone. She was here, now. To kill or to die. Shifting around to his left, where he couldn't see. He had to turn his whole body to follow. How long could he last? His clothes were already sodden and dark with blood.

Her mouth was dry, her throat raw. She forced herself to sing the words.

'Pádraig Colm O'Coughlan.'

Soft and sweet. Like a mother's lullaby. Maybe it caught a distant memory; it made him pause. She struck again. Aiming for his neck, but he pulled away and her knife sank into the skin above his shoulder.

Edging away before he could hurt her.

'Pádraig Colm O'Coughlan.' She shouted it this time. Loud enough for her words to echo off the brickwork across the street.

He was failing, she saw it in his face. He had enough strength for one final charge. Through her. Knock her down and he'd be free. The Irishman hunched his shoulders.

The pistol shot broke the night.

A moment of utter silence. Then women started to scream and men were shouting. Families pushed every which way to try and find safety.

Jane's eyes stayed on the Irishman. He swayed. His hand opened and he dropped his knife, then slowly toppled to the floor. She was ready to leap on him, to give him the killing blow.

Before she could move, the watchman was there. The gun was still smoking in his hand. He crouched, placing a hand against the Irishman's neck.

'Still alive.' He nodded to the two large men with him.

'Get out of the way,' Jane said. The watchman looked at her with contempt.

Simon came out of the crowd, Rosie two steps behind him.

The men from the watch started to drag the Irishman off.

'I want him,' Jane said. 'He's mine.'

The inspector turned. 'I don't give a sliver of damnation what you want, girl.'

'He owes me for what he did.'

'You?' He pointed to one of the men pulling O'Coughlan. The Irishman was moaning, muttering something in the language he remembered. 'Do you see him? Do you?'

She didn't want to answer, but the word came anyway. 'Yes.'

'His name's Griffin. That man killed his brother. Don't tell me that he owes you a thing.' His anger flamed. Spittle flew from his lips as he spoke. 'It's done now. You stopped him.'

She saw him nod to Simon and he marched away, following his men.

'Did you tell them about tonight?' Jane asked.

He looked straight at her. 'Yes.'

Jane gazed down at her knife. Very slowly and carefully, she wiped the blood from the blade on her dress then slid it in her pocket.

'Why?'

'You know why,' he said. 'We needed help to beat someone like him.'

'I hurt him. He wouldn't have survived.'

'I couldn't take that chance. Rosie and I weren't able to force our way through to you in time. He might have killed you. I daren't risk that.'

'No,' she said. 'He was mine.'

She turned and walked away.

Her head was a torment. Her body screamed at her, pain rolled around in her skull, and she couldn't quiet it.

Simon had betrayed her. Tried to protect her like one of his children. It didn't matter what he believed, that he thought it was for the best; it was what had happened. She'd had no chance to strike that last blow, to beat the Irishman this final time. To see the life leave his eyes.

It hurt to walk. She hobbled. Jane felt the demons dance around her. She ignored them.

It would pass. It would all pass.

She slipped through to the small garden in front of the cottage. A light was still burning inside. Jane opened the door. Mrs Shields looked up. Horror filled her face.

'Oh, child . . . what have they done to you?'

THIRTY

Simon watched her go. The excitement was fading. All around, sound was growing as people cautiously returned to the night market.

'I . . .' he began, then shook his head. He couldn't find the words for what he was thinking.

'You did the right thing,' Rosie told him. She put her arm through his and began to steer him towards home. Her dress swished against her legs as she walked. 'We both know he could have killed her. He might have killed all of us.'

He was furious with himself. The bitterness in Jane's voice . . . 'I did it all wrong.'

'No.' Her hand tugged on his wrist. 'The way you arranged things made sense. Do you care who ended up killing him?'

'I don't,' he admitted. 'But—'

'No buts,' Rosie said. 'Would you rather have him dead, or Jane?'

He narrowed his eyes and turned to look at her. 'No need to ask, is there?'

'Of course not. What you did was try to make sure she stayed alive. It worked.'

'I took away the one thing she wanted.'

'You made a difficult choice. If she doesn't see that, I know Mrs Shields will. She'll show her.'

Maybe she was right. But he'd never forget that final look Jane gave him before she left. All the trust they'd built up over the years turned to dust in an instant. He'd caused that. It was his fault and his alone. He'd betrayed her.

Time, that was what she needed. A few days while her anger cooled. Some weeks for her to heal, the swelling around her nose to subside and all those bruises become a memory. After that they might be able to pick up once more. But if it happened, he knew it would be fragile. It could shatter so easily. She'd no longer be willing to do whatever he needed. She wouldn't risk her life for him the way she had.

In his heart Simon knew he couldn't blame her. The Irishman was dead, but it felt hollow, no victory at all. A killer was gone, but it was the constable's men who'd finished the job.

'No more brooding,' Rosie said. 'We're going to collect the boys and take them home.'

Simon was out early, prowling through a Sunday morning. He'd slept badly, caught in worries and dark dreams. All the traces of the market had gone from the site by Holy Trinity Church. Hardly a soul on the streets. A coach arrived, crossing Leeds Bridge and hurrying up Briggate to the Talbot.

No more body snatchers. For now, at least. Soon someone else would have the idea and take up the trade; maybe they already had. But this gang was finished. Ackroyd hung by the mob, the Irishman disposed of by the watch. His body would never be found, Simon was certain of that.

Kingsley was in gaol, waiting for his trial and sentence. Just the misdemeanour of digging up and selling corpses. A short spell in prison.

He'd kept quiet, rather than implicate Amanda Parker. What had she promised him? A word with the judge to lighten his sentence? Money after he was released? She knew her charms and how to use them; the man had fallen for it. She sat above it all, still untouchable.

He'd done everything he could. It wasn't right, it wasn't enough. But it was finished. It was over.

When he arrived home, Rosie was wearing a sky-blue gown with a bodice of navy and white stripes. She had a pale, thin shawl of light wool around her shoulders, and soft leather shoes on her feet. All dressed up.

'Where are you going?' he asked, bemused.

'I have to make a social call. Duty.' She drew her visiting card from a small reticule and smiled. Occasionally she did go to see people on a Sunday, the only day in the week when people weren't working. Rarely quite so dressed up, though. She kissed his cheek. 'Take the boys somewhere. See if you can wear them out.'

'All right,' he said as she put her hat on her head, finding the right angle and pinning it deftly into place.

*　　*　　*

Jane was sitting, trying to read *Sense and Sensibility*. But the words seemed too light. They floated off the page and out through her mind.

After she came home, Mrs Shields had cradled her. Put ointment on her bruised body, over all the wounds the Irishman had given her. Everywhere except her face.

'Better to let that heal by itself,' she said as she studied the nose. 'Rosie put it back in place?'

'Yes.'

A nod. 'She did a good job. You'll still be able to see it was broken, but it won't be bad.'

Jane didn't care about how she looked. Why would that matter? Fury at Simon burned inside her. He'd taken away the thing that was important to her.

'Drink this.' Catherine Shields handed her a mug. She sipped. A bitter taste that made her mouth pucker. She tried to hand it back. 'All of it, child. You need it.'

The draught worked. She fought it, but it pulled her in. Rest helped. Her body felt stronger this morning. Still arrows of pain whenever she touched her face, but not the fire it had been the day before.

But she was empty inside. Simon had ruined it all. Before she fell asleep, Jane had tried to cry for the loss of a friendship. It had been the first dependable thing in her life. But she'd schooled herself too well. The tears wouldn't flow.

A knock at the door. She started to rise, feeling her muscles complain, but Mrs Shields waved her back down. Silence, and the next thing was Rosie crouching beside her chair, wearing an expensive gown, eyes examining her.

'I'm sorry.'

The apology made her pay attention.

'I know you must hate Simon. Both of us.' Her expression shifted. 'I don't think you're right, but I do understand *why*. It was wrong to do it without telling you. I think Simon would see that if he'd let himself look. You know what men are like.'

'Yes.'

'Do you still feel you could take a walk with me? Doing what we discussed yesterday? It's not far. Nothing to tax you too much.'

She'd forgotten about it. Pushed it all the way out of her

thoughts. But Rosie was here, so earnest and hopeful. Her eyes pleaded.

'Yes,' Jane said. 'I can.'

They came out on to the Head Row, surrounded by the quiet of the Sabbath. The pavements were almost empty, barely a cart on the road. Rosie slipped Jane's arm through hers and set off down the hill. A sedate, ladylike pace.

'This is the only way Gwendolyn Jordan will see any proper justice,' Rosie said.

As they approached Burley House, Jane paused for a moment to gaze at the building.

'We're only going to visit for a minute or two,' Rosie told her. Her eyes glittered. Something dark lingered under her words.

They didn't go through the gate and up the drive. Instead, Rosie led the way through the woods.

'The back way. This is a time to be informal and unseen.'

'The servants . . .'

'I asked a few questions,' Rosie said. 'She can only afford two now, and they're both off today.'

'There's the coachman,' Jane told her.

A tight smile. 'We'll have to make sure he doesn't see us.'

The door to the kitchen was locked. Jane watched as Rosie took out Simon's picks and worked them. She wasn't as skilled as her husband, but in less than a minute they were inside. A finger to the lips.

Everything in the place had been scoured clean. Saucepans hanging, tile floor swept and mopped. They tiptoed through, into the hall.

A twist of the gold ring as she let Rosie lead.

Amanda Parker looked up as they entered. It was warm outside, but a fire was burning in the hearth. Her eyes widened in panic.

'What are you doing here? I never receive visitors on a Sunday.' She glared at Jane. 'Why is she with you?'

'You'll have to make an exception this time. We both came to talk about some people you know. Gwendolyn Jordan, for one.' Rosie's voice had turned to ice.

'Who?' Mrs Parker narrowed her eyes.

'Those people you helped, the body snatchers. They dug her out of the ground and sold her body to a doctor in Edinburgh so his pupils could dissect her. I'd have thought you'd remember that. But it was just one of quite a few, wasn't it?'

'That's slander. If you ever say it to people, I'll sue you.'

Rosie shook her head. 'There's no need. Peter Kingsley will be going before the magistrate. I'm sure he'll gladly talk to make sure he receives a shorter sentence.'

'There's—'

'No need? Everything already ordered. Is that what you were going to say? It's handy for you that the other two are dead, isn't it?' She paced around behind Amanda Parker's chair. The woman had to strain her head around to watch her. 'Shall I remind you of their names? Harold Ackroyd and—'

'Pádraig Colm O'Coughlan.' Jane was happy to spit it from her mouth.

'I don't know who they are.'

'You might be the only person in Leeds who doesn't.' A long pause, the sound of her shoes on the parquet floor. 'All because of Tom Rawlings, wasn't it? He had to ruin things by wanting that whore. Did you tell them to kill him?'

'No one knows where he is.' Her voice was defiant.

'I saw his body,' Jane said. 'In Garland's Court. That's when we knew you were trying to use us.'

'What do you want?' Amanda Parker asked. 'I can pay you a little—'

'I'm not after your money.' Rosie stood in front of her. 'I'm going to destroy you. Piece by little piece, I intend to let out everything I know about this. Soon you won't have a name to protect. No one will receive you. They'll all pretend they never knew you.'

'Why? What good does that do?'

'I just gave you her name: Gwendolyn Jordan.'

'I never saw her. I didn't know who she was until you said it.'

'You didn't care, either. My husband seems to imagine you're untouchable. I know he's wrong, and I know exactly how to hurt you. I can ruin you in society and I will. I'll make you pay, and you'll find that bill waiting for you every single day for the rest of your life.'

Rosie turned to leave. Jane was in front of her, close to the door as it burst open. Frank the coachman, still wearing the dirty bandage around the wound on his left hand.

'I heard voices. I want to make sure nothing was . . .'

His words tailed away as he saw Jane, then Rosie. A grin as he took out his knife.

'You broke in here.'

Jane already had her blade in her hand. She felt nothing, no anger, no fear, no danger. He'd come after her for weeks. She'd done exactly what Simon asked. Given him chances, sent him packing. Wounded him, when it would have been simpler just to kill. None of it had worked, Now he wanted a fight; she'd give him one. But no holding back this time, no stopping. It was all or nothing. Release some of her rage over the Irishman.

She let him come. He believed he was good with a knife, but he had no skill. None at all. He could lunge and parry. That was it.

Jane watched him prance back and forth, preening like a dancing master. How long? Ten seconds? A minute? She didn't know. She waited until he launched himself forward, then slipped to the side. As easy as that. A cut to his neck and he fell to the floor, the blood spurting like a fountain.

She stared down at him. He'd brought it on himself, trying to be a bigger man than he was. In the end, there was no satisfaction in seeing him die. It wasn't the solace she craved.

Suddenly she was aware of a sound behind her. A chair pushed back. Amanda Parker had pulled a knife from somewhere. Moving forward, but Rosie didn't give an inch. She was ready.

'I had to learn to use this when I worked on Briggate.'

No reply. Jane circled, ready to help, but Rosie waved her away.

She could only watch as Amanda Parker rushed forward, arm extended, flailing with her blade. Rosie took a gliding step and stabbed. Pushed the woman backwards and watched her topple.

'You should have remembered your lessons.' She wiped the steel clean on Mrs Parker's gown. The light was already fading in the woman's eyes.

A final glance around and Jane followed Rosie out of the room.

As they went back through the woods, Jane asked, 'What are we going to do now?'

'We're going home,' Rosie said. She took a deep breath and

examined her clothes. Not a single speck of blood. 'We went out for a walk and a talk, that was all.'

'The servants will find them when they come back.'

She nodded. 'They will. They'll call the constable. He'll find two bodies, and Leeds will have a scandal and a mystery. The lady and the coachman.' She smiled 'Let them make of it what they will, eh? We were never here.'

Close to Green Dragon Yard, Jane asked, 'Would you really have done it? Spread the rumours and ruined her?'

Rosie's eyes were glittering again. 'Of course. I didn't go there to kill her. I wanted her to keep suffering for years and years.' Before she turned away, she put a hand on Jane's arm. 'Thank you for coming with me today.'

THIRTY-ONE

Monday morning and the talk exploded around the coffee cart. Everyone had a theory about the deaths. Simon listened, a suspicion growing in his mind.

Rosie had said nothing when she returned the day before. She looked satisfied, but he thought little about it. Soon enough, they'd eaten dinner, and spent a Sunday afternoon as families did. Everything ordinary.

He understood why she'd done it. But he'd never ask her. She might tell him one day; more likely she'd keep it all to herself. She'd have been careful, nothing that could lead back to her. Now it really was done. Almost all.

Clark Foundry was bustling at the start of a week. The air was loud with men and machines, the deep ring of metal on metal, and ripe with the smell of heat.

'I'm sorry to keep you waiting, Mr Westow,' Joseph Clark said as he entered. Behind him, timid, not sure whether he wanted to be here, came Harmony Jordan. Both in their old work clothes, covered with thick leather aprons. 'Do you have some news?'

Funny how simple it was to put it all into a few sentences, he thought. Clark listened, nodding.

'Kingsley is the one who arranged everything?' he asked. Jordan stood, silent, motionless.

'Yes. He sold the bodies and arranged shipment. He'll be standing trial this week.'

'Did you talk to him?' Clark said.

'I asked him where he sent Gwendolyn.'

He heard Jordan draw a sharp breath as he told them. Wanting to know and scared to hear.

'Thank you.' The words crept out when he heard. Jordan hurried out of the office.

'I'll write to someone I know in Edinburgh today. Maybe . . .' Clark spread his hands. The white cuffs of his shirt were burned and singed. 'You've done well, Mr Westow. I'm grateful. We both are. I'll come by tomorrow to pay you.'

Maybe at least one of the dead would rise.

July, 1824

Jane hesitated before taking the package from the chest. She unknotted the string and opened the brown paper. Held the dress against herself and closed her eyes for a second.

Once it was on and pulled so it fell flatteringly around her body, she stood and looked in the mirror. The bruises had all gone, the pains and deep aches with them. She'd always have a bump on her nose, but everything had healed. Everything on the surface. No one saw what was inside. She'd always keep all that out of sight.

Jane picked up a brush and began to pull it through her hair. Again and again, the way she'd work a whetstone and a blade. She'd done a pair of jobs for Simon in the last month. Small things, easy tasks, simple money to add to her handsome share of Clark's fee. Simon had been tentative when he approached her; she was cautious, not certain whether to accept. Everything went smoothly. But the future . . . the future would take care of itself.

Her hair shone in the sunlight through the window. She sighed. She knew she'd never be one of the Bennet sisters or the Dashwoods, but she could be Miss Truscott. Miss Jane Truscott.

Jane opened the door and stepped into the room, standing until Mrs Shields turned to look at her.

'Do you still think it suits me?'

'Child, of course I do. It looks as lovely as it did the first time you wore it for me.' The old woman pursed her lips, curious. 'Why have you put it on now? Are you going somewhere?'

'I am.' Jane extended her arm. 'We are.'

The phaeton was waiting on the Head Row. Coach and driver engaged for the day. Carrying them around Leeds, so Catherine Shields could see the way it had grown, The old streets and the new. The woman gazed like an eager child, pointing out places from her past. Houses she'd lived in, little glimpses into her history.

A little after noon they pulled up at the corner of Briggate

and Boar Lane. Jane bought food from Kate the pie-seller, intro-
ducing the women to each other. From there to Quarry Hill,
where she brought Miss Dawlish from her shop to meet the
woman she'd once known. Jane listened as they talked, a litany
of names from all the years gone by.

She kept an eye on Mrs Shields, finally moving on, over
Leeds Bridge and into Hunslet. Mrs Shields had known another
shopkeeper here, Miss Spinks. During the winter, the woman had
promised a visit. Now it could happen.

By the middle of the afternoon, the old woman was tiring.
Home once more. Catherine Shields embraced her. Her eyes were
wet with tears.

'Thank you, child. You've given me one of the best days of
my life.'

'I'm glad.' She meant the words. 'You deserve to be happy.'

'I am, child. I truly am.'

Jane smiled. Maybe for the very first time, she felt content.

AFTERWORD

Until the Anatomy Act changed everything in 1832, there was a market for what the body snatchers – the resurrection men – offered. Not the Burke and Hare idea of murdering people to supply the corpses, but digging up those who died. The supply to be used for anatomy was limited to those who had been executed, and the rise in medical and anatomy schools, especially in the 1820s, meant increased demand. As always, there was someone willing to supply.

It was a lucrative business. Twelve pounds for a body was common, equivalent to almost £1,200 today. Leeds wasn't immune from the trade. In 1831, the corpse of Thomas Rothery was taken from Wortley parish church and brought to a house in Sheepscar, the home of a solicitor's clerk called John Craig Hodgson. He was one of a gang of body snatchers and kept corpses at his house until he could find a buyer. When arrested, he had a four-hour trial, was fined and sentenced to six weeks in prison at York Castle (as stated in the book, the crime was just a misdemeanour). The house is long since gone, although an old photograph of it can be seen on the excellent Leodis website; it became known as Resurrection Cottage.

Other bodies were discovered in coaching offices as they passed through Leeds, some packed in such small boxes that it seemed impossible for them to contain human remains.

Leeds had no Saturday market; the space by Holy Trinity Church really was used by visiting circuses. The inspiration came from Henry Mayhew's *London Labour and the London Poor* and its vivid description of a Saturday night market there.

I'm grateful to all the people at Severn House, from top to bottom. But especially Sara Porter, my editor there, a woman with an eye for every detail that's often saved me from embarrassment. Then there's Lynne Patrick, who's edited every book in this series, and my others, and probably knows these characters as well as I do.

Thank you to all the bloggers and reviewers who've helped

to spread the word. To libraries and bookshops everywhere that stock the books, and above all, to the readers. You are wonderful.

Last, but far from least: my love to Penny Lomas, who puts up with these people, and with me, every day.

4/23